Situational Crime Prevention and Crime Reduction

Situational Crime Prevention and Crime Reduction

G. S. BAJPAI
Professor & Chairperson
Centre for Civil & Criminal Justice Administration
National Law Institute University, Bhopal (MP), India

SERIALS PUBLICATIONS
NEW DELHI (INDIA)

First Published - 2011

ISBN 978-81-8387-357-4

Published by

SERIALS PUBLICATIONS
4830/24, Prahlad Street, Ansari Road
Darya Ganj, New Delhi-110002 (India)
Phone : 23245225 Fax : 91-11-23272135
E-mail: serials@sify.com

CONTENTS

1

Introduction

Over the last few decades, crime has accelerated markedly, and so have its costs. Nations are spending increasing amounts on health and property as well as on the police, prosecution, court and prisons. Crime control uses up about 5 per cent of gross domestic product (GDP) in developed countries and up to 14 per cent in developing countries, according to recent estimates. But this spending has done little to reverse crime rates or reform offenders. The number of repeat offenders, rates of all serious crimes and level of fear of crime in the community remains discouragingly high. *(http://www.uncjin.org).*

Safe living and quality of life are the objectives aspired by every society. Crime undermines the both. This has prompted us to devise ways and means to deal with crime in the society. Crime control through formal institutions and crime prevention emerged as the possible responses. Criminologists have recognized the significance of crime prevention practices. Acting before the occurrence of crime has always considered more appropriate than acting afterwards. Crime prevention can have several varieties. The two major forms are: social prevention and situational crime prevention. They correspond to the two main ways of preventing crime- reducing criminal motivation and reducing crime opportunities. Later is known as situational crime prevention (SCP).

The criminals, by and large, are of two varieties. One, those who are biologically, sociologically or psychologically motivated and the other are those who are opportunists and are enticed by the availability of opportunities for seeking unlawful gains. In other words, the motivation in them is situationally triggered. This category of offenders often outnumbers the former one. And situational crime prevention can be immensely effective in this case.

The SCP has a practical focus. It is based on opportunity reduction. The wider acceptability of this practice was due to various factors. This may include the virtual failures of the traditional methods of crime prevention and control and consistently eroding confidence of people in the traditional styles of performance of criminal justice agencies. Typically in India, the discussion centered largely on how the police could be made more result oriented and justice dispension a quicker one. The pursuits like these took enormous time but the results were still not very convincing. The people and sections of the society seem to crave for something that could bring an instant and visible check on criminal practices taking place in their immediate environs. The measures of situational crime prevention were able to satisfy these expectations of people to a great extent in many nations.

The focus in situational crime prevention remains in the setting and context of crime rather than on criminals. It makes the criminal action difficult by making the target inaccessible through several techniques based on the manipulation of environment and applications of technology. The SCP works on the premises that the crime reduction is possible if the opportunities for crime are significantly reduced. This objective is achievable through various ways. Sometimes it may be by making the target inaccessible and invulnerable ('target hardening'), by increasing the natural and techno-surveillance or by making criminal action more risky and gains less rewarding.

Paradoxically, the lead in all such initiatives is not taken by the criminal justice agencies as the SCP techniques may be implemented by a 'multi agencies partnership' of all basic community institutions such as school, municipals, health centers, transport authority, business enterprise, communication departments, entertainment centers like cinema, clubs, theatres etc. This kind of arrangement exists in the UK and is known as Crime Reduction (CR).

Situational crime prevention uses up-to-date technology, surveillance and building design to ward off potential criminals. The result has been a sharp rise in the private policing and security industries, increased surveillance by local residents or non-police professionals and the widespread use of technical aids, such as closed-circuit television and speed cameras.

SCP is about the practical ways to reduce crime. The business establishment, banks, public transporters, shopping centers, housing society managers, entertainment industries, factory owners and residents in the community etc are always concerned with the security against any offending practices. They tend to seek for measures those could immediately deliver the results. They look for ways and means capable of visibly discouraging criminals' movements. The emergence of CCTV, electronic alarms, swipe cards, computer chips for identification, password, screening devises, secured parking systems, hidden cameras are the product of the growing concern to quickly respond to crime problem. Remarkably, these situationally effective measures have had a history of efficient performance in all parts of the world.

THEORETICAL FRAMEWORK OF SITUATIONAL CRIME PREVENTION

The key concepts in SCP, according to Gilling, (1997), are opportunity and physical environment. SCP is defined as those interventions designed to prevent the occurrence of crimes, especially by reducing opportunities and increasing risk. (Tony and Ferrington, 1995). The concept of situational crime prevention traces its origin in the UK (Clarke, 1997). Though the Newman's 'defensible space' and Jeffrey's work on crime prevention through environmental design emerged in the US but they really did not take shape in resulting in to any crime prevention methodology until recently.

KEY CONCEPTS & THEORIES

The present structure of SCP is essentially based on some crime theories developed with situational perspectives in crime occurrence. A brief overview of these is as follows.

Routine Activity Theory–that explains that crime is often a result of a triangle–victim, offender and lack of capable guardian. The convergence of these three variables: a *likely offender*, a *suitable target*, and the *absence of a capable guardian* against crime are invariably result in crime occurrence.

A capable guardian is anything, either a person or thing that restricts crime from taking place. These can be formal or informal.

Some examples of capable guardians could be: police patrols, security guards, Neighbourhood Watch schemes, door staff, locks, fences, barriers, lighting, alarm systems, vigilant staff and co-workers, friends, neighbours, Close Circuit Television (CCTV) systems etc.

Of *VIVA* and *CRAVED*

The likelihood of a target becoming prone for offending practices depends upon many things. In other words, a target causes criminal temptation due to a combination of factors. This statement takes us to 'hot products, person and object'.

The VIVA (Clarke, 1999) is about a characteristic model indicating 'hot factor' approach.

Value: The basic value of the object may be of interest to the motivated offenders.

Inertia: The items of lighter weight (CD Player, jewellery etc.) are more preferred by offenders than the items of high weight.

Visibility: The objects in display become more suitable targets.

Access: The easy access to the object causes ripe situation for crime commission.

This model was replaced by another model explaining the cases of theft. This is "CRAVED", identifying six important properties: these products are generally Concealable, Removable, Available, Valuable, Enjoyable and Disposable.

Rational Choice Theory–this assumes that offending behaviour is designed to benefit the offender in some way. It seeks to understand how the offender makes crime choices, driven by a particular motive within a specific setting, which offers the opportunities to satisfy that motive. The focus of modus operandi here is closely linked to Situational Crime Prevention.

Situational Crime Prevention-although not strictly a theory, this approach takes an offender's motives and propensities as given and therefore seeks to influence the offender's decision or ability to commit crimes at particular places and times.

Opportunity Theory-seeks to re-emphasise opportunity as a cause of crime, regardless of criminal inclinations. Opportunity is necessary and is the single principle that governs the theory of how settings cause crime. The easy or tempting opportunities entice people into criminal action. Felson & Clarke (1998) elaborated the opportunity and crime model by suggesting ten principles. These are as under:

1 Opportunities play a role in causing all crime
2 Crime opportunities are highly specific
3. Crime opportunities are concentrated in time and space
4. Crime opportunities depend on everyday movements
5. One crime produces opportunities for another
6. Some products offer more tempting crime opportunities
7. Social and technological changes produce new crime opportunities
8. Opportunities for crime can be reduced
9. Reducing opportunities does not usually displace crime
10. Focussed opportunity reduction can produce wider declines in crime

Displacement Theory-classifies the types of crime displacement that may occur when a crime is prevented. Reviews of displacement suggest that displacement occurs much less frequently or fully than previously thought, but it is still a consideration in crime prevention work *(www.crime reduction.gov.uk).* The displacement is of several (Clarke and Felson, 1998) types:

- crime can be moved from one location to another (geographical displacement);
- crime can be moved from one time to another (temporal displacement);
- crime can be directed away from one target to another (target displacement);
- one method of committing crime can be substituted for another (tactical displacement);
- one kind of crime can be substituted for another (crime type displacement).

Clarke (1997) proposed the following set of measures of situational crime prevention.

Sixteen Opportunity Reduction Techniques in Situational Crime Prevention

Increase the perceived effort of crime	*Increase the perceived risks of crime*	*Reduce the anticipated rewards of crime*	*Remove excuses for crime*
1. Harden targets: *steering column locks, anti-robbery screens*	5. Screen entrances and exits: *electronic merchandise tags, baggage screening*	9. Remove targets: *phone cards, removable car radios, women's refuges*	13. Set rules: *hotel registration, customs declaration, codes of conduct*
2. Control access to targets: *entry phones, electronic access to garages*	6. Formal surveillance: *red light and speed cameras, security guards*	10. Identify property: *vehicle licensing, property marking, car parts marking*	14. Alert conscience: *roadside speedometers, "idiots drink-and-drive" signs*
3. Deflect offenders from targets: *bus stop location, street closings, segregation of rival fans*	7. Surveillance by employees: *park attendants, CCTV on double deck buses*	11. Reduce temptation: *rapid repair of vandalism, off-street parking*	15. Control disinhibitors: *drinking age laws, car ignition breathalyser, V-chip in TV*
4. Control crime facilitators: *photos on credit cards, plastic beer glasses in pubs*	8. Natural surveillance: *street lighting, defensible space architecture*	12. Deny benefits: *ink merchandise tags, PIN for car radios, graffiti cleaning*	16. Assist compliance: *litter bins, public lavatories, easy library check-out*

Source: Clarke, Ronald. V. (Ed.). 1997. *Situational Crime Prevention: Successful Case Studies, Second* Edition. Albany, NY: Harrow & Heston.

INGREDIENTS

SCP mainly draws upon the aforementioned theories SCP is therefore a specific target oriented approach to crime prevention that utilises managerial techniques, design and manipulation of environment for reducing the criminal risks. The probable criminal actions are also made risky and less rewarding by this technique. The ideas like these are traceable to the seminal works by Clarke. Infact, the studies by Clarke laid a firm foundation for application of this approach in actual setting. Clarke talked of several ways and means to apply SCP. He mainly talked of four strategies and sixteen techniques of the SCP. The four main strategies are as under:

1. increasing the effort needed to commit the crime;
2. increasing the risks associated with the crime;
3. reducing the rewards of crime; and
4. removing excuses or creating embarrassment

The theories and ideas analysed above make a case for crime prevention by way of the following approaches:

1. Problem oriented policing
2. Defensible space architecture
3. Crime prevention through environmental designs
4. Situational crime prevention

Conceptual Differences: The following Table indicates the mutual differences in certain new approaches that are recently emerging in the area of crime reduction.

Approaches	*Focus*	*Methods*
Situational Crime prevention	Elimination of criminogenic situations	Managerial techniques, design and manipulation of environment
Crime & Disorder Reduction	Multi agency approach	Action relating to several areas falling under community agencies
Community Policing	Enlisting citizen support for crime prevention and image building	Service oriented programmes
Problem oriented policing	Specific crime problems	Target oriented and evidence based problem solving
Broken window	Neighbourhood in disorders and deterioration	Upkeep of neighbourhood and focused policing
Community Safety	Wider view of crime reduction	Collective and comprehensive interventions

SITUATIONAL CRIME PREVENTION TECHNIQUES

Apparently, SCP comprises specially customized measures to reduce the opportunity for specific crimes. SCP techniques or measures signify the control, planning and manipulation of the immediate environment or setting in as systematic and permanent a manner as possible. The measures are meant to transmit a massage to likely offenders that the attempts required to execute crime and the risks associated have amplified, and that the pay offs that can be attained through crime have significantly diminished.

SCP applies highly specific techniques in the opportunity reduction for any offending behaviour. Ranges of such technological and managerial initiatives have shown encouraging results in the UK. The performance of these initiatives was made visible in several evaluation studies carried out in the UK. Clarke (1997) has developed a sixteen techniques model for opportunity reduction that is being used everywhere with appropriate modifications. In a paper developed by the Surrey Community Safety Unit (structure of this model is based on the Clarke's model), the results of opportunity reductions have been discussed. It would be interesting to have a look as to how these techniques are put in to practice.

Target Hardening

Securing the target with the help of technologies/designs/ tactics is called target hardening. This is also about making targets more resistant to attack or more difficult to remove or damage. The use of locks, screen, and shields are some popular ways. The use of a slur rejecter devise has significantly reduced the use of slur in parking machines and London Underground trains. Likewise, the use of transparent screen and anti-bandit screens are considered to have cut down assaults incidence and robberies in the UK by 40 percent. The target hardening has a success story in case of postal stores robberies too. Many stores in England have small postal counters in a corner of the store. These handle a lot of money and are attractive targets for robbers. In the early

1980s, the postal counters in London had a bigger problem than usual with robberies, even though most of them had "anti-bandit" screens. Most of the robberies involved people trying to break down the screens with sledgehammers or their bare hands, pointing guns at the staff behind the screens, or attacking other staff or customers outside the secure area and forcing the staff behind the screen to let the robbers in. After upgrading the screens to be more resistant to attack, robberies dropped by 40% (Ekblom, 1987). This further facilitated the target hardening. A mention of electronic surveillance in target hardening will be appropriate here. The Electronic article surveillance (EAS) is a method to discourage shoplifting. Introduced in 1968-69, this technology has proved to be an effective anti-shoplifting measure. This electronic technique is about an electronically detectable element that is attached on the article. The transmitters and receivers at the exit of shops can immediately detect the article if someone tries to take it away (Dilonarado, 1997).

Access Control

This measure is applied to 'defend space' by checking the offenders' access to offices, factories, apartments or in any buildings. In the UK this has resulted in good amount of risk reduction. The measures like use of PIN numbers for accessing bank accounts or computer, installation of entry phones, dialling the code to gain access have considerably cut the incidence of burglary, thefts, and robberies in the UK.

Deflecting Offenders

This situational measure applies the logical segregation or exclusion of likely offenders. For instance, the rival groups of fans in football matches in Britain segregated in the stadia to avoid violent clashes. To avoid the incidence of brawls in the closing time of pubs, the scheduling of last buses with the closing time of pubs has worked significantly. Street closures, separate public facilities for women and rescheduling the conveyance routes at the time of public functions are similar such measures.

Controlling Facilitators

The studies in the Britain of injury of potential kinds of broken glass have led to recommendations that toughened or plastic material glasses be used in the pubs and beer bars. Disabling the stolen cell phones or similar goods was found be another effective way in this regard.

Entry/Exit Screening

The electronic methods of screening in entry and exit checking are in use in all important points in the UK.

Formal Surveillance

The police, security guards or detective personnel provide this form of surveillance. The use of burglar alarm and CCTV is being prominently used. The country wide use of Home office sponsored CCTV initiatives have minimised the crime incidence to its lowest ever. According to sources (*www.crimereduction.gov.uk*), under the Crime Reduction Programme of CCTV Initiative around £170 million will be spent on 684 CCTV schemes. The findings to this effect have been shown in some CCTV evaluation studies. Existing Home Office Research and other evaluations indicate that CCTV can be effective in reducing crime and fear of crime and in helping the police detect crime and convict criminals as part of an overall strategy. Studies, for example, show a 41% overall decrease in vehicle crime in car parks where CCTVs were installed - contributing to the Governments overall target of a national 30% reduction in vehicle crime by 2004. Infact, the CCTV has emerged one of the most powerful situational crime prevention tools. This has saved the community, people and establishment throughout the UK. Some of the live case studies can be seen at- *http://www.crimereduction.gov.uk/cctvminisite28.htm*. The major areas of intervention by this tool are- missing persons, weapons incidents, assaults, smuggling, intelligence gathering, street management, counter terrorism etc. The latest remote monitoring technology has come in now that enables the pictures transmition down the phone lines to a Central Monitoring Station. The guards can then move cameras, deliver audio warnings and switch on lights all from a remote location.

Another measure in the same category is that of alarms. The utilisation of this technique in planned ways has already delivered effective outcomes in crime reduction in the developed part of world. Intruder detection systems have proved immensely effective for warning of the presence of an intruder in residential premises, commercial official and school buildings. In many cases, police respond quickly enough so that the offender or offenders are caught. If they are not caught, they are at least discouraged from coming back and often leave the property they were attempting to steal behind. There are now improved versions of various alarms like Tecom® system. It has the capacity to provide more than just intruder detection. This system has the capacity for additional devices such as smoke or glass break detectors to be incorporated to support other preventative measures against specific problems such as broken windows or arson attacks. Intruder detection systems have traditionally used the telephone line as their sole means of communication. With the development of Telstra's Mobile Data® network, there is a more economical tamper proof alternative. Mobile Data® uses the UHF radio digital data network to provide a secure, fast and economical means of communication

Surveillance by Employees

The incidence of vandalism was cut down in the UK because of resident caretakers. The two third reduction was also seen in offences following the appointment of attendants in the parking area during high-risk time.

Natural Surveillance

There are host of people in a position to observe and see around. They may be neighbours, staff, students or parents, hall hirers, sports clubs or in fact anyone who has a legitimate reason to be on the site. Creating the opportunity to see involves: creation of a surveillance zone through trees and shrubs, where trees are pruned up and shrubs are trimmed down to provide a corridor of visibility; ensuring that shrubs and trees do not shield buildings from nearby premises and roads; ensuring that lighting enhances surveillance by illuminating clearly all buildings and areas in the school and target directed lighting, target hardening, territorial re-enforcement.

General measures like neighbourhood upkeep in terms of good amount of street lights and whistle making can have wide ranging applications. Appearing pretty simple and routine, these measures do contribute in situational crime prevention. The researches in the UK have shown that because streets were lighter there were fewer opportunities for offenders. The street lighting played a part in generating a more cohesive community; people had more pride in their area. The benefits of street lighting continued into adjacent areas.

Target Removal

This is about reducing the vulnerability by shifting or removing the target from risk situation. The use of phone cards and steel cover in public phones has reduced the attacks on them. The removal of gas and electronic coin meters that were the frequent target of thefts reduced the incidence significantly.

Identifying Properties

Identifying properties by marking or engraving useful details helped the detection in large among of thefts and burglary. The marking of postcode on goods also give an idea of their location when the same are recovered as stolen goods.

Denying Benefits

During the California Gold Rush, more than 150 years ago, stagecoach robberies were plaguing silver mine. So they started casting the silver into 400-pound blocks. These blocks were too heavy for a bandit on horseback, or even a gang of them, to carry off.

The offenders normally get frustrated when they fail to make use of stolen goods.

The cases of credit cards fraud have always been a serious problem in Britain. In the year 2000 alone the cost of such frauds was £ 425 million. The new technology of computer aided chip and use of pin in credit card has produced good results in denying the benefits to cheaters and frauds. The SCP worked remarkably against thefts and burglaries in the UK. Notably, theft and burglaries are major offences in the UK. Using the 'denying benefit' approach, attention is being paid to effect a crackdown on the markets and transactions of stolen goods. This technique is known as 'market reduction approach' discourages the thieves when they find no conduits to sell the stolen goods (Sutton *et al*, 2001). The graffiti cleaning and use of speed humps are in the same direction. The displays of one piece of shoe or part of a devise that cannot of any use are the example of this technique.

Reducing Frustration and Stress

At crowded places, the efficient queuing and polite handling by the dealers are capable of managing the situational bursts out. The expanded and convenient seating, passage, and soothing effect of music on such public or semi public places tend to cut down the possibilities of individual or collective aggression.

The Other Situational Measures

There are several other efficient measures that have produced good results. Rule setting, peer pressure, post instructions, alert conscience, assist compliance, control of drug and alcohol are a few of them.

Many ordinary people commit less-serious crimes, despite realizing that they shouldn't. They are motivated by reasoning like "This store is more costlier," or "I always work overtime and don't get paid enough," or "This store is so big, they won't miss this one pair of pants."

The following set of crime prevention techniques involves increasing the pressure on people to do what they know is right in the first place.

(1) Set Rules or Procedures that Explain Acceptable Conduct-For example, implementing a refund policy at a retail store can reduce the amount of refund fraud.

(2) Remind People that the Offence is Wrong-Signs in New York City's Port Authority bus terminal read "Smoking here is illegal, selfish, and rude."

(3) Limit Access to Things that Reduce People's Abilities to Think-The best example of this is alcohol.

(4) Make it Easy for People to "Do the Right Thing."- Put a cash register right by the door, or put a garbage can just outside your small grocery so people won't litter so much.

Fixing broken window: In their work, James Q. Wilson and George Kelling have explained as to how a sense of neglect of community in terms its upkeep and order affects the chain of crimes. Restoring order in possible manners can be of immense value to crime reduction efforts.

CRIME PREVENTION THROUGH ENVIRONMENTAL DESIGN (CPTED)

The basic idea in CPTED is that the physical environment can be changed or manipulated to produce behavioural effects and changes leading to the resultant reduction in the incidence and fear of crime, thereby improving the quality of life, and enhancing profitability for business. Like all situational crime prevention strategies, CPTED has as one of its primary aims to reduce the opportunity for specific crimes to occur. Where CPTED differs from traditional target hardening strategies is that the techniques employed seek to use environmental factors to affect the perceptions of all users of a given space - addressing not only the opportunity for the crime but also perceptions of fear on the part of those who may otherwise be victims.

Drawing heavily on behavioural psychology, CPTED concepts and strategies take advantage of the relationships that exist between people and their environments. The way we react to an environment is more often than not determined by the cues we are picking up from that environment. Those things that make normal or legitimate users of a space feel safe (such as good lighting), make abnormal or illegitimate users of the same space feel unsafe in pursuing undesirable behaviours (such as stealing from motor vehicles). *(http://www.cpted.com.au/)*

THE 'HOT' ANALYSIS

The identification and elimination of vulnerable or 'hot' locations and objects is the key approach in SCP. The crime 'reductionists' have developed remarkable understanding in this area. A software exploring hot spot is also available now (*http://www.crimestat.com/*). The main contention in the approach is that much crime can be avoided if resources and managerial planning is timely employed. Following are some significant measures in this process (Clarke, 1999).

(i) Exploration of Hot points - the places with higher level of incidents concentration.

(ii) Identification of Hot places–the geographic locations, which attract larger criminal attention due several vulnerability factors.

(iii) Analysis of Hot routes–certain routes are relatively unsafe. They facilitate criminal movement.

(iv) Identification of Hot objects–crime is also directed in greater amount towards special goods and substances due their value and access. Electronic instruments and objects are, for instance, come in this category.

(v) Recognizing Hot people–certain people are more prone to criminal offending behaviour. They may be targeted more frequently due their peculiar set of characteristics.

NEW DEVELOPMENTS

The SCP is about managerial skills and tactical planning. Recently, the companies involved in the manufacturing of security devises have shown immense interests in developing new solutions to the crimonogenic problems experienced by the people in their day-to-day life. The use of personal alarms, for example, amongst the foreign female students in urban towns is getting popular as this gives them a confidence that in the event of any street crime or offending advancements the same can be used to attract public attention. This small devise has become an article in the bags of such persons who require much of their time away from home. The Observer (April 27, 2003) reported that Karrysafe, the first company in Europe to design bags and fashion accessories, which protect users against street crime, was launched in 2001. It created bags with built in alarms. The bags guard against the four top methods of street theft: 'dipping' (by pickpockets), grabbing, lifting and slashing. If grabbed, for example, the strap gives way, allowing the thief to take the bag without resorting to violence. Then it triggers a 138-decibel alarm that they cannot turn off.

Anti-crime measures have been taken to the level of fabric too. 'Techno-textiles' are increasingly being used to foil criminals, with polymers such as Kevlar and Nomex, which are stab-, slash-, and bulletproof, incorporated into bag and jacket designs. Levi's has already produced an 'e-wear' jacket, in conjunction with Philips. Pioneered at MIT in Boston, 'e-wear' has become a strong interest area for electronics and clothing manufacturers. With street crime on the rise, a key issue is the portability and visibility of items such as mobile phones, personal stereos and computers. The Levi's jacket was an attempt to design a garment that could both carry, with comfort, these items, while protecting the wearer.

This is just the tip of the iceberg. Many designers see a day when the victim of a street assault may be able to ward off an attacker with ease. They cite fabrics that can change state to become 'anti-touch' (suddenly sharp for example), or light up and emit an alarm. These garments could be made from impenetrable fabrics and, on attack, release a permanent stain to mark out the perpetrator.

REVIEW OF RESEARCH AND DEVELOPMENTS IN SITUATIONAL CRIME PREVENTION AND CRIME REDUCTION

There have been studies in the recent past on different aspects of situational crime prevention in many parts of the world. A few studies could be cited here to reflect the focus on this subject. Lewis and Sullivan [1979] carried out a study on citizen attitudes relevant in crime prevention. Laycock [1985] was of the view that property marking plays a deterrent role to domestic burglary. Similarly, public lighting and women's experience on fear of crime was studied by Painter [1990] and Atkins *et al.* [1991]. Police patrolling in hot spots [Sherman and Weisburd, 1995], repeat burglary [Anderson *et al*, 1995), prevention of burglary [Stockdale and Gresham, 1995), case studies on CCTV in town centers [Brown, 1995], police handling of crime [Marvell and Moody, 1996] are some of the studies focusing upon various situational dimension in reducing crime. Smith [1996] highlighted the role of crime prevention through environmental design in preventing vehicle theft. A conceptual interpretation of crime prevention was carried out by Sherman *et al.* (1997). Lab (1997) examined the crime prevention approaches by evaluation methods. A similar study has also been carried out by Jordan [1998]. Reducing theft from shopping bags in city center markets by Poyner and Webb [1997], crime and small-scale places [Taylor 1998], preventing of residential burglary [Bennett and Durie 1999], perceptions of safety at night in different lighting conditions [Boyce *et al.* 2000], survey of stolen goods [Allen 2000] are some of the more studies highlighting the importance of situational crime prevention. Witte and Witt [2000] carried out economic theories of crime causation. Blake and Coupe [2001] studied the impact of single and two-officer patrols in arresting burglars. Market reduction approach [Sutton *et al.* 2001], police response time [Di Tella and Schargrodsky 2001], Street lighting and crime [Farrington and Welsh, 2002], crime and midsize cities [Goodman 2002], Effects of CCTV [Welsh and Farrington 2002], patterns in residential burglary [Martin, 2002], effect of police crackdowns [Scott, 2003] and [Skogan & Frydl 2003], evaluation of the target hardening project [Casey. *et al.* and Segessenmann, 2003], intelligence and policing [Cope 2004], decision-making by Offenders [Hearnden and Magill, 2004], management of crime scene [Williams 2004] and market reduction approach by Australian Institute of Criminology (2005) are some more studies suggesting the situational approach in crime prevention.

The situational crime prevention is relatively a new practice. The major developments in this area are presented in the following heads:

International Status

Since 1980 onwards crime prevention moved from being of trivial intellectual interest to become a major concern of governments in most of the nations. The discernible trend is that the governments, in the recent past, in several nations apparently promoted the policies leading to community safety and crime reduction and not essentially launching 'crackdown on crime' type approach.

As stated earlier that SCP practice has been massively nurtured and improvised in the UK and subsequently it has emerged as a frontline technique to combat crime. The Kirkholt project in Britain, for instance, paved the way to undertake situational crime prevention measures in a big way. This project began in 1989 involving variety of professionals like city officials, police, social workers and the university in tackling repeat victimization on the Kirkholt housing estate in Rochdale. The project personnel organized a neighbourhood watch programme to surround victimized homes and encouraged residents to upgrade locks and bolts as well as remove coin-operated electric and gas meters (to reduce readily available cash).

The Kirkholt programme resulted in a 75 per cent drop in burglaries within a period of three years. Lower gas/electricity meter losses and the reduced amount of property/cash stolen covered the programme's costs. And it saved about $3.84 for every dollar invested in police time, detection, sentencing, probation and detention costs. The Kirkholt and other successful crime prevention programmes convinced the British government in 1998 to adopt the Crime and Disorder Act, which joined local authorities and police with other agencies-including social services, education, probation, child protection and the courts.

Prompted by the success of such initiatives, the Home Office in the UK that is primarily responsible for developing the policies and programmes and their implementation, has subsequently launched its 'Crime Reduction' programme in 2000's. The host of measures targeting virtually all sorts of offences are now being undertaken. A sum to the tune of £450 million is being spent on these programmes.

Besides UK, US and Australia are the two other countries where significant works in this area have been conducted. We can review the country wise review of some significant studies conducted in this area.

United Kingdom

It seems an uphill task to review and document all works on the subject conducted in the UK. There is a chronology of incidents and developments in the UK that is responsible for the matured progression of SCP. A Tabular display as given below documents important landmark development in this field.

Key Development in Crime Prevention Since 1975

Crime as opportunity	1976
Designing out crime	1980
Coordinating crime prevention efforts	1980
Situational crime prevention	1980
First British Crime survey report	1983
Crime prevention unit set up	1983
Home office standing conference	1983
First crime prevention unit paper	1985
Five Town Initiative	1986
Gas and suicide	1988
Safer Cities	1988
Crimc Concern 1988	1988
First Kirkholt Report	1988
Crash Helmets & motor bike theft	1989
Home Office Circular 44/99	1990
Morgan report	1991
Police Research Group set up	1992
First CCTV challenge	1995
Repeat Victimization task Force set up	1996
First issue of International Journal of Risk,	1996

Contd...

Security and Crime Prevention	
Policing and Reducing Crime Unit set up	1998
'Opportunity Makes the Thief'- PRS- 98	1998
Crime & Disorder Act	1998
Beating Crime	1998
Crime Reduction Programme	1999
Safety in Numbers	1999
Crime targets Task Force	1999
Calling Time on Crime	2000
The Home Office Policing and Crime Reduction Directorate	2000
Appointment of Regional Crime Directors	2000
Tool kit for Crime Reduction	2001
Launch of Community Safety Journal	2002
Community Safety Partnership, The Audit Commission Report	2003

Initiatives

The following section would present a gist of certain SCP based initiatives undertaken in the UK.

Secured by Design (SBD) is a police initiative to encourage the building industry to adopt crime prevention measures in development of design to assist in reducing the opportunity for crime and the fear of crime, creating a safer and more secure environment.

The Building Safer Communities (BSC) fund, announced by the Home Secretary in January 2003, is a key element of the Government's crime reduction strategy.

Reducing Burglary Initiative (RBI) Home Office. Some 247-burglary reduction projects were sanctioned that covered 2.1 million households that have suffered around 110,000 burglarioes. The evaluation carried out by the independent agencies and experts were reported by Kodz and Pease, (2003). The findings in the SDPs area showed that burglaries rates fell in 40 of the 55 SDPs areas. The rates of burglaries were compared with non-project areas and it was found that the rates the project areas achieved 15% to 20% reduction (Kodz and Pease, 2003).

Vehicle Crime Reduction Team(VCRT): In 1998, this scheme was launched. The trends in crime against vehicles in the UK have always been disturbing. The current figures (2002-3) of all types of vehicle crimes, as per BCS estimates, are 23.66 million. This scheme is a strategic initiative to cut the incidence. The target was to reduce this crime by 30 per cent (Sallybanks & Brown, 1999).

Hot product Focus: The products that are lucrative for stealing are called hot products. Clarke (1999) reported that certain ways, based on hot product focus, to prevent theft in many studies. The list includes parts marking (Rhodes, 1997), electronic key systems (Hazelbaker, 1997), vehicle tracking devices (Ayres and Levitt, 1998), and security-coded radios (Braga and Clarke, 1994). An even wider range of successes has been reported in reducing robberies for cash, including in banks (Gabor,1990; Grandjean, 1990; Clarke et al., 1991), sub-post offices (Ekblom,1987), betting shops (Clarke and McGrath, 1990), convenience stores (Hunter and Jeffery (1997) and buses (Stanford Research Institute, 1970). This apart, the growing use of plastic cards for payment and the ATM are also in the same direction.

Street Crime Initiatives (SCI): This was started in March 2002 involving ten police forces. This programme resulted in substantial crime reduction. There has been, for example, a 10% reduction in the number of robberies compared to last year;

CCTV Initiatives: A brief account of CCTV initiative has already presented in the Report. The CCTV performance and planning can also be seen at a special *website- http://www.crimereduction.gov.uk/cctvminisite1.htm.* There are 684 CCTV schemes in the UK worth over £17omillion. Evaluation Studies show a 41% overall decrease in vehicle crime in car parks where CCTV has been installed - contributing to the Government's overall target of a national 30% reduction in vehicle crime by 2004.

Designing out Crime: The crime reduction based on the environmental panning and space management fall in this category. The Bristol City Council and local police Architectural Liaison Officers (ALOs) have jointly developed a set of guidelines that ensures that the principles of Crime Prevention Through Environmental Design (CPTED).

Other Crime Reduction Initiatives of the Home Office: Following are the other initiatives for reducing crime initiated by the Home office.

- Rural Crime
- Safer Schools
- Safer Hospitals
- Technologies for Improving Home Security
- Communities against Drugs
- Small Retailers in Deprived Areas.
- Crime stoppers
- The Safer Communities Initiative (SCI)
- Safe Street

Electronic article surveillance (EAS) is a method to discourage shoplifting. Introduced in 1968-69, this technology has proved to an effective anti-shoplifting measure. This electronic technique is about an electronically detectable element that is attached on the article. The transmitters and receivers at the exit of shops can immediately detect the article if someone tries to take it away.

Focusing on specific crime problems, several studies could be referred here those applied various methods of situational crime prevention in tackling the problems successfully.

Gloria Laycock highlighted role of Property Marking (1985) and SCP applications in reducing burglary from chemists' shops (1985) in the UK. Southall and Ekblom (1985) discussed about SCP and car security while measures against Prepayment Coin Meters were explored by Nigel Hill (1986). Clarke and Lester (1989) discussed the situational aspects of suicide prevention. 'Opportunity Makes the Thief' was the title that attracted wider attention. This publication by Felson & Clarke (1998) elaborated the opportunity and crime model by suggesting ten principles. Notably, Clarke (1997) has published an edited volume from US comprising a sixteen techniques model for opportunity reduction that is being used everywhere with appropriate modifications. The main techniques in SCP were: *controlling facilitator* in case of credit card and fraud (Masuda,1997), *deflecting offenders* in case of shop thefts in city centers (Poyner and Webb, 1997), *denying benefits* by reducing the rewards in shoplifting (DiLonardo & Clarke, 1996), *formal surveillance* in case of thefts by employees (Masuda, 1996),target hardening in case of robberies in post office (Ekblom, 1997).

In a study by Husain and Storey (1991) found the effect on street light on the likelihood of crime incidence in the community. The problem of repeat burglaries and their prevention was highlighted in a study by Chenery and Pease (1994). Poyner and Webb (1997) made a study showing the SCP's effects on theft from shopping bags. There can be hot products attracting greater criminal concentration. A study showing this feature by Clarke (1999) is worth mention here. Read and Tilley (2000) elucidated as to how the crime reduction could be made applicable by the law enforcement agencies. Curtin et al (2001) showed the process of developing crime reduction plans. A different approach to situational crime prevention in terms of ethical and social aspects has also been presented in a study by Hirsch, Garland & Wakefield (2000). Sutton *et al* (2001) discussed about the impact of market reduction approach on cases of theft. Studies by *Clarke* and John (2003) Bullock &Tilley (2003) on problem solving methods and crime reduction respectively are also remarkable. The application of SCP measures was also studied in case of alcohol reduction (Plant and Harrison, 2003). The CCTV, a major SCP application, was found to be significantly effective in preventing crimes in cases of 22 evaluations carried out by Welsh and Ferrington (2003). Similarly, the improved street lighting was found to be deterrent for crimes in a study by Ferrington and Welsh (2002).

US: The basic ideas rooted in the environmental design aspects in situational crime prevention are inspired by the pioneering works by Oscar Newman who was instrumental in bringing architect aspect in crime prevention tasks. His ideas of 'defensible space' (1972) and several other studies later laid the foundation of Environmental Criminology in the later years. Jeffrey was also working in the same direction and his study (1971) was also remarkable. The most recent studies (Schneider (2000) and Timothy (2000) in this field in the US link themselves with these works. Interestingly enough, the UK might be the birthplace of practice of SCP. But all the theories in the root of SCP were developed in the US. The Routine Activity Theory (Cohen and Felson, 1979), Rational Choice Theory (Cornish and Clarke, 1986,Clarke and Felson,1993) and Life style Theory (Gottfredson and Hirschi, 1990) are also in the same vein. Specifically on situational crime prevention, the study by Felson (1994) is cited to be of high reckoning. The compilation of successful case studies of SCP by Clarke (1993) is one of the most cited works in this area.

In the 2000's, lot of interest was shown towards Kelling and Cole's (1996) idea of 'fixing broken window'. This preventive approach explained as to how a sense of neglect of community in terms its upkeep and order affects the chain of crimes. Restoring order in possible manners can be of immense value to crime reduction efforts.

Lately, two books (Catch Me If You Can: The True Story of a Real Fake by Redding & Abagnale (2000) and The Art of the Steal : How to Protect Yourself and Your Business from Fraud, *America's #1 Crime* by Abagnale (2002) published in the US stirred the people and media. They talked about the real life experiences of Abagnale in deceiving the business and corporate sectors.

Other countries: The Australian Institute of Criminology has conducted some studies with a focus on situational crime prevention. They can be seen at- *http://www.aic.gov.au/publications/crimprev/* Geason and Wilson(1992) examined how situational crime prevention can be used by in a variety of retail establishments to combat robbery. Roderick (1995) discussed about crime prevention against business while Indermaur (1999) explored SCP in case of violent crime. The International Crime Prevention Centre, Montreal, Canada, has also published good amount of publications on several aspects of crime prevention. There exits international network of UN crime prevention agencies in various countries of the world.

But the focus of these agencies has not thus far on the situational aspects of crime prevention.

Many resources and on line publications on situational crime prevention are also available at- *http://crimeprevention.rutgers.edu/resources/resources.htm*

(ii) National Status: There are general studies on crime prevention in India. However, on the aspects of situational crime prevention or crime reduction, there is a visible dearth of works in India. Regrettably, no study strictly falling in the domain of the proposed work could be found. This acute penury of research in this domain underscores the need to undertake this kind of works in India.

ORIGIN OF THE RESEARCH PROBLEM

The origin of research problem could be traced in the virtual failures of existing criminal justice agencies in bringing the crime down to the optimum level of public satisfaction. The need to look for methods that could quickly result in crime reduction is indeed crucial in the present day situations. We have lived quite long with the experience that the police performance is not going to ameliorate overnight. Nor does the justice dispensing is going to be improved. The appointed commission/committees too have a frustrating past owing to non-implementation of suggested recommendations. Criminologists have also been almost unable to suggest any actionable prescription that could be readily used by the law enforcement agencies. The pursuits of locating causes of crime in the biology or sociology of offenders have seldom resulted in any practical solutions to cut the day-to-day crime that are experienced by the people. The all-pervasive climate of disillusionment presses for something that could *work instantaneously*.

The basic thrust of the proposed research is also backed by the Model Police Bill proposed by the National Police Commission that says that one of the duties of the police must be to: (i) identify problems and *situations* that are likely to result in commission of crimes; (ii) *reduce the opportunities* for the commission of crimes through preventive patrol and other prescribed police measures

The answers to this grim scenario seem to lie in the applications of crime reduction and situational crime prevention practices. The merit of these practices are that they visibly and instantly show the amount of crime reduced by the application of a particular set of measures.

THE PRESENT STUDY: STATEMENT OF PROBLEM

The present study intends to examine the notion of situational crime prevention. The idea is to analyze the opportunity theory and various measures of crime reduction. The exercise mainly intends to identify the presence of situational element in certain crimes against property thereby exploring the possibility of framing SCP measure in Indian context. With the help of a sample survey, the present study aims at highlighting the factors and combinations making the targets situationally vulnerable for crime. A critical review of concept and theoretical structure pertaining to SCP has also made in this study.

OBJECTIVES

Following are the main objectives of this study.

1. To assess the extent and type of crimes that could be attributed to the ten principles of opportunity developed by R V Clarke.
2. To explore the situational dimensions attributable to the occurrence of crime in the selected sites.
3. To consider the opportunity theory model in case of selected types of crimes.
4. To assess the situational attributes in crime occurrence with the help of the perceptions of crime victims

METHODOLOGY

Sampling Design

To approach the objectives of the study, a sample of 400 crimes took place in the chosen town areas viz. Bhopal and Sagar in the state of Madhya Pradesh have been considered. The cases of thefts and burglary and some other property offences have been included in the universe of the study. To examine the applicability of opportunity theory, the victims of these cases have been interviewed with the help of an interview schedule entailing the essentials of the concept in question.

Tools Used

The literature survey as well as online resources on this subject have been explored and then tools for collection of data have been devised. These tools were developed for conducting the survey. In this connection "Interview schedule" was formulated which include, crime scene variables, owner's behavior variables, victims related variables, general indicators of the locality, general indicators of vehicle theft as well as opinion survey.

Data Collection

The data have been collected in the two cities of Madhya Pradesh viz. Bhopal and Sagar. The first phase included secondary data that were collected through the police stations of Bhopal and Sagar. Both the cities have been divided into two halves i.e. Hot Spot and Cool Spot. These breakups have been made on the criteria of crime-population ratio. Accordingly, two hot spot police stations and two cool spot police stations have been identified in both the cities. After identifying the eight police stations (four each from the two cities comprising of two each hot and cool spot locations) of Bhopal and Sagar, the secondary data have been collected, which included the cases of Theft, Burglary, Dacoity, Robbery, Pick pocketing, Vehicle theft during the year 2006. The information from the secondary sources included name and address of the victim, date and time of occurrence, place of occurrence, act under which case was registered, loss of property due to crime as well as accused arrested or not. After collecting the secondary data, the survey of victims in these crimes was conducted in both the cities. A sample of 200 victims in each city Bhopal and Sagar [100 from cool spot locations as well as 100 from hot spot locations) was contacted for data collection. The Process of collecting data was informal interview as well as focused discussions held with the individual victims of crime.

EXTENT OF DATA COLLECTION

Amount of Information Sought form Respondents

Survey Town	*Hot spot area*	*Cool spot area*	*No. of Question applied per Respondents*	*Total No of Questions asked*
Bhopal	100	100	67	67 X 200 = 13,400
Sagar	100	100	67	67 X 200 = 13,400
Total	200	200	-	26,800

DATA ANALYSIS

The data collected in the study was subjected to advanced statistical analysis. The process of data analysis involved the transferring of coded data on the Statistical Package for Social Sciences [SPSS] spread sheet and then the appropriate tools and tests have been identified for analyzing the data. The major tests applied were: Chi square test, Kendall tau b, correlation test, regression analysis, unstandardized β, standard error, standardized β, t-value, analysis of variance [ANOVA], correlations co-efficient [R], coefficient of determination [R^2], Adjusted R^2, standard error of the estimate, F-ratio, pearson chi-square, likelihood ratio, linear-by-linear association, mann-whitney U, wilcoxon W, kruskal-wallis test. There were 67 variables in the study which generated 53 frequency tables, 20 cross-tabulation tables and 54 tables concerning advanced tests.

Tabulation Plan

Type of Tables	*No of Tables Generated*
Frequency tables	53
Cross-tabulation [Chi square test, Kendall tau b]	20
Association of independency & dependency [Chi-square, correlation]	16
Regression analysis [unstandardized β, standard error, standardized β, t-value]	22
Analysis of variance [ANOVA]	21
Model Parameters [Correlations co-efficient [R], coefficient of determination [R^2], Adjusted R^2, standard error of the estimate, F-ratio]	21
Pearson chi-square, likelihood ratio, linear-by-linear association	18
Mann-whitney U, wilcoxon W, kruskal-wallis test	54
Total	225

Significance of the Study: The significance of the present study could be elucidated in the following statements.

1. The subject under study is virtually non-existent in researches in criminology in India.
2. The proposed project could help in action based exercises for developing and examine the efficacy of situational crime prevention intervention.
3. It is likely to contribute to enhancing the capability of police and satisfaction of beneficiaries and stakeholders.
4. The project may lead to the development of tools based on managerial, environmental designing and technological inputs in crime reduction.
5. The theoretical understanding about SCP would also be enhanced by the outcome of the study.

LIMITATIONS OF THE STUDY

1. The study is limited to the Bhopal and Sagar cities of Madhya Pradesh.
2. The study is limited to cases of Theft, Burglary, Dacoity, Robbery, Pick pocketing, Vehicle theft only.
3. The study is limited to registered cases of crime in both the cities.
4. The study is limited to the hot spot and cool spot locations of both the cities.
5. The study is limited to the situational crime prevention variables.

PICTURESQUE OF THE STUDY

For the sake of convenience of readers, the present study is divided into nine chapter, *First:* Introduction, *Second:* Situational Correlates of Crime, *Third*: Contextual Analysis of Situational Crime, *Fourth*: Analysis of Situational Crime Variables Part-I, *Fifth*: Analysis of Situational Crime Variables Part-II, *Sixth*: Advanced Analysis of Situational Correlates of Crime, *Seventh*: Opinions of Victims on Situational Crime Factors, *Eighth*: Summary & Conclusions and References.

2

SITUATIONAL CORRELATES OF CRIME

The present chapter offers the preliminary analysis of data collected from the two cities i.e. Bhopal and Sagar in respect of several situational correlates of crime. The findings have been discussed by classifying the cities in terms of hot and cool spot locations. The hot spot refers to the places where the concentration of crime exceeds the average rate of crime of that city and cool spot denotes the locations where the rate of crime is markedly lower than the average rate of crime of the concerned city. The findings in this chapter are regarding the frequency distribution of main variables of the study. The key variables pertain to crime, owners' traits, victim characteristics, objects of theft and opinion of victims.

CRIME SCENE VARIABLES

An attempt has been made to find out the situational crime prevention variables in the hot spot and cool spot areas of Bhopal and Sagar cities. Table 1 shows the frequency and percentage distribution of data collected from various police stations of Bhopal and Sagar Towns.

Table 2 shows crime category variables in the hot spot and cool spot locations of Bhopal and Sagar cities. This Table denotes that in hot spot location of Bhopal. Maximum crime is of theft from shop and business places [37 per cent] while minimum crime occurrence was of vehicle theft [30 per cent]. In case of Bhopal cool spot places, the maximum crime occurrence was of vehicle theft [51 per cent] as compared to minimum crime occurrence of theft from residence [6 per cent]. In case of Sagar hot spot locations, it has been observed that maximum crime is of vehicle theft [49 per cent] as compared to minimum crime of theft from residence. In case of Sagar cool spot places, the maximum crime occurrence was of vehicle theft [42 per cent] as compared to minimum crime occured of burglary from shop [1 per cent].

Table 1
Showing Distribution of Data from Police Stations of Bhopal and Sagar Cities

Bhopal			*Sagar*		
Police Station	*Frequency*	*Per cent*	*Police Station*	*Frequency*	*Per cent*
Bhopal Kotwali	60	30.0	Civil Lines	21	10.5
Mangalwara	40	20.0	Gopal Gang	59	29.5
T. T. Nagar	56	28.0	Kotwali Sagar	60	30.0
Jahangirabad	44	22.0	Motinagar	39	19.5
Cant	21	10.5			
Total	200	100.0	Total	200	100.0

Table 2
Showing Crime Distribution in Police Stations of Bhopal and Sagar Cities

	Bhopal		*Sagar*	
Crime Category	*Hot Spot*	*Cool Spot*	*Hot Spot*	*Cool Spot*
Theft from shop/ Business Place	37	43	27	33
Theft from residence	33	6	24	24
Burglary from shop				1
Vehicle theft	30	51	49	42
Total	100	100	100	100

Table 3 shows the frequency distribution of crime occurrence week in various police stations of Bhopal and Sagar cities. It has been observed from the study that most crime occur in first week [29 per cent], whereas crime occurrence was minimum in third week [22 per cent] in the hot spot a locations of Bhopal as compared to cool spot maximum crime occur in second week [29 per cent], where as minimum crime occur in fifth week [4 per cent]. In case of

Sagar city hot spot the maximum crime occur in second week [28 per cent], where as minimum crime occur in fifth week [7 per cent] as compared to cool spot maximum crime occur in second week [26 per cent], whereas minimum crime occur in fifth week [6 per cent].

Table 3
Showing Distribution of Crime Occurrence as per Week

	Bhopal		*Sagar*	
Week of Occurrence	*Hot Spot*	*Cool Spot*	*Hot Spot*	*Cool Spot*
First Week	29	17	23	25
Second Week	23	29	28	26
Third Week	22	23	22	20
Fourth Week	26	27	19	22
Fifth Week		4	7	6
Total	100	100	99	99
NA/NR			1	1
Total	100	100	100	100

Table 4
Frequency Distribution of Crime Occurrence as per Time

	Bhopal		*Sagar*	
Time of Occurrence	*Hot Spot*	*Cool Spot*	*Hot Spot*	*Cool Spot*
6 to 11.59 AM	3	4	11	3
12.0 to 5.59 PM	25	28	30	18
6 to 11.59 PM	37	31	22	32
12 to 5.59 AM	34	36	36	44
Total	99	99	99	97
NA/ NR	1	1	1	3
Total	100	100	100	100

Table 4 describes the frequency distribution of time of crime occurrence in various police stations of Bhopal and Sagar town. It has been observed that in case of Bhopal hot spot most crime incidents take place during night 6 to 12 PM [37 per cent] where as a few crime occur in morning 6 to 12 AM [3 per cent] as compared to cool spot location the most crime incidents take place at night 12 to 6 AM [36 per cent] where as a few crime occur in morning 6 to 12 AM [4 per cent]. In case of Sagar hot spot location, the most crime incidents take place during night 12 to 6 AM [36 per cent] where as a few crime occur in morning 6 to 12 AM [11 per cent] as compared to cool spot location the most crime incidents take place at night 12 to 6 AM [44 per cent] where as a few crime occur in morning 6 to 12 AM [3 per cent].

Table 5
Frequency Distribution of Crime Scene Locations

	Bhopal		*Sagar*	
Location of Scene of Crime	*Hot Spot*	*Cool Spot*	*Hot Spot*	*Cool Spot*
Open	62	77	70	57
Indoor/ Close	37	23	28	42
Office/ Institution	1		2	
Total	100	100	100	99
NA/ NR				1
Total	100	100	100	100

Table 5 shows the frequency distribution of crime scene locations falling within various police stations of Bhopal and Sagar city. Table denotes that in hot spot locations of Bhopal city maximum crime occured in open area [62 per cent] followed by 37 percent in indoor location. In case of cool spot places of Bhopal city the maximum crime occured in open area [77 per cent] as compared to minimum crime occured in indoor area [23 per cent]. Similar trend was noticed in case of hot and cool spot locations in Sagar city as well.

Table 6 shows the frequency distribution of outdoor scene of crime locations in various police stations of Bhopal and Sagar cities. It has been observed that most incidence of crime in densely populated area took place in outdoor location [37 per cent], whereas in thinly populated [12 per cent] location of Bhopal attracted lesser crime incidence as compared to cool spot locations. In case of Sagar, hot spot locations and densely populated area had the highest incidence of crime [29 per cent], where as minimum crime occur in thinly populated [17 per cent].

Table 6
Frequency Distribution of Outdoor Scene of Crime Locations Variable

	Bhopal		Sagar	
Nature of outdoor scene of crime	*Hot Spot*	*Cool Spot*	*Hot Spot*	*Cool Spot*
Densely Populated	37	52	29	28
Moderately Populated	23	29	26	21
Thinly Populated	12	2	17	9
Total	72	83	72	58
NA/ NR	28	17	28	42
Total	100	100	100	100

Table 7
Frequency Distribution of Lighting Arrangement on the Immediate Street

	Bhopal		Sagar	
Lighting arrangement on the immediate street	*Hot Spot*	*Cool Spot*	*Hot Spot*	*Cool Spot*
Inadequate	18	8	17	25
Adequate	54	49	25	26
Moderate	8	12	19	22
Total	80	69	61	73
NA/NR	20	31	39	27
Total	100	100	100	100

Table 7 describes the frequency distribution of lighting arrangement adjacent to the areas falling under various police stations of Bhopal and Sagar city. It has been observed in the context of Bhopal hot spots that the lighting arrangements were adequate [54 per cent] whereas lighting arrangements were moderate in some cases [8 per cent]. As compared to cool spot locations, the maximum lighting arrangement on the immediate street were adequate [49 per cent] whereas lighting arrangement, on the immediate street were inadequate [8 per cent]. In case of Sagar hot spot locations, the lighting arrangement, on the immediate street were adequate [25 per cent] where as lighting arrangement on the immediate street were inadequate [17 per cent] as compared to cool spot location, the lighting arrangement, on the immediate street do not show any significant difference in these categories.

Table 8
Frequency Distribution of Lighting Arrangement on the Premises

	Bhopal		*Sagar*	
Lighting arrangement in the premises	*Hot Spot*	*Cool Spot*	*Hot Spot*	*Cool Spot*
Inadequate	19	20	23	30
Adequate	50	31	19	17
Moderate	10	18	20	28
Total	79	69	62	75
NA/NR	21	31	38	25
Total	100	100	100	100

Table 8 shows the availability of lighting arrangement on the premises in crime locations in the area following within the police stations of Bhopal and Sagar District. In the Bhopal hot spot location, the lighting arrangement on the premises were adequate [50 per cent] where as the lighting arrangement on the premises were moderate [10 per cent] as compared to cool spot location the maximum lighting arrangement, on the premises were adequate [31 per cent] whereas lighting arrangement on the premises were moderate [18 per cent]. In case of Sagar hot spot locations, the lighting arrangement, on the premises were more or less similar in these three categories as compared to cool spot location where the lighting arrangement, on the premises were inadequate [30 per cent] where as the lighting arrangement, on the premises were adequate [17 per cent].

Table 9
Frequency Distribution of the Variable "Was it Easy for Offender to Commit this Crime"

	Bhopal		*Sagar*	
Was it easy for offender to commit this crime?	*Hot Spot*	*Cool Spot*	*Hot Spot*	*Cool Spot*
Yes	42	34	45	41
No	58	66	55	57
Total	100	100	100	98
NA/ NR				2
Total				100

Table 9 shows the responses of subject on "was it easy for offender to commit this crime"? It has been observed that maximum respondents of Bhopal hot spot location viewed that it was not easy for offender to commit this crime [58 per cent], while many respondents found that it was easy for offender to commit this crime [42 per cent]. In the cool spot locations almost similar trend was noticed. In case of Sagar hot spot as well as cool spot locations, there was not any significant difference in this regard.

Table 10
Frequency Distribution of the Variable Location of Crime Scene

	Bhopal		*Sagar*	
Location of crime scene	*Hot Spot*	*Cool Spot*	*Hot Spot*	*Cool Spot*
Hot Spot	99	3	100	1
Cool Spot	1	97	0	99
Total	100	100	100	100

In order to evaluate the situational factor in crime, attempt has been made to classify the crime locations into hot and cool spot categories. Hot spot refers to area where the maximum concentration of crime was found and cool spot was the place attracting lesser number of crimes. Table 10 indicates the frequencies of crime in both the locations.

Table 11
Frequency Distribution Predominant Characteristics of Locality

	Bhopal		*Sagar*	
Predominant characteristic of locality	*Hot Spot*	*Cool Spot*	*Hot Spot*	*Cool Spot*
Residential	40	13	43	39
Commercial	31	33	17	18
Mixed	21	53	22	42
Others	7	1	18	1
Total	99	100	100	100
NA/NR	1			
Total	100			

Nature of crime occurrence varies according to character of the locality. Table 11 displays the hot and cool spot locations in four major types of localities. Majority of hot spot locations in Bhopal [40%] and Sagar [43%] were situated in the residential settings whereas the ratio of these locations was 31 and 17 per cent in the commercial locality. The presence of cool spot in Sagar city was up to 39 per cent in residential settings and it was only 13 per cent in case of Bhopal. The cool spot locations were 33 per cent in commercial setting in the city of Bhopal and the corresponding figure was 18 per cent in case of Sagar city.

Table 12
Frequency Distribution of Surveillance/Security Arrangements

	Bhopal		*Sagar*	
Surveillance/Security arrangements	*Hot Spot*	*Cool Spot*	*Hot Spot*	*Cool Spot*
Satisfactory	14	3	0	0
Average	34	51	34	23
Unsatisfactory	50	46	65	77
Others	1	0	1	0
Total	99	100	100	100
NA/NR	1			
Total	100			

The presence of surveillance and security measures is a situational deterrent to criminals. Table 12 surveys the availability of such measures across hot and cool spot locations. There were only a negligible percentage of respondents in the hot spot location in Bhopal [14%] showing satisfaction to surveillance measures and no one was satisfied with these measures in the city of Sagar. In fact, there was average satisfaction with these security measures among the respondents in Bhopal [85%] and in Sagar [57%]. Majority of the respondents in Bhopal and Sagar were unsatisfied [50 to 77 %] with these measures.

OWNER'S BEHAVIOUR

Table 13 shows the frequency distribution of the variable as to how much time victim spent at home. In Bhopal hot spot locations, most victims spend 6 to 10 hours time in home [71 per cent] and in cool spot locations most victims spent 6 to 10 hours time in home [80 per cent]. In case of Sagar hot spot locations, most victims spent 11 to 15 hours time in home [50 per cent]. In cool spot locations, 55 per cent victims spent 6 to 10 hours time in home, while only 8 per cent victims spent 16 to 20 hours time at home.

Table 13
Showing Distribution of "How Much Time Victim Spent at Home"

	Bhopal		*Sagar*	
Average time spent at home	*Hot Spot*	*Cool Spot*	*Hot Spot*	*Cool Spot*
1 to 5 Hours	1	1	1	
6 to 10 Hours	71	80	44	55
11 to 15 Hours	23	18	50	37
16 to 20 Hours	5	1	4	8
Total	100	100	99	100
NA/ NR			1	
Total			100	

Table 14
Frequency Distribution of "How Much Time Victim Remains Away from the Target"

	Bhopal		*Sagar*	
How much time remains away from the target	*Hot Spot*	*Cool Spot*	*Hot Spot*	*Cool Spot*
1 to 5 Hours	52	51	64	59
6 to 10 Hours	15	31	28	24
11 to 15 Hours	2	1	1	
16 to 20 Hours	31		3	6
Total	100	83	96	89
NA/NR		17	4	11
Total		100	100	100

Table 14 shows as to how much time victim remained away from the target. It has been observed that in Bhopal hot spot locations, 52 per cent victims remained away from the target from1 to 5 hours. In case of Sagar hot spot locations, considerable number of victim [64 per cent] remained away from the target for 1 to 5 hours. In Sagar cool spot locations also 59 per cent victims remained away from the target for 1 to 5 hours. It can be calculated that the victims being away from target did not vary significantly in the cool or hot spots locations of the two cities.

Table 15
Frequency Distribution of Distance Between Workplace and Crime Scene Among Various Police Stations of Bhopal and Sagar Cities

	Bhopal		*Sagar*	
Distance between workplace and crime scene	*Hot Spot*	*Cool Spot*	*Hot Spot*	*Cool Spot*
Within 5 Km.	61	62	80	88
6 to 10 Km.	28	25	18	11
11 to 15 Km.	5	12	1	
More than 16 Km.	6	1	1	
Total	100	100	100	99
NA/NR				1
Total				100

The absence of capable guardian makes a target vulnerable for crime. It was attempted to examine as to whether distance makes crime target vulnerable in any manner. As almost equal frequencies existed in all hot and cool spots locations of both the cities [Bhopal Hot/Cool spot 61 and 62 per cent respectively and Sagar Hot/Cool Spot 80 and 88 per cent respectively]. It is therefore inferred that distance did not matter in the occurrence of crime. Table 15 shows the frequency distribution of the variable distance between workplace and crime scene in various police stations of Bhopal and Sagar cities. It has been observed that in Bhopal hot spot locations, the maximum distance between workplace and crime scene was within 5 kilometers [61 per cent] and minimum distance between workplace and crime scene was 11 to 15 kilometers [5 per cent] where as in cool spot locations the maximum victims distance between workplace and crime scene was within 5 kilometers [62 per cent] and minimum victims distance between workplace and crime scene was more than16 kilometers [5 per cent]. In case of Sagar hot spot locations, the maximum victims distance between workplace and crime scene was within 5 kilometers [80 per cent] and minimum victims distance between workplace and crime scene was more than 11 kilometers [2 per cent] where as in cool spot locations the maximum victims distance between workplace and crime scene was within 5 kilometers [88 per cent] and minimum victims distance between workplace and crime scene was more than 6 to 10 kilometers [11 per cent].

Table 16
Frequency Distribution of "Distance between Crime Target and Owner at the Time of Crime Commission"

	Bhopal		*Sagar*	
Distance between crime target and owner at the time of crime commission	*Hot Spot*	*Cool Spot*	*Hot Spot*	*Cool Spot*
No Distance	31	19	17	23
Within 1 Km.	43	49	60	47
1 to 2 Km.	4	12	8	14
2 to 3 Km.	3	3	6	3
Above 3 Km.	19	17	9	12
Total	100	100	100	99
NA/ NR				1
Total				100

Table 16 shows the frequency distribution of the variable distance between crime target and owner at the time of crime commission in various police stations of Bhopal and Sagar cities. It has been observed from the study that in Bhopal hot spot locations the maximum victims were at the distance [1 kilometers] from crime target at the time of crime commission was 43 per cent and minimum distance from crime target and owner at the time of crime commission was 2 to 3 kilometers [3 per cent] where as in cool spot locations the maximum victims were at distance from crime target at the time of crime commission [1 kilometers] 49 per cent and 3 per cent victims were at 2-3 km distance from crime target at the time of crime commission. In case of Sagar hot spot locations the maximum victims 60 per cent were at 1 km distance from crime target and owner at the time of crime commission while victims distance from crime target and owner at the time of crime commission was 2 to 3 kilometers [6 per cent] where as in cool spot locations the victims distance from crime target and owner at the time of crime commission was within 1 kilometers [47 per cent] and a few victims had at distance from crime target and owner at the time of crime commission was 2 to 3 kilometers [3 per cent].

Table 17
Frequency Distribution of the Variable "Did Crime Occur in the Absence of Victim"

	Bhopal		*Sagar*	
Did crime occur in the absence of victim owner at the time of crime commission?	*Hot Spot*	*Cool Spot*	*Hot Spot*	*Cool Spot*
Yes	70	81	81	75
No	30	19	19	25
Total	100	100	100	100

In the parlance of situation crime prevention, the 'capable guardian' was missing in 70 to 80 per cent cases, as the victims were not present close to the target of crime. Table 17 shows the frequency distribution of absence of victim. The general trend is that 70 to 80 per cent crime occurred in the absence of victim while 20 to 30 per cent crime occurred in the presence of victim.

Table 18
Frequency Distribution of "What was Victim Doing at the Time of Crime Occurrence"

	Bhopal		*Sagar*	
What was victim doing at the time of incidence?	*Hot Spot*	*Cool Spot*	*Hot Spot*	*Cool Spot*
Sleeping	31	35	41	40
Working	14	11	21	16
Leisure	6	16	19	21
Other (Specify)	45	38	19	20
Total	96	100	100	97
NA/ NR	4			3
Total	100			100

The victim engagement at the time of crime commission determines the vulnerability situation. The figures shown in Table 18 show that the victims were asleep in majority of the cases.

Table 19
Frequency Distribution of "Whether the Victim Resisted Crime"

	Bhopal		Sagar	
Did the victim resist crime owner at the time of crime commission?	*Hot Spot*	*Cool Spot*	*Hot Spot*	*Cool Spot*
Yes	3	4	7	9
No	97	96	93	90
Total	100	100	100	99
NA/ NR				1
Total				100

Table 19 shows the relevant data. It has been observed as general trend in both the locations that most victims [90 to 97 per cent] did not have opportunity to resist crime while few of them 3 to 9 per cent could do so.

VICTIMS RELATED VARIABLES

Table 20 shows the frequency distribution of the age of victims among various police stations of Bhopal and Sagar cities. It has been observed from that in Bhopal hot spot locations maximum victims were of age group 21 to 30 [33 per cent] while only 2 per cent victims were of age group up to 20 years. In cool spot locations, the 52 per cent victims were of age group 31 to 40 and only 3 per cent victims were of age group up to 20 years. In case of Sagar hot spot locations, 34 per cent were in the age group of 21 to 30 years while only 7 per cent victims were of age group up to 20 years. In cool spot locations of this city, the maximum victims were of age group 31 to 40 [34 per cent] only few victims [3 per cent] were of age group up to 20 years.

Table 20
Frequency Distribution of the "Age of Victims"

	Bhopal		Sagar	
Age of the victim	*Hot Spot*	*Cool Spot*	*Hot Spot*	*Cool Spot*
Up to 20 Years	2	3	7	3
21 to 30 Years	33	25	34	29
31 to 40 Years	31	52	27	34
41 to 50 Years	21	12	19	21
Above 50 Years	13	8	13	13
Total	100	100	100	100

Table 21
Frequency Distribution of the "Sex of Victims"

Sex of the victim	*Bhopal*		*Sagar*	
	Hot Spot	*Cool Spot*	*Hot Spot*	*Cool Spot*
Male	78	92	96	89
Female	22	8	4	11
Total	100	100	100	100

Table 21 shows the frequency distribution of the sex of victims among various police stations of Bhopal and Sagar Cities. It has been observed from that in Bhopal hot spot locations 78 per cent victims were males while only 22 per cent victims were females, whereas in cool spot locations the 92 per cent victims were males while only few 8 per cent victims were females. In case of Sagar hot spot locations 96 per cent victims were males and only few victims 4 per cent were females. In cool spot locations most of the victims [89 per cent] were males and few victims [11 per cent] were females. The crime incidence studied in this exercise was predominantly a male dominated affair and it did not vary much in hot or cool spot locations in the two cities covered in this study.

Table 22
Frequency Distribution of the "Occupation of Victims"

Occupation of victim	*Bhopal*		*Sagar*	
	Hot Spot	*Cool Spot*	*Hot Spot*	*Cool Spot*
Student	11	8	25	9
Service Class	48	13	34	16
Businessman	19	62	28	55
Wage earner	12	10	5	8
Other (Specify)	10	6	8	12
Total	100	99	100	100
NA/NR		1		
Total		100		

Does the experience of victimization vary along with the nature of occupation held by the victims? The data presented in Table 22 indicate that service class was the key target of various crimes in the hot spot locations of both the cities [48 and 34 per cent] and it was the business class who victimized quite frequently in cool spot locations [62 and 55 per cent].

Table 23
Frequency Distribution of "Was any Implement Used in the Commission of Crime"?

	Bhopal		*Sagar*	
Was any implement used in the commission of crime?	*Hot Spot*	*Cool Spot*	*Hot Spot*	*Cool Spot*
Yes	60	73	72	75
No	39	25	27	25
Total	99	98	99	100
NA/NR	1	2	1	
Total	100	100	100	

Situationally triggered theft or burglary often utilize some implements. It was attempt to know in this study if any such things were used in committing theft or burglary. The data indicated in Table 23 bear it out that in 60 to 75 per cent cases in both the cool and hot spot localities of two cities some implements were also used.

Table 24
Frequency Distribution of "What Made Target Lucrative"?

	Bhopal		*Sagar*	
What made target lucrative?	*Hot Spot*	*Cool Spot*	*Hot Spot*	*Cool Spot*
Cost/ Value	24	34	11	19
Easy Availability	23	14	23	17
Easy Access	50	47	62	53
Others	3	5	4	11
Total	100	100	100	100

This is generally held in the research on situational crime prevention that some exterior trait of the target makes it lucrative for theft and burglary. Table 24 shows easy access to crime scene in the hot spot area of the two cities [i.e. Bhopal and Sagar 50 and 62 per cent respectively] and cost of the object [24 and 11 per cent respectively] and easy availability [23 and

23 per cent respectively] made them lucrative for crime. Almost similar trend was also noted in cool spot locations.

Table 25
Frequency Distribution of "Description of Crime Scene"

	Bhopal		*Sagar*	
Description of crime scene	*Hot Spot*	*Cool Spot*	*Hot Spot*	*Cool Spot*
Easily Approachable	43	20	33	32
Secured	2	1	3	1
Unguarded	41	61	55	54
Other	13	18	9	13
Total	99	100	100	100
NA/ NR	1			
Total	100			

The nature of crime scene in terms of its accessibility for the offender makes the opportunity for crime commission more easier. Table 25 delineates the nature of crime scene and occurrence of crime in the cities of Sagar and Bhopal. The data indicate that the crime scene was found to be easily approachable by majority of the offenders in hot spot locations of Bhopal and Sagar cities [43 and 33 per cent respectively]. As many as 41 per cent and 55 per cent offenders in the same locations found crime scene unguarded. The corresponding per centage for the same variable in the cool spot locations was 61 and 55 per cent. The scene of crime was regarded as secured by only negligible number of respondents.

Table 26
Frequency Distribution of "Presence of Security Measures at Crime Scene"

	Bhopal		*Sagar*	
Presence of security measures at crime scene	*Hot Spot*	*Cool Spot*	*Hot Spot*	*Cool Spot*
Inadequate	74	72	80	85
Adequate	9	6	1	1
Moderate	16	22	19	13
Total	99	100	100	99
NA/ NR	1			1
Total	100			100

The perceived security measures in the locality are significant pointer to vulnerability for crime. The respondents up to 85 per cent felt the security measures at the crime scene to be inadequate. Only a negligible number of respondents had a satisfaction with the security measures.

Table 27
Frequency Distribution of "Crime Scene Visible to Others"

	Bhopal		*Sagar*	
Crime scene visible to others	*Hot Spot*	*Cool Spot*	*Hot Spot*	*Cool Spot*
Yes	34	42	53	47
No	39	28	23	30
Not Known	19	28	18	18
Total	92	98	94	95
NA/NR	8	2	6	5
Total	100	100	100	100

The crime reduction approaches confirm that visibility of crime scene is deterrence to the potential offenders. The data collected is the study [Table 27] bear it out that in 67 per cent cases in Bhopal and 53 per cent cases in Sagar, the crime scene was not visible to others. In fairly large number of cases the crime scene is visible to others.

Table 28
Frequency Distribution of "Locking Arrangements at Crime Scene"

	Bhopal		*Sagar*	
Locking arrangement	*Hot Spot*	*Cool Spot*	*Hot Spot*	*Cool Spot*
Inadequate	23	30	44	51
Adequate	24	17	7	3
Moderate	22	26	31	27
Total	69	73	82	81
NA/NR	31	27	18	19
Total	100	100	100	100

The locking arrangement at crime scene is an indicator of 'target hardening'. Table 28 displays that the locking arrangements were inadequate in 95 per cent cases in Sagar and 53 per cent cases in Bhopal. These were adequate in 10 per cent cases in Sagar and 41 per cent cases in Bhopal.

Table 29
Frequency Distribution of "Quality of Lock at Crime Scene"

	Bhopal		*Sagar*	
Quality of Lock	*Hot Spot*	*Cool Spot*	*Hot Spot*	*Cool Spot*
Good	22	19	6	3
Average	28	26	33	29
Poor	17	28	43	49
Total	67	73	82	81
NA/ NR	33	27	18	19
Total	100	100	100	100

In continuation to the above Table, Table 29 describes the quality of lock used at various crime locations in the selected cities. The quality of lock was poor in 92 per cent cases in Sagar city and 40 per cent cases in Bhopal city.

Table 30
Frequency Distribution of "Was there is Police Patrolling at Crime Scene"?

	Bhopal		*Sagar*	
Was there police patrolling?	*Hot Spot*	*Cool Spot*	*Hot Spot*	*Cool Spot*
Regular	21	21	2	0
Occasionally	44	50	30	16
Never	33	28	68	84
Total	98	99	100	100
NA/NR	2	1		
Total	100	100		

The patrolling measures in the locality of crime scene are supposed to deter situational crime commission. On surveying the periodicity of police patrolling, it was found [Table 30] that in a large number of cases in both the cities, the patrolling was never under taken [68 per cent and 84 per cent in Sagar as well as 33 and 28 per cent in Bhopal].

Table 31
Frequency Distribution of the Variable "Presence of People Around, When Crime Occurred"

	Bhopal		*Sagar*	
Presence of people around, when crime occurred	*Hot Spot*	*Cool Spot*	*Hot Spot*	*Cool Spot*
Yes	41	44	52	48
No	44	27	27	38
Do not know	15	29	21	14
Total	100	100	100	100

Table 31 shows the frequency distribution of the variable of presence of people around, when crime occurred in various police stations of Bhopal and Sagar cities. It has been observed from the study that in Bhopal hot spot locations most of the time [41 per cent] there was presence of people around, when crime occurred and only a few [15 per cent] did not know about it. In cool spot locations, the most of the time [44 per cent] there was presence of people around, when crime occurred and in 27 per cent there was not any presence of people around, when crime occurred. In case of Sagar hot spot locations most of the time [52 per cent] there is not any presence of people around, when crime occurred while only 21 per cent cases the victim didn't know it. In cool spot locations as [48 per cent] and there was presence of people around, when crime occurred and in 14 per cent cases victim did not know about it.

SITUATIONAL INDICATORS OF VEHICLE THEFT

Table 32 shows the crime location in respect of type of vehicle stolen. The two-wheelers were found to be highly prone for theft in hot and cool spot locations [93.9 and 95.2 per cent] respectively in case of Sagar city. The corresponding per centage was 86.7 and 78.4 per cent respectively in the city of Bhopal. The four wheelers were not the frequent targets in these locations in the two cities.

The places of parking from where the vehicles have been stolen are of crucial importance in the situational analysis of the crime. The data shown in the Table 33 make it clear that vehicle that were parking in unauthorized places were more likely to be stolen in Bhopal and Sagar regardless of hot or cool spots. The vehicles parked at authorized place were less likely to be taken away. The pattern did not vary in terms of hot and cool spot locations in the two cities.

Table 32
Frequency Distribution of Type of Vehicle Stolen

	Bhopal		*Sagar*	
Type of Vehicle	*Hot Spot*	*Cool Spot*	*Hot Spot*	*Cool Spot*
Two Wheelers	26	40	46	40
	[86.7%]	[78.4%]	[93.9%]	[95.2%]
Four Wheelers	4	11	3	2
	[13.3%]	[21.6%]	[6.1%]	[4.8%]
Total	30	51	49	42
	[100%]	[100%]	[100%]	[100%]

Table 33
Frequency Distribution of "Place of Vehicle Parking at the Time of Theft"

	Bhopal		*Sagar*	
Place of Parking	*Hot Spot*	*Cool Spot*	*Hot Spot*	*Cool Spot*
Official Parking	3	3	1	0
	[10.0%]	[5.9 %]	[2.0%]	[0.0%]
Parked in unauthorized place	16	17	30	25
	[53.3%]	[33.3%]	[61.2%]	[59.5%]
At market place	5	19	6	9
	[16.7%]	[37.3%]	[12.2%]	[21.4%]
Railway/Bus stand	0	2	2	2
	[0.0%]	[3.9%]	[4.1%]	[4.8%]
Other	6	10	10	6
	[20.0%]	[19.6%]	[20.4%]	[14.3%]
Total	30	51	49	42
	[100%]	[100%]	[100%]	[100%]

Table 34 shows the causes of vehicle theft. The maximum victims believed that place of parking was unsafe in [Bhopal 27.5 average of hot and cool spot] and in Sagar 47.5 per cent victims also felt the same.

Table 34
Frequency Distribution of "What Causes the Theft of Vehicle"

	Bhopal		*Sagar*	
What causes the theft of vehicle?	*Hot Spot*	*Cool Spot*	*Hot Spot*	*Cool Spot*
Was not locked	2	0	2	3
	[6.7%]	[0.0%]	[4.2%]	[7.1%]
Lock wasn't good	3	14	7	5
	[10.0%]	[27.4%]	[14.3%]	[11.9%]
Place was unsafe	10	11	22	21
	[33.3%]	[21.6%]	[44.9%]	[50.0%]
Vehicle was attractive	6	11	5	6
	[20.0%]	[21.6%]	[10.2%]	[14.3%]
Any other	9	15	13	7
	[30.0%]	[29.4%]	[26.5%]	[16.7%]
Total	30	51	49	42
	[100%]	[100%]	[100%]	[100%]

Table 35
Frequency Distribution of "Do you Think Two-wheelers are More Prone for Theft than Four-wheelers"

	Bhopal		*Sagar*	
Do you think two-wheelers are more prone for theft than four-wheelers?	*Hot Spot*	*Cool Spot*	*Hot Spot*	*Cool Spot*
Yes	15	32	41	35
	[50.0%]	[62.7%]	[83.6%]	[83.3%]
No	6	8	4	3
	[20.0%]	[15.7%]	[8.2%]	[7.1%]
Can't Say	9	11	4	4
	[30.0%]	[21.6%]	[8.2%]	[9.6%]
Total	30	51	49	42
	[100%]	[100%]	[100%]	[100%]

Table 35 shows the frequency distribution of the variable- 'do you think two-wheelers are more prone for theft than four-wheelers among various police stations of Bhopal and Sagar cities?' It has been observed from the study that in Bhopal and Sagar locations that there is general trend that most of the owners were of view that two-wheelers are more prone for theft than four-wheelers.

OPINION SURVEY

The instances and exposure to risk situation affect the perception of the local residents about victimization. An exercise has been done in this study to assess the perceptions of respondents regarding their sense of security and their opinions about the opportunity and prevalence of crime in the locality they reside.

Table 36
Showing Response on: "Do You Find this Area Safe"?

	Bhopal		*Sagar*	
Do you find this area safe?	*Hot Spot*	*Cool Spot*	*Hot Spot*	*Cool Spot*
Yes	28	36	30	17
No	61	59	68	82
Can't Say	11	5	2	1
Total	100	100	100	100

Table 36 shows the opinions of victims about their perceived safety irrespective of crime locations, majority of respondent [59 to 80 per cent] felt their neighborhood to be unsafe.

Table 37
Showing Response on: "Do You Feel that Opportunity to Commit the Crime in this Locality are in Abundance"?

	Bhopal		*Sagar*	
Do you feel that opportunities to commit the crime in this locality are in abundance?	*Hot Spot*	*Cool Spot*	*Hot Spot*	*Cool Spot*
Yes	66	59	67	83
No	28	36	26	17
Can't Say	6	5	7	0
Total	100	100	100	100

How do the victims feel about the availability of opportunity to commit crime in their locality? Table 37 clearly brings out that 59 to 83 per cent victims found the easy availability of opportunity to commit crime in their localities.

Table 38
Showing Response on: "Do You Consider that there is Crime Problem in Your Neighborhood"?

	Bhopal		*Sagar*	
Do you consider that there is crime problem in your neighborhood?	*Hot Spot*	*Cool Spot*	*Hot Spot*	*Cool Spot*
Yes	57	56	66	80
No	33	37	31	20
Can't Say	9	7	3	0
Total	99	100	100	100
NA/NR	1			
Total	100			

Table 38 is about the perceived prevalence of crime in the neighborhood. As many as 56 to 80 per cent respondents confirmed the existence of crime in their localities.

Table 39
Showing Response on: "Nature of Crime Existed in the Locality"?

	Bhopal		*Sagar*	
Nature of crime problem	*Hot Spot*	*Cool Spot*	*Hot Spot*	*Cool Spot*
Burglary	25	9	18	18
Robbery	8	17	14	20
Petty Theft	21	36	30	42
Street attack/assault	3	0	4	4
Serious hurt	0	1	0	0
Any Other (Specify)	10	6	4	1
Total	67	69	70	85
NA/NR	33	31	30	15
Total	100	100	100	100

Table 39 takes stock of the perceiveds nature of crime problem in the locality. Most respondent 57 per cent in Bhopal and Sagar [72 per cent] found instances of petty theft to be most recurrent followed by burglary. The respondents did not find the cases of assault or serious hurt to be a serious issue in their locality.

The factors that are perceived by the victims to be responsible for crime are quite crucial in the situational explanation of crime. Table 40 conveys that the movement of strangers in the area (hot spot [43%] and cool spot [30%]) in the city of Bhopal was the prime factor perceived by the respondents making the neighborhood crime prone. The correspondence per centage in case of Sagar city was 24 and 18 per cent respectively. The presence of bad characters in the locality was equally felt crucial by the respondents.

Table 40
Showing Response on: "What Makes the Neighborhood Crime Prone"?

	Bhopal		*Sagar*	
What makes the neighborhood crime prone?	*Hot Spot*	*Cool Spot*	*Hot Spot*	*Cool Spot*
Strangers movement in the area	33	30	24	18
Suspicious looking person living as tenant in the area	9	11	14	15
Antisocial and bad characters roaming in the area	28	26	32	35
Drinkers roaming in the locality	11	12	4	13
Operation of gambling dens	5	4	1	6
Total	86	83	75	87
NA/ NR	14	17	25	13
Total	100	100	100	100

Table 41
Showing Response on: "Do You Feel Opportunities for Crime can be Reduced by"?

	Bhopal		*Sagar*	
Do you feel opportunities for crime can be reduced by-	*Hot Spot*	*Cool Spot*	*Hot Spot*	*Cool Spot*
Increasing of police patrolling	40	41	45	41
Greater Surveillance	46	48	32	45
Community Policing	9	7	16	9
Other	5	4	6	5
Total	100	100	99	100
NA/NR			1	
Total			100	

Table 41 shows that 32 to 48 per cent respondents felt that opportunity for crime can be reduced by greater surveillance and increased patrolling by police [41 to 55 per cent]. The popular alternative of community policing was not adequately endorsed by the respondents in this regard.

Table 42
Showing Response on: "Do You Think Most of the Crimes of Theft/ Burglary Occur Because of the Negligence of the Victim"?

	Bhopal		*Sagar*	
Do you think most of the crimes of theft/ burglary occur because of the negligence of the victim?	*Hot Spot*	*Cool Spot*	*Hot Spot*	*Cool Spot*
Yes	57	66	72	74
No	27	26	24	21
Can't Say	15	8	4	5
Total	99	100	100	100
NA/NR	1			
Total	100			

Negligence giving rise to situational occurrence of crime has been perceived [57 to 74 per cent] as key factor in causing theft and burglary.

Table 43
Showing Response on: "Do You Think Victim Create Opportunity for Crimes'"?

	Bhopal		*Sagar*	
Opinion about victim create opportunity for crimes by	*Hot Spot*	*Cool Spot*	*Hot Spot*	*Cool Spot*
Public display of money and other valuables	32	26	25	24
Negligence	59	67	73	75
Any Other (Specify)	8	5	1	1
Total	99	98	99	100
NA/NR	1	2	1	
Total	100	100	100	

The respondents in this study also expressed their opinions about the creation of opportunity by the victims. The data shown in Table 43 highlight that negligence was rated to be the main way of causing opportunity in hot spot areas of Bhopal and Sagar city [59 and 73 per cent respectively]. The corresponding percentage in cool spot area of these cities was 67 and 75 percent respectively. In these cities the victims belonging to hot spot area found public display of valuables as a key promoter of opportunity [26 and 24 per cent].

Table 44
Showing Response on: "Opportunity Makes the Thief"?

	Bhopal		*Sagar*	
Opportunity makes the thief?	*Hot Spot*	*Cool Spot*	*Hot Spot*	*Cool Spot*
Yes	74	78	95	95
No	4	6	2	1
Can't Say	22	16	3	4
Total	100	100	100	100

The perception "Opportunity makes the thief" as advocated by Clark was also examined. Table 44 confirms that respondents [74 to 95 per cent] in different locations attributed to this.

Table 45
Showing Response on: "Do You Generally Avoid Traveling Alone in a Public Transport in Late Evening or Night"?

	Bhopal		*Sagar*	
Opinion about avoid traveling alone in a public transport in late evening or night?	*Hot Spot*	*Cool Spot*	*Hot Spot*	*Cool Spot*
Yes	43	33	25	24
No	56	67	74	76
Total	99	100	99	100
NA/NR	1		1	
Total	100		100	

In cool and hot spot areas of Bhopal and Sagar cities 24 to 43 per cent victims expressed [Table 45] that they avoided traveling alone in a public transport in late evenings. On the other hand 56 to 76 per cent respondents did not have any such effect.

Table 46
Factors Causing Avoidance of Traveling Alone in Public Transport in Late Evening or Night

Factors	*Bhopal*		*Sagar*	
	Hot Spot	*Cool Spot*	*Hot Spot*	*Cool Spot*
Possibility of misbehavior of fellow passengers and staff	3	3	2	4
Pick Pocketing	11	10	9	8
Possibility of theft	20	10	7	2
Attack/Kidnapping	1	0	0	2
Possibility of sexual harassment	1	3	0	2
Possibility of being bullied in public transport	9	11	7	7
Any Other (Specify)	4	1		1
Total	49	38	25	26
NA/NR	51	62	75	74
Total	100	100	100	100

Table 46 displays the factors responsible for restricting the movement of respondents. As many as 20 per cent and 18 per cent respondents in hot and cool spot area of Bhopal avoided traveling alone in public transport because possibility of theft. In the same locations the respondents [11 to 10 per cent] did so because of possibility of pick pocketing. Similar trend was observed in Sagar cities.

Table 47
Showing Response on: "Do You Avoid Visiting Certain Places and Areas of the City Because of Possibility of Crime or Violence"?

Opinion about avoid visiting certain places and areas of the city because of possibility of crime or violence?	*Bhopal*		*Sagar*	
	Hot Spot	*Cool Spot*	*Hot Spot*	*Cool Spot*
Yes	51	37	25	24
No	44	57	70	74
Can't Say	5	6	4	2
Total	100	100	99	100
NA/ NR			1	
Total			100	

The perceived risk of crime was fairly high among the respondents. This perception was shared by 51 per cent respondent in the hot spot area of Bhopal as against 57 per cent in cool spot area. The corresponding per centages in the city of Sagar were 25 and 74 per cent.

Table 48
Showing Response on: "What are the Measures Behind Avoiding Visiting Certain Places in the City"?

	Bhopal		*Sagar*	
Factors	*Hot Spot*	*Cool Spot*	*Hot Spot*	*Cool Spot*
Hooliganism	36	20	19	13
Terrorist attack	3	2	0	3
Rape	2	3	0	3
Kidnapping or murder risk	1	0	2	3
Any Other	14	15	8	4
Total	56	40	29	26
NA/ NR	44	60	71	74
Total	100	100	100	100

The victims avoided visiting certain places because of various factors. In the hot spot areas of Bhopal and Sagar 36 and 19 per cent respectively opted not to visit certain places in the cities due to Hooliganism in those area. The other factors were also operational.

Table 49
Showing Response on: "No One is Safe in this City"?

	Bhopal		*Sagar*	
Response Categories	*Hot Spot*	*Cool Spot*	*Hot Spot*	*Cool Spot*
Strongly agree	14	6	7	6
Agree	26	26	23	26
Undecided	17	14	15	12
Disagree	28	47	41	43
Strongly disagree	15	7	14	9
Total	100	100	100	96
NA/ NR				4
Total				100

The perceived sense of safety of the victims in the locality was extracted by having their opinion "No one is safe in this city". Table 49 shows the respondents in hot spot area of Bhopal were divided almost equally [26 and 28 per cent] in terms of 'agree' and 'disagree' whereas 14 per cent were 'strongly agree'. In the cool spot area of this city 26 per cent 'agreed' to this notion and 47 per cent did not. In case of Sagar city the division was almost equal in both the locations in terms of 'agree' and 'disagree'.

Table 50

Showing Response on: "Have You ever been Harassed or Assaulted by Anybody Because of Your Caste, Class, Religion or Sexual Status"?

	Bhopal		*Sagar*	
Opinion about ever been harassed or assaulted by anybody because of your caste, class, religion or sexual status?	*Hot Spot*	*Cool Spot*	*Hot Spot*	*Cool Spot*
Yes	19	15	9	12
No	81	85	91	88
Total	100	100	100	100

Does victimization and perceived risk of victimization has any thing to do with racial or class prejudice? On asking about experience of being harassed because of caste, class, religion or sexual status [Table 50], majority of the victims denied any such happening but 19 and 15 per cent respondents in hot and cool spot areas of Bhopal city confirmed this experience. The corresponding percentage was 9 and 12 percent in the city of Sagar.

Table 51 depicts the perceived increase in crime in the neighborhood. As many as 64 and 69 per cent respondents in hot and cool spot areas of Bhopal city found crime to have increased in the last five years in their neighborhood. The corresponding per centage was 81 and 88 per cent respectively in case of Sagar city. It is interesting to note that a very insignificant number of victims found crimes to have decreased during this period. A sizeable number of victims found crime rate to have remained unchanged.

Table 51
Showing Response on: "Do You Think that during the Last Five Years, the Crime in the Neighborhood"?

	Bhopal		Sagar	
Opinion about during the last five years, the crime in the neighborhood has	*Hot Spot*	*Cool Spot*	*Hot Spot*	*Cool Spot*
Increased	64	69	81	88
Decreased	2	2	0	0
Remained unchanged	34	29	18	10
Total	100	100	99	98
NA/NR			1	2
Total			100	100

Table 52
Showing Response on: "In Case, Crime has Increased, Please Specify the Crimes"?

	Bhopal		Sagar	
Type of crime registered increase in last 5 years	*Hot Spot*	*Cool Spot*	*Hot Spot*	*Cool Spot*
Dacoity	1	0	1	2
Robbery	18	21	22	19
Petty theft	18	12	13	14
Grand theft	28	33	44	49
Rape	0	1	1	0
Hooliganism	6	6	2	8
Sexual assault	0	1	0	0
Any other	2	3	0	0
Total	73	77	83	92
NA/ NR	27	23	17	8
Total	100	100	100	100

The respondents were also asked about the type of crime, which has really increased in the recent past. The perusal of Table 52 clearly shows that robbery, theft or petty theft were increasingly regarded to have increased significantly in all the locations of selected cities. The respondent did not find dacoity or sexual assault to have risen significantly.

The respondents were asked to report the crime, which has increased significantly in their locality. Table 53 find the respondent attributing theft to have increased quite significantly followed by serious hurt. The occurrence of other kinds of crime was not noted significantly by the respondents in the selected cities.

Table 53
Showing Response on: "Could You Indicate which of the Following Crimes Occur Mostly in Your Area"?

	Bhopal		*Sagar*	
Opinion about 'could you indicate which one or two of the following crimes occur mostly in your area'?	*Hot Spot*	*Cool Spot*	*Hot Spot*	*Cool Spot*
Serious hurt	21	11	16	11
Theft	55	75	64	69
Dacoity	1	1	2	2
Street attack	6	2	7	10
Communal violence	0	0	1	0
Political violence	0	0	1	0
Cheating	4	6	0	5
Rape	0	0	1	0
Any other	7	5	1	1
Total	94	100	93	98
NA/NR	6		7	2
Total	100		100	100

3

Contextual Analysis of Situational Crime

Certain crime categories (theft from shop, residence or business place, burglary and vehicle theft) have been focused in the present study to examine the situational factors operating in their occurrence. It is needless to state the identification of situational factors is ultimately exploited in framing the situational crime prevention strategy. In the present chapter crime category as independent variable has been examined in the context of several other variables. The cross-tabulation has been performed to ascertain the association between the variables.

The above Table shows the relative distribution of "crime category" and "week of occurrence" variables. The most cases of theft [26.5 per cent] occurred in second week while few cases of theft [4.3 per cent] occurred in fifth week. It was found that Vehicle theft cases were [43.0 per cent] highest in the second week of the month [13 per cent] and were lowest in third week [7.8 per cent]. In all the weeks of the month while Burglary from shop cases [0.3 per cent] was lowest occurrence. The percentage of all kinds of crime was consistently lowest in the fifth week of the month whereas all categories of offences showed fairly high distribution of per centage in the remaining four week. In other words there was no identifiable pattern indicating the concentration of any particular crime category in any specific week of the month. The Chi-Square value is non-significant [$\chi^2 = 10.217$, $P<0.806$] as well as Kendall's tau-b is also non significant.

Table 1

Cross Tabulation of Variables "Crime Category" and "Week of Occurrence"

	Week of Occurrence						
Crime Category	*First Week*	*Second Week*	*Third Week*	*Fourth Week*	*Fifth Week*	*NA/ NR*	*Total*
Theft from shop/	32	35	35	32	5	1	140
Business Place	8.0%	8.8%	8.8%	8.0%	1.3%	.3%	35.0%
Theft from	24	19	20	19	4	1	87
residence	6.0%	4.8%	5.0%	4.8%	1.0%	.3%	21.8%
Burglary from	0	0	1	0	0	0	1
shop	.0%	.0%	.3%	.0%	.0%	.0%	.3%
Vehicle theft	38	52	31	43	8	0	172
	9.5%	13.0%	7.8%	10.8%	2.0%	.0%	43.0%
Total	94	106	87	94	17	2	400
	23.5%	26.5%	21.8%	23.5%	4.3%	.5%	100.0%

$\chi^2 = 10.217$, df = 15, P< 0.806 K tau b = P< 0.955, Nonsignificant

Table 2

Cross Tabulation of Variables "Crime Category" and "Time of Occurrence"

	Time of Occurrence					
Crime Category	*6 to 11.59 AM*	*12.0 to 5.59 PM*	*6 to 11.59 PM*	*12 to 5.59 AM*	*NA/ NR*	*Total*
Theft from shop/	6	32	49	51	2	140
Business Place	1.5%	8.0%	12.3%	12.8%	.5%	35.0%
Theft from residence	3	16	7	58	3	87
	.8%	4.0%	1.8%	14.5%	.8%	21.8%
Burglary from shop	0	1	0	0	0	1
	.0%	.3%	.0%	.0%	.0%	.3%
Vehicle theft	12	52	66	41	1	172
	3.0%	13.0%	16.5%	10.3%	.3%	43.0%
Total	21	101	122	150	6	400
	5.3%	25.3%	30.5%	37.5%	1.5%	100.0%

$\chi^2 = 50.674$, df = 12, P< 0.001 K tau b = P< 0.002, Significant

Time of crime commission is generally regarded as a prime situational factor. In the cases covered in this study, an attempt was made to underscore the extent to which this factor had any situational role to play. Table 2 shows that most of crime incidents took place between 12 to 5.59 AM [37.5 per cent] and 6 to 11.59PM [30.5 per cent]. The theft from shop or business place mostly occurred during this time interval [25.1 per cent] and similarly the vehicle theft took place during the same time frame [26.8 per cent]. The chi square value is significant [χ^2 = 50.674, P< 0.001] as well as Kendall's tau-b is also significant.

Table 3
Cross Tabulation of Variables
"Crime Category" and "Location of Scene of Crime"

	Location of Scene of Crime				
Crime Category	*Open*	*Indoor/ Close*	*Office/ Institution*	*NA/NR*	*Total*
Theft from shop/	86	51	2	1	140
Business Place	21.5%	12.8%	.5%	.3%	35.0%
Theft from residence	10	77	0	0	87
	2.5%	19.3%	.0%	.0%	21.8%
Burglary from shop	0	1	0	0	1
	.0%	.3%	.0%	.0%	.3%
Vehicle theft	170	1	1	0	172
	42.5%	.3%	.3%	.0%	43.0%
Total	266	130	3	1	400
	66.5%	32.5%	.8%	.3%	100.0%

χ^2 = 211.23, df = 9, P< 0.001
K tau b= P< 0.001, Significant

The significance of place of occurrence of crime has always been a matter of interest to environmental Criminologists and this assumes even greater importance in a study focusing upon the situational factors in crime. Table 3 shows that almost all the crime categories included in this study had open scene of crime [66.5 per cent] where as those crime that took place in the indoor location were 32.5 per cent of the total. The chi square value is significant [χ^2 = 211.23, P< 0.001] as well as Kendall's tau-b is also significant.

Several studies referred to earlier in this report bear it out that adequate lighting arrangement in the vicinity could discourage potential criminals. This situational instigator of crime has been examined in the present study. Table 4 shows during the time of occurrence of crime there was adequate lighting arrangement in 38.5 per cent cases whereas this arrangement was moderate and inadequate in 15.3 per cent and 17 per cent respectively. The chi-square value is significant [$\chi^2 = 40.13$, $P < 0.001$] while Kendall's tau-b is non-significant.

Table 4
Cross Tabulation of Variables "Crime Category" and "Lighting Arrangement on the Immediate Street"

	Lighting arrangement on the immediate street				
Crime Category	*Inadequate*	*Adequate*	*Moderate*	*NA/NR*	*Total*
Theft from shop/	11	70	21	38	140
Business Place	2.8%	17.5%	5.3%	9.5%	35.0%
Theft from residence	26	21	22	18	87
	6.5%	5.3%	5.5%	4.5%	21.8%
Burglary from shop	0	0	0	1	1
	.0%	.0%	.0%	.3%	.3%
Vehicle theft	31	63	18	60	172
	7.8%	15.8%	4.5%	15.0%	43.0%
Total	68	154	61	117	400
	17.0%	38.5%	15.3%	29.3%	100.0%

$\chi^2 = 40.13$, df = 9, $P < 0.001$
K tau b= $P < 0.917$, Non-significant.

Table 5
Cross Tabulation of Variables "Crime Category" and "Lighting Arrangement in the Premises"

	Lighting arrangement on the immediate street				
Crime Category	*Inadequate*	*Adequate*	*Moderate*	*NA/NR*	*Total*
Theft from shop/	19	50	33	38	140
Business Place	4.8%	12.5%	8.3%	9.5%	35.0%
Theft from residence	31	17	20	19	87
	7.8%	4.3%	5.0%	4.8%	21.8%
Burglary from shop	0	0	0	1	1
	.0%	.0%	.0%	.3%	.3%
Vehicle theft	42	50	23	57	172
	10.5%	12.5%	5.8%	14.3%	43.0%
Total	92	117	76	115	400
	23.0%	29.3%	19.0%	28.8%	100.0%

$\chi^2 = 26.74$, df = 9, $P < 0.002$ K tau b = $P < 0.551$, Non-significant

Table 5 shows that the all types of crime were significantly higher [23 per cent] where lighting arrangement on the premises was inadequate and 19 per cent cases of crime also took place where such arrangement was only moderate. This significantly depicts the situational role played by this factor in the crime categories covered in this study. The chi-square value is significant [$\chi^2 = 26.74$, $P < 0.002$] while Kendall's tau-b is non-significant.

Table 6
Cross Tabulation of Variables "Crime Category" and "Average Time Spent at Home"

	Average time spent at home					
Crime Category	*1 to 5 Hours*	*6 to 10 Hours*	*11 to 15 Hours*	*16 to 20 Hours*	*NA/ NR*	*Total*
Theft from shop/	2	94	35	8	1	140
Business Place	.5%	23.5%	8.8%	2.0%	.3%	35.0%
Theft from residence	0	45	35	7	0	87
	.0%	11.3%	8.8%	1.8%	.0%	21.8%
Burglary from shop	0	1	0	0	0	1
	.0%	.3%	.0%	.0%	.0%	.3%
Vehicle theft	1	110	58	3	0	172
	.3%	27.5%	14.5%	.8%	.0%	43.0%
Total	3	250	128	18	1	400
	.8%	62.5%	32.0%	4.5%	.3%	100.0%

$\chi^2 = 16.13$, df = 12, $P < 0.186$
K tau b= $P < 0.827$, Non-significant

The main thesis of situational criminologists is that crime occurs when the capable guardian is not present. To verify this, an effort was made in this study to examine as to in how many instances the owner was absent from the scene or was not in a position of guarding the same. Table 6 show the cross tabulation between the "Crime Category" and "Average time spent at home" variables. The data indicate that lesser the absence of owner from home, greater were the chances of crime commission. Crime was most likely to occur when the owner was away from the target [11.3 per cent theft from residence and most importantly 30.5 per cent vehicle theft took place when the owner was not close to the target of crime]. The chi-square value is [$\chi^2 = 16.13$, $P < 0.186$] and Kendall's tau-b both shows non-significant value.

Table 7
Cross Tabulation of Variables "Crime Category" and "Distance Between Workplace and Crime Scene"

	Distance between workplace and crime scene					
Crime Category	*Within 5 Km*	*6 to 10 Km.*	*11 to 15 Km.*	*More than 16 Km.*	*NA/ NR*	*Total*
Theft from shop/	94	32	8	2	4	140
Business Place	23.5%	8.0%	2.0%	.5%	1.0%	35.0%
Theft from residence	74	12	0	0	1	87
	18.5%	3.0%	.0%	.0%	.3%	21.8%
Burglary from shop	1	0	0	0	0	1
	.3%	.0%	.0%	.0%	.0%	.3%
Vehicle theft	122	38	10	0	2	172
	30.5%	9.5%	2.5%	.0%	.5%	43.0%
Total	291	82	18	2	7	400
	72.8%	20.5%	4.5%	.5%	1.8%	100.0%

$\chi^2 = 15.61$, df = 12, P< 0.210,
K tau b= P< 0.555, Non-significant

It may be relevant to understand as to whether the distance between the location of crime and victim's workplace affected the occurrence of crime. This is could be situationally causative factor for crime. Table 7 gives the insight about role of "distance between workplace and crime scene" in relation to "crime category". It has been observed from the study that most [72.8 per cent] crime occurred when the distance between workplace and crime scene was within 5 Km only 0.5 per cent crime occurred when the distance between workplace and crime scene was more than 16 Km. While considering the distance, the size of city is also relevant. The chi-square value is [$\chi^2 = 15.61$, P< 0.210] and Kendall's tau-b both shows non-significant value.

Table 8 exhibits the relation between "crime category" and "distance between crime target and owner at the time of crime commission". It has been observed from the study that almost 50 per cent of crime occurred when victim was within 1 Km range of the crime target. Almost one-fifth of the theft from shop or business place occurred when victim was at no distance or within1 Km distance from crime target. Only in negligible

Table 8
Cross Tabulation of Variables "Crime Category" and "Distance between Crime Target and Owner at the Time of Crime Commission"

	Distance between crime target and owner at the time of crime commission						
Crime Category	*No Distance*	*Within 1 Km.*	*1 to 2 Km.*	*2 to 3 Km.*	*Above 3 Km*	*NA/NR*	*Total*
Theft from shop/ Business Place	47	32	17	11	32	1	140
	11.8%	8.0%	4.3%	2.8%	8.0%	.3%	35.0%
Theft from residence	31	24	6	3	23	0	87
	7.8%	6.0%	1.5%	.8%	5.8%	.0%	21.8%
Burglary from shop	1	0	0	0	0	0	1
	.3%	.0%	.0%	.0%	.0%	.0%	.3%
Vehicle theft	11	143	15	1	2	0	172
	2.8%	35.8%	3.8%	.3%	.5%	.0%	43.0%
Total	90	199	38	15	57	1	400
	22.5%	49.8%	9.5%	3.8%	14.3%	.3%	100.0%

$\chi^2 = 156.61$, df = 15, P< 0.001
K tau b= P< 0.251, Non-significant

cases [3.8 per cent] occurred when the victim was 2 to 3 Km from crime scene. The chi-square value is significant [χ^2 = 156.61, P< 0.001] while Kendall's tau-b is non-significant.

Table 9
Cross Tabulation of Variables "Crime Category" and "Did Crime Occur in the Absence of Victim"

	Did crime occurs in the absence of victim		
Crime Category	*Yes*	*No*	*Total*
Theft from shop/Business Place	88	52	140
	22.0%	13.0%	35.0%
Theft from residence	56	31	87
	14.0%	7.8%	21.8%
Burglary from shop	1	0	1
	.3%	.0%	.3%
Vehicle theft	162	10	172
	40.5%	2.5%	43.0%
Total	307	93	400
	76.8%	23.3%	100.0%

χ^2 = 52.22, df = 3, P< 0.001
K tau b= P< 0.001, Significant

Though in the crime categories covered in this study, it is implied that these incidents took place when the victim was practically away or not in control of the object or target of the theft. Nevertheless, an attempt was made to exactly assess the situation. It is observed from Table 9 that in 76.8 per cent of crime cases, the victim was absent while in 23.3 per cent cases the victim was present. Almost 35 per cent cases of theft from shop, business places and residence occurred in the absence of victim. In case of vehicle theft 40.5 per cent occurred in the absence of victim while in 2.5 per cent cases victim was around. The chi square value [χ^2 = 52.22, P< 0.001] as well as Kendall's tau-b is significant.

Victim's engagement at the time of crime commission assumes significance in any study focusing upon situational aspects. Table 10 describes the relation between "crime category" and "what the victim was doing at the time of crime". It has been observed from the study 36.8 per cent victim were sleeping at the time of crime commission while 31 per cent victims were working or were at leisure. Almost 25 per cent of cases of theft from shop, business places and residence occurred when victim was sleeping. In case of vehicle theft, no clear-cut pattern was observed. The chi-square value is significant [$\chi^2 = 45.75$, $P < 0.001$] while Kendall's tau-b is non-significant.

Table 10
Cross Tabulation of Variables "Crime Category" and "What the Victim was Doing at the Time of Crime"

	What was victim doing that time?					
Crime Category	*Sleeping*	*Working*	*Leisure*	*Other (Specify)*	*NA/ NR*	*Total*
Theft from shop/	56	15	15	48	6	140
Business Place	14.0%	3.8%	3.8%	12.0%	1.5%	35.0%
Theft from residence	43	10	5	29	0	87
	10.8%	2.5%	1.3%	7.3%	.0%	21.8%
Burglary from shop	0	1	0	0	0	1
	.0%	.3%	.0%	.0%	.0%	.3%
Vehicle theft	48	36	42	45	1	172
	12.0%	9.0%	10.5%	11.3%	.3%	43.0%
Total	147	62	62	122	7	400
	36.8%	15.5%	15.5%	30.5%	1.8%	100.0%

$\chi^2 = 45.75$, df = 12, $P < 0.001$
K tau b= $P < 0.812$, Non-significant

As most kinds of theft occur without the knowledge of the victim, the chances of resistance of any sort from his/her side are rare. However, at times the victim might be becoming aware about theft being committed and it could be meaningful to study if any resistance from the victim at that point of time makes any difference. Table 11 describes the cross tabulation between "crime category" and "Did the victim resist crime". It has been observed from the study that in 94 per cent cases victim did not have occasion to resists crime while in 5.8 per cent cases the victim could resists the crime. Almost in 50 per cent of cases of theft from shop, business places and residence, it was found that victim did not resist crimes. In case of vehicle theft, 42 per cent cases, the victim did not resist the crime while in 1 per cent case victim did resist the crimes. The chi-square value is non-significant [$\chi^2 = 10.40, P< 0.109$] while Kendall's tau-b is significant.

Table 11
Cross Tabulation of Variables "Crime Category" and "Did the Victim Resist Crime"?

	Did the victim resist crime?			
Crime Category	*Yes*	*No*	*NA/NR*	*Total*
Theft from shop/	14	125	1	140
Business Place	3.5%	31.3%	.3%	35.0%
Theft from residence	5	82	0	87
	1.3%	20.5%	.0%	21.8%
Burglary from shop	0	1	0	1
	.0%	.3%	.0%	.3%
Vehicle theft	4	168	0	172
	1.0%	42.0%	.0%	43.0%
Total	23	376	1	400
	5.8%	94.0%	.3%	100.0%

$\chi^2 = 10.40$, df = 6, P< 0.109
K tau b= P< 0.013, Significant

Table 12
Cross Tabulation of Variables "Crime Category" and "Age of the Victim"

	Age of the victim					
Crime Category	*Up to 20 Years*	*21 to 30 Years*	*31 to 40 Years*	*41 to 50 Years*	*Above 50 Years*	*Total*
Theft from shop/	2	35	49	30	24	140
Business Place	.5%	8.8%	12.3%	7.5%	6.0%	35.0%
Theft from residence	2	22	25	24	14	87
	.5%	5.5%	6.3%	6.0%	3.5%	21.8%
Burglary from shop	1	0	0	0	0	1
	.3%	.0%	.0%	.0%	.0%	.3%
Vehicle theft	10	64	70	19	9	172
	2.5%	16.0%	17.5%	4.8%	2.3%	43.0%
Total	15	121	144	73	47	400
	3.8%	30.3%	36.0%	18.3%	11.8%	100.0%

$\chi^2 = 58.13$, df = 12, P< 0.001 K tau b= P< 0.001, Significant

Age of a person could be crucial in the situational analysis of crime. Table 12 describes that the relation between age of the victim and nature of crime. It has been observed from the study that most victims [33.5 per cent] were in the age group of 21 to 40 years while only 3.8 per cent victims were of age below 20 years. Almost one-fifth with the victims of the cases of theft from shop, business place and residence occurred with the person in the age group of 21 to 40 years. The chi square value is significant [$\chi^2 = 58.13$, $P< 0.001$] as well as Kendall's tau-b is also significant.

Table 13

Cross Tabulation of Variables "Crime Category" and "Sex of the Victim"

	Sex of the victim		
Crime Category	*Male*	*Female*	*Total*
Theft from shop/Business Place	115 28.8%	25 6.3%	140 35.0%
Theft from residence	71 17.8%	16 4.0%	87 21.8%
Burglary from shop	1 .3%	0 .0%	1 .3%
Vehicle theft	168 42.0%	4 1.0%	172 43.0%
Total	355 88.8%	45 11.3%	400 100.0%

$\chi^2 = 24.41$, df = 3, $P< 0.001$
K tau b= $P< 0.001$, Significant

Table 13 examines if the sex of victim had anything to do with the nature of crime. It is exhibited from Table that 88.8 per cent victims were male while 11.3 per cent victims were female. The theft from shop, business place and residence occurred where male victims [46.6 per cent] were involved where as in this category, only 10.3 per cent female victims were involved. In case of vehicle theft there were 42 per cent male victims and only 1 per cent female victims were found. The chi square value is significant [$\chi^2 = 24.41$, $P< 0.001$] as well as Kendall's tau-b is also significant.

Table 14 examines the relation between crime category and occupation of victim. It is displayed in Table that most [41.1 per cent] of the victims were of business class, while 27.8 per cent victims were of service class and only 8.8 per cent victims were wage earners. In one-fifth of the cases of theft from shop, business place and residence, the victims were businessman. Most [19.3 per cent] of the vehicle theft occurred with businessmen The chi square value [$\chi^2 = 27.34$, P< 0.007] and Kendall's tau-b is significant.

Table 14
Cross Tabulation of Variables "Crime Category" and "Occupation of Victim"

	Occupation of victim					
Crime Category	*Student*	*Service Class*	*Business man*	*Wage earner*	*Other (Specify)*	*Total*
Theft from shop/	12	36	59	15	18	140
Business Place	3.0%	9.0%	14.8%	3.8%	4.5%	35.1%
Theft from residence	8	30	27	10	12	87
	2.0%	7.5%	6.8%	2.5%	3.0%	21.8%
Burglary from shop	0	0	1	0	0	1
	.0%	.0%	.3%	.0%	.0%	.3%
Vehicle theft	33	45	77	10	6	171
	8.3%	11.3%	19.3%	2.5%	1.5%	42.9%
Total	53	111	164	35	36	399
	13.3%	27.8%	41.1%	8.8%	9.0%	100.0%

$\chi^2 = 27.34$, df = 12, P< 0.007
K tau b= P< 0.001, Significant

Table 15
Cross Tabulation of Variables "Crime Category" and "Locking Arrangement"

	Locking arrangement			
Crime Category	*Inadequate*	*Adequate*	*Moderate*	*Total*
Theft from shop/	22	18	22	62
Business Place	7.2%	5.9%	7.2%	20.3%
Theft from residence	36	15	23	74
	11.8%	4.9%	7.5%	24.3%
Burglary from shop	0	0	0	0
	0	0	0	0
Vehicle theft	90	18	61	305
	29.5%	5.9%	20.0%	62
Total	148	51	106	305
	48.5%	16.7%	34.8%	100.0%

$\chi^2 = 13.24$, df = 4, P< 0.010
K tau b= P< 0.223, Non-significant

The quality and nature of locking arrangements indicate the 'target hardening' value of the target that becomes situationally more resistant to crime. Table 15 shows the adequacy of locking arrangement and chances of crime occurrence. It is clear from Table that Inadequate locking arrangement have higher crime [48.5 per cent] while 34.8 per cent incidents took place where the locking arrangement were moderate and 16.7 per cent incidents occurred where the locking arrangements were found to be adequate. In case of vehicle theft more or less similar trend has been observed. The chi-square value is Significant [χ^2 = 13.24, P< 0.010] and Kendall's tau-b shows non-significant value.

Table 16

Cross Tabulation of Variables "Crime Category" and "Was There Police Patrolling"

	Was there police patrolling			
Crime Category	*Regular*	*Occasionally*	*Never*	*Total*
Theft from shop/	21	59	57	137
Business Place	5.3%	14.9%	14.4%	34.5%
Theft from residence	1	24	62	87
	.3%	6.0%	15.6%	21.9%
Burglary from shop	0	0	1	1
	.0%	.0%	.3%	.3%
Vehicle theft	22	57	93	172
	5.5%	14.4%	23.4%	43.3%
Total	44	140	213	397
	11.1%	35.3%	53.7%	100.0%

χ^2 = 24.07, df = 6, P< 0.001
K tau b= P< 0.096, Non-significant.

Surveillance or chances of discloser of identity of likely offenders serve as deterrent to crime. It is in this context, it was attempted to know if the police patrolling had any effect as situational deterrent to crime. Table 16 indicates that more than half of the crime occurred in the places where there was no police patrolling [53.7 per cent]. Regular police patrolling areas had least crime occurrence [11.1 per cent] where as occasionally patrolled area attracted moderate [35.3 per cent] crime occurrence. Similar trend occurs in case of vehicle theft.

The chi-square value is Significant [$\chi^2 = 24.07$, $P< 0.001$] and Kendall's tau-b shows non-significant value.

Table 17
Cross Tabulation of Variables "Crime Category" and "Presence of People Around, when Crime Occurred"

	Presence of people around, when crime occurred			
Crime Category	*Yes*	*No*	*Do not know*	*Total*
Theft from shop/	65	50	25	140
Business Place	16.3%	12.5%	6.3%	35.0%
Theft from residence	11	56	20	87
	2.8%	14.0%	5.0%	21.8%
Burglary from shop	1	0	0	1
	.3%	.0%	.0%	.3%
Vehicle theft	108	30	34	172
	27.0%	7.5%	8.5%	43.0%
Total	185	136	79	400
	46.3%	34.0%	19.8%	100.0%

$\chi^2 = 70.89$, df = 6, $P< 0.001$
K tau b = $P< 0.023$, Significant

Visibility is a crucial deterrent to the potential thieves and burglars Investigation in this study has been made to know if the presence of people around had any impact on the occurrence of crime. The finding of this study [Table 17] shows that most victim [46.3 per cent] were of the opinion that there was presence of people while 34 per cent found that there was no one around crime scene where as 19.8 per cent "did not know" about it. In case of vehicle theft 27 per cent of them said that there were people around crime scene where as "No" opinion and "Do not know" opinion were found to be 7.5 and 8.5 per cent respectively. The chi-square [$\chi^2 = 70.89$, $P< 0.001$] and Kendall's tau-b shows significant value.

History of earlier attempts of theft with the same target is crucial to be subsequent occurrence of crime. Table 18 shows the cross tabulation of variables "crime category" and "history of earlier attempts". The data show that almost 91 per cent of victims did not report any earlier attempt while only 9 per cent victims said that there were earlier attempts. It implies that in the cases covered in the selected townships the recurrence of crime was not found. In case of vehicle theft 4.8 per cent victims were had earlier attempts while 38.2 per cent victims had not reported earlier attempt of vehicle theft. The chi-square value and Kendall's tau-b however, did not convey significant relationship between the two variables.

Table 18
Cross Tabulation of Variables "Crime Category" and "History of Earlier Attempts"

	History of earlier attempts		
Crime Category	*Yes*	*No*	*Total*
Theft from shop/ Business Place	7	133	140
	1.8%	33.4%	35.2%
Theft from residence	10	76	86
	2.5%	19.1%	21.6%
Burglary from shop	0	1	1
	.0%	.3%	.3%
Vehicle theft	19	152	171
	4.8%	38.2%	43.0%
Total	36	362	398
	9.0%	91.0%	100.0%

$\chi^2 = 4.47$, df = 3, P< 0.215 K tau b= P< 0.058, Non-significant

Table 19
Cross Tabulation of Variables
"Crime Category" and "Location of Crime Scene"

	Location of crime scene				
Crime Category	*Hot Spot Bhopal*	*Cool Spot Bhopal*	*Hot Spot Sagar*	*Cool Spot Sagar*	*Total*
Theft from shop/	38	42	27	33	140
Business Place	9.5%	10.5%	6.8%	8.3%	35.0%
Theft from residence	33	6	25	23	87
	8.3%	1.5%	6.3%	5.8%	21.8%
Burglary from shop	0	0	0	1	1
	.0%	.0%	.0%	.3%	.3%
Vehicle theft	31	50	49	42	172
	7.8%	12.5%	12.3%	10.5%	43.0%
Total	102	98	101	99	400
	25.5%	24.5%	25.3%	24.8%	100.0%

$\chi^2 = 29.72$, df = 9, P< 0.001 K tau b= P< 0.099, Significant

Table 19 examines whether the location of crime affected the nature of crime. The data indicate that the total incidence of crime was equally distributed in the hot/cool spot locations of the towns Bhopal and Sagar. There was not any clear pattern emerges from the data shown in the Table. The chi-square value is Significant [$\chi^2 = 29.72$, $P<0.001$] and Kendall's tau-b also shows significant value.

Table 20
Cross Tabulation of Variables "Crime Category" and "Surveillance / Security Arrangements"

	Surveillance/Security arrangements				
Crime Category	*Satis-factory*	*Average*	*Unsatis-factory*	*Others*	*Total*
Theft from shop/	6	64	67	2	139
Business Place	1.5%	16.0%	16.8%	.5%	34.8%
Theft from residence	2	15	70	0	87
	.5%	3.8%	17.5%	.0%	21.8%
Burglary from shop	0	0	1	0	1
	.0%	.0%	.3%	.0%	.3%
Vehicle theft	9	63	100	0	172
	2.3%	15.8%	25.1%	.0%	43.1%
Total	17	142	238	2	399
	4.3%	35.6%	59.6%	.5%	100.0%

$\chi^2 = 27.57$, df = 9, $P< 0.001$
K tau b = $P< 0.405$, Non-significant

The arrangements of security serve the purpose of 'target hardening' to any crime target. As situational factor, the role of surveillance and security arrangements were examined in this study. The data shown in the Table 20 depict that maximum crime [59.6 per cent] was reported from the locations devoid of satisfactory arrangements of surveillance/security whereas the incident was lowest [4.3 per cent] where these were satisfactory. The chi-square value is significant [$\chi^2 = 9$, $P< 0.001$] and K.

4

Analysis of Situational Crime Variables—Part-I

The situational factors identified and studied in respect the city of Bhopal have been further subjected to advanced statistical analysis so that the interaction of various variables could be ascertained. This section deals with the application of ANOVA and Regression analysis of certain variables pertaining to the study.

CRIME SCENE VARIABLES

Distance Analysis Among Crime-scene Variables (Association of Independency)

Table 1 shows the proximity matrix (dissimilarity) among the crime scene variables. The association of independency has been examined through chi square test. This analysis has been done to find out the interaction among the independent crime scene variables. The chi-square is useful to test whether variables differ significantly or not, also useful to determine the extent of association between cross-tabulated variables. The result of chi-square shows that there is statistically significant difference between time of occurrence and lighting arrangement in the premises; time of occurrence and lighting arrangement on the immediate street; week of occurrence and outdoor scene of crime; time of occurrence and outdoor scene of crime. The chi square value gives significance level between

Table 1
Chi-square Matrix Among Crime Scene Variables

Independent Crime Scene Variables → ↓	*Week of Occurrence*	*Time of Occurrence*	*Location of Scene of Crime*	*In case of outdoor scene of crime*	*Lighting arrange-ment on the immediate street*	*Lighting arrange-ment in the premises*	*Was it easy for offender to commit this crime*
Week of Occurrence		9.295	7.845	15.763	14.517	14.703	7.950
Time of Occurrence	9.295		5.546	15.186	17.336	17.796	6.785
Location of Scene of Crime	7.845	5.546		9.789	12.122	12.444	5.686
In case of outdoor scene of crime	15.763	15.186	9.789		20.982	21.124	13.743
Lighting arrangement on the immediate street	14.517	17.336	12.122	20.982		4.582	12.392
Lighting arrangement in the premises	14.703	17.796	12.444	21.124	4.582		12.779
Was it easy for offender to commit this crime	7.950	6.785	5.686	13.743	12.392	12.779	

* This is a dissimilarity matrix

cross-tabulated variables. It shows that the chi-square value is of highest independency in case of time of occurrence and lighting arrangement in the premises, whereas it is lowest of independency in case of lighting arrangement on the immediate street and lighting arrangement in the premises. There is enough evidence [χ = 12.444] that lighting arrangements close to the crime scene location especially in cases like thefts and burglary are quite crucial. From the viewpoint of situational theorists, the lights uncover the identity and causes what is called 'de individualization' which surely works as facilitator to commit crime with impunity.

Distance Analysis Among Crime Scene Variables (Association of Dependency)

Table 2 shows the proximity matrix (similarity) among the crime-scene variables. The association of dependency has been examined through correlation analysis. This analysis has been done to find out the co-linearity among the independent crime scene variables. It is evident from the Table that lighting arrangement on the immediate street and lighting arrangement in the premises were highly correlated. The variables of location of scene of crime and outdoor scene of crime were also found to be significant correlated. The results show that four variables i.e. lighting arrangement on the immediate street, lighting arrangement in the premises, location of scene of crime, outdoor scene of crime are mutually correlated and hence there would be individual contribution as well as interacting effect amongst the variables in question. This Table also gives hierarchy of the crime scenes variables by arranging the correlation values in descending order i.e. lighting arrangement on the immediate street, lighting arrangement in the premises, location of scene of crime, outdoor scene of crime, time of occurrence, was it easy for offender to commit this crime and last week of occurrence.

Regression Co-efficient Between Crime Scene Variables and Crime Category

The regression analysis is performed to find out the extent, direction and strength of relationship between several

Table 2
Correlation Matrix Among Crime Scene Variables

Independent Crime Scene Variables → ↓	*Week of Occurrence*	*Time of Occurrence*	*Location of Scene of Crime*	*In case of outdoor scene of crime*	*Lighting arrange-ment on the immediate street*	*Lighting arrange-ment in the premises*	*Was it easy for offender to commit this crime*
Week of Occurrence		.050	-.030	.064	.055	.076	-.014
Time of Occurrence	.050		.274	.199	-.545	-.560	-.101
Location of Scene of Crime	-.030	.274		.730	-.146	-.129	-.053
In case of outdoor scene of crime	.064	.199	.730		-.128	-.114	-.061
Lighting arrangement on the immediate street	.055	-.545	-.146	-.128		.970	-.098
Lighting arrangement in the premises	.076	-.560	-.129	-.114	.970		-.104
Was it easy for offender to commit this crime	-.014	-.101	-.053	-.061	-.098	-.104	

* This is a similarity matrix

variables and a dependent variable. Table 3 shows the co-efficient of regression model within crime scene variables and crime category. Table shows the value within five parameters. These are unstandardized β, standard error, standardized β, t-value and level of significance.

Table 3
Regression Coefficients Between Crime Scene Variables and Crime Category

Crime Scene Variables	*Unstandardized Coefficients B*	*Std. Error*	*Standardized Coefficients Beta*	*t*	*Sig.*
(Constant)	6.130	.806		7.606	.000
Week of Occurrence	-2.216E-03	.100	-.001	-.022	.982
Time of Occurrence	5.197E-02	.139	.030	.375	.708
Location of Scene of Crime	-1.523	.364	-.392	-4.182	.000
In case of outdoor scene of crime	-6.520E-02	.053	-.113	-1.227	.221
Lighting arrangement on the immediate street	.130	.151	.219	.857	.393
Lighting arrangement in the premises	-.137	.152	-.235	-.902	.368
Was it easy for offender to commit this crime	-.764	.241	-.202	-3.163	.002

** *Dependent Variable:* Crime Category.

The un-standardized β values explains on to what degree each predictor [independent] effects the out-come [dependent], if the effects of all other predictors are held constant or we can say this value as representing the change in outcome associated with a unit change in the predictor.

The standardized β values tell us the number of standard deviations that the outcome [dependent variable] will change as a result of one standard deviation change in the predictor [independent variable]. These β values are in many ways easier to interpret because they are not dependent on the units of measurement of the variable. The β value has associated standard error indicating to what extent these values would vary across different samples.

The error means the difference between observed values to actual value. These standard errors are used in determining whether or not the β value differs significantly from zero. The t-static tests are useful measures of whether the predictor [independent variable] is making a significant contribution to the model. Here model means the relation between all the crime scene variables and crime category. Therefore, if the t-test associated with a β value is significant then the predictor is making a significant contribution to the model. The smaller the value of significance (less than 0.05) and larger the value of t means the greater contribution of that predictor [independent variable].

The value of unstandardized β_1 is -0.0022, this means week of occurrence influences -0.0022 or -0.22 per cent of crime category variable, while other predictor is held constant. All the un-standardized β value can be interpreted in the same way.

The standardized β_1 is -0.001 and this value indicates that as week of occurrence scale increases by unit standard deviation, crime category increases by -0.001 standard deviations. All the standardized β value can be interpreted in the same way. The t-value for location of Scene of Crime -4.182 ($P < 0.001$) and 'was it easy for offender to commit this crime' is -3.163 ($P < 0.002$) is significant predictor of crime category, while week of occurrence and time of occurrence is non-significant predictor of crime category. It denotes that the perception of victims that offender had easy chances to commit crime was found to be significantly correct.

Analysis of Variance (ANOVA) Between Crime Scene Variables and Crime Category

The analysis of variance [ANOVA] has the advantage that it can be used to analyse situations in which there are several independent variables. ANOVA shows how the independent variables interact with each other and what effects these interactions have on the dependent variable. We need to know how much of this variation the regression model can explain (Model sum of square, SSM) as well as how much of the variation cannot explain by the model (Residual sum of squares, SS_R). The regression model is intended to apply to measure the strength of relation between all crime scene variables and crime category. The strength of association between crime scene variables and crime category is known in statistical terms as model sum of square that means how much of this variation the regression model can explain, while non-associated strength between crime scene variables and crime category is known in statistical terms as residual sum of square that means how much of this variation remains unexplained by this model.

The most important part of Table 4 is the F-ratio, which is 9.601 is significant at $P < 0.001$. In this case, there is a probability of .001 that an F ratio of this size would occur by chance (that's only a 0.1% chance), hence, because the observed significant value is less than .05 we can say that the regression model overall predicts crime category significantly well. SST = SSM + SSR. This value conveys that regression value is greater than residual than the variable has significant contribution for crime category or if residual value is greater than regression value than these crime scene variables has non-significant contribution for crime category.

Table 4
Analysis of Variance [ANOVA] Between Crime Scene Variables and Crime Category

Model Parameters	*Sum of Squares*	*df*	*Mean Square*	*F*	*Sig.*
Regression	175.306	7	25.044	9.601	.000
Residual	500.849	192	2.609		
Total	676.155	199			

* *Predictors:* (Constant), Was it easy for offender to commit this crime, Week of Occurrence, Location of Scene of Crime, Lighting arrangement in the premises, Time of Occurrence, In case of outdoor scene of crime, Lighting arrangement on the immediate street.

** *Dependent Variable:* Crime Category.

However, the ANOVA does not tells about the individual contribution of variables in the model yet it tells us whether the model overall results in a significant good degree of prediction of the outcome variable.

Model Showing Summary Between Crime Scene Variables and Crime Category

Table 5 describes whether the model is successful is predicting crime category. This summary table provides the value of R and R^2 for the model that has been derived. The model means effect of all crime scene variables and crime category and nature of relationship between them. Table shows the value of multiple correlations co-efficient [R], coefficient of determination [R^2], Adjusted R^2, standard error of the estimate and F-ratio. The R is a measure of the multiple correlations between the predictors and the outcome and that R^2 indicates the variable in the outcome for which the predictors account. The adjusted R^2 value indicates the loss of predictive power or shrinkage. The R has a value of 0.509 and this value represents the multiple correlations between crime scene variables and crime category. The value of R^2 Coefficient of determination is 0.259, which tells us that crime scene variables account for 25.9 per cent of the variation for crime category.

The adjusted R^2 gives some idea of how well the model generalizes and ideally its value to be the same or very close to the value of R2 (coefficient of determination). The difference between coefficient of determination [R^2] and adjusted R^2 shows the loss of predictive power across different samples. In fact the difference between the values is 0.259 - 0.232 = 0.027 (about 2.7 per cent). This means across different samples in same population the loss of prediction is 2.7 per cent.

Table 5
Model Showing Summary Between Crime Scene Variables and Crime Category

R	*R Square*	*Adjusted R Square*	*Std. Error of the Estimate*	*R Square Change*	*F Change*
.509	.259	.232	1.62	.259	9.601

* *Predictors:* (Constant), Was it easy for offender to commit this crime, Week of Occurrence, Location of Scene of Crime, Lighting arrangement in the premises, Time of Occurrence, Lighting arrangement on the immediate street

This shrinkage means that if the model were derived from the population rather than a sample it would account for approximately 2.7 per cent variance in the outcome.

Regression Coefficient Between Crime Scene Variables and Target vulnerability

Table 6 shows the result of regression. The value of β_0 is 2.114, which means that all the variables are excluded then this model predicts 2.114 of target vulnerability. The value of β_1 is 0.00117, which can be interpreted in the way that with every unit increase in the week of occurrence scale, the target vulnerability is increased by 0.00117 units. This interpretation is true only if the effects of other crime scene variable are held constant. All other unstandardized β value interpreted in the same way.

The value of standardized β_1 is 0.001 that means that week of occurrence scale target vulnerability are increased per 0.001 unit standard deviation. This interpretation is true only if the effects of other crime scene variable are held constant. All other standardized β value is interpreted in the same way.

The t-statistic value for the outdoor scene of crime is 2.775 (level of significance = .006, $P<0.05$) are the significant predictor of target vulnerability while t value for the week of occurrence variable is .021 (Level of significance = .983, $P > 0.05$) are the non-significant predictor of target vulnerability. The similar way all other t statistic value can be interpreted for this model.

Table 6
Regression Coefficients Between Crime Scene Variables and Target Vulnerability

Crime Scene Variables	*Unstandardized Coefficients B*	*Std. Error*	*Standardized Coefficients Beta*	*t*	*Sig.*
(Constant)	2.114	.449		4.713	.000
Week of Occurrence	1.170E-03	.056	.001	.021	.983
Time of Occurrence	4.720E-02	.077	.054	.612	.541
Location of Scene of Crime	-5.211E-03	.203	-.003	-.026	.980
Lighting arrangement on the immediate street	4.366E-03	.084	.015	.052	.959
Lighting arrangement in the premises	9.970E-03	.084	.034	.118	.906
Was it easy for offender to commit this crime	-.183	.134	-.096	-1.364	.174

** *Dependent Variable:* What made target lucrative.

Analysis of Variance (ANOVA) Between Crime Scene Variables and Target Vulnerability

Table 7 exhibits an analysis of variance (ANOVA) that tests whether the model is significantly better at predicting the outcome. This analysis shows the three values i.e. variation explained by the model [model sum of squares (SSM)], variation unexplained by the model [residual sum of squares (SSR)] and total variation of the model [total sum of square (SST)]. The result of ANOVA shows that model sum of squares (SSM) is 16.777, while residual sum of squares (SSR) is 155.098 whereas total sum of square (SST) is 171.875. The value of F-ratio [2.967, p<0.006] explains that the independent crime scene variables have significant contribution in dependent variable [target vulnerability]. It shows that the situational likelihood was significantly contingent upon the situational variables like time, location of crime scene, visibility of crime scene and perceived easiness to commit crime.

Table 7
Analysis of Variance [ANOVA] Between Crime Scene Variables and Target Vulnerability

Model Parameters	*Sum of Squares*	*df*	*Mean Square*	*F*	*Sig.*
Regression	16.777	7	2.397	2.967	.006
Residual	155.098	192	.808		
Total	171.875	199			

* *Predictors:* (Constant), Was it easy for offender to commit this crime, Week of Occurrence, Location of Scene of Crime, Lighting arrangement in the premises, Time of Occurrence, In case of outdoor scene of crime, Lighting arrangement on the immediate street

** Dependent Variable: What made target lucrative

Model Summary Between Crime Scene Variables and Target Vulnerability

Table 8 shows that the value of R (multiple correlation coefficient) is 0.419, which describes the level proportional associations [0.312] between crime scene variables and target vulnerability. The co-efficient of determination (R2) value is 0.098; if we convert this value into percentage then it can be said that crime scene variables account for 9.8 per cent of the variability in target vulnerability. The adjusted R2 value is 0.065 and the difference between R2 is (0.098 - 0.065 = 0.033) which means loss of predictive power is 3.3 per cent (across different samples in the same population).

Table 8
Model Summary Between Crime Scene Variables and Target Vulnerability

R	*R Square*	*Adjusted R Square*	*Std. Error of the Estimate*	*Change Statistics R Square Change*	*F Change*
.312	.098	.065	.90	.098	2.967

* *Predictors:* (Constant), Was it easy for offender to commit this crime, Week of Occurrence, Location of Scene of Crime, Lighting arrangement in the premises, Time of Occurrence, In case of outdoor scene of crime, Lighting arrangement on the immediate street.

Regression Co-efficient Between Crime Scene Variables and Safeness of the Area

Table 9 shows the results of regression. The value of β_0 is 1.578 that conveys the all crime scene variables are excluded and this model predicts 1.578 per unit of safeness of the area. The value of β_1 is -0.02149 that explains that with every unit increase in the week of occurrence variable scale, the safeness of the area variable is increased by -0.02149 units. This must be true if the effects of other crime scene variable are held constant.

Table 9
Regression Coefficients Between Crime Scene Variables and Perceived Safeness of the Area

Crime Scene Variables	*Unstandardized Coefficients B*	*Std. Error*	*Standardized Coefficients Beta*	*t*	*Sig.*
(Constant)	1.578	.295		5.352	.000
Week of Occurrence	-2.149E-02	.037	-.043	-.585	.559
Time of Occurrence	-2.346E-02	.051	-.042	-.463	.644
Location of Scene of Crime	.154	.133	.125	1.156	.249
In case of outdoor scene of crime	-2.858E-04	.019	-.002	-.015	.988
Lighting arrangement on the immediate street	-1.712E-02	.055	-.091	-.310	.757
Lighting arrangement in the premises	2.612E-02	.055	.141	.471	.638
Was it easy for offender to commit this crime	4.629E-02	.088	.038	.524	.601

** *Dependent Variable:* Do you find this area safe.

The value of standardized β_1 is -0.043, which means that week of occurrence scale is increased by unit standard deviation; safeness of the area variable is increased by -0.043 standard deviations. This interpretation is true only if the effects of other crime scene variables are held constant. All other un-standardized β values and standardized β value are interpreted in the same way.

The t value for the variable location of scene of crime is 1.156 (Level of significance 0.249, P > 0.05) and in a moderate significant predictor of safeness of the area, while t-value for the variable In case of outdoor scene of crime is -0.015 (Level of significance = 0.988, P < 0.05) is a non-significant predictor of area of safety variable. All other value of t-static can be interpreted in the same way.

Analysis of Variance (ANOVA) Between Crime Scene Variables and Perceived Safeness of the Area

Table 10 denotes the components of analysis of variance (ANOVA). The result of ANOVA shows that model sum of square (SSM) is 1.471 (explained variance) and residual sum of squares (SSR) is 67.009 (unexplained variance) where as total sum of squares (SST) is 68.480 (total variance). The F ratio value is 0.602 (Level of significance = 0.754, P > .05), which shows non-significant results. This means in this model there is much un-explained variance than explained variance.

Table 10
Analysis of Variance [ANOVA] Between Crime Scene Variables and Perceived Safeness of the Area

Model Parameters	*Sum of Squares*	*df*	*Mean Square*	*F*	*Sig.*
Regression	1.471	7	.210	.602	.754
Residual	67.009	192	.349		
Total	68.480	199			

* *Predictors:* (Constant), Was it easy for offender to commit this crime, Week of Occurrence, Location of Scene of Crime, Lighting arrangement in the premises, Time of Occurrence, In case of outdoor scene of crime, Lighting arrangement on the immediate street.

** *Dependent Variable:* Do you find this area safe.

Model Summary Between Crime Scene Variables and Perceived Safeness of the Area

Table 11 describes the multiple correlations co-efficient (R) that are 0.147; define the level of association between crime scene variables and perceived safety of area. The coefficient of determination (R2) is 0.021 that means 2.1 per cent of the variability by crime scene variables account for perceived safety of area. The adjusted R2 value is -0.014 and the difference between R2 is [0.021 - (-0.14) = 0.35] which means across different samples loss of predictive power is 35 per cent.

Table 11
Model Summary Between Crime Scene Variables and Perceived Area of Safety

R	*R Square*	*Adjusted R Square*	*Std. Error of the Estimate*	*Change Statistics R Square Change*	*F Change*
.147	.021	-.014	.59	.021	.602

* *Predictors:* (Constant), Was it easy for offender to commit this crime, Week of Occurrence, Location of Scene of Crime, Lighting arrangement in the premises, Time of Occurrence, In case of outdoor scene of crime, Lighting arrangement on the immediate street.

OWNER'S BEHAVIOR VARIABLES

Distance Analysis Among Owner's Behavior Variables (Association of Independency)

Table 12 shows the dissimilarity matrix within owner's behavior variables. This analysis is necessary to find out the relation within variables. This matrix also gives a clear picture about the independent association among them. It exhibits from the table that "distance between crime target and owner at the time of crime commission" and "how much time remains away from the target"; "what was victim doing that time" and "how much time remains away from the target" have significant chi-square value.

Table 12
Chi-square Matrix of Owner's Behavior Variables

→ ↓ *Independent Ow.ers Behavior Variables*	*Average time spent at home*	*How much time remains away from the target*	*Distance between workplace and crime scene*	*Distance between crime target and owner at the time of crime commission*	*Did crime occur in the absence of victim*	*What was victim doing that time*	*Did the victim resist crime*	*Did the offender over power victim*
Average time spent at home		14.151	8.392	9.040	4.226	8.871	3.560	3.276
How much time remains away from the target	14.151		14.695	18.270	10.312	15.076	14.661	14.464
Distance between workplace and crime scene	8.392	14.695		11.705	7.256	10.142	8.423	8.166
Distance between crime target and owner at the time of crime commission	9.040	18.270	11.705		9.891	13.652	7.745	7.874
Did crime occur in the absence of victim	4.226	10.312	7.256	9.891		8.075	4.631	4.198
hat was victim doing that time	8.871	15.076	10.142	13.652	8.075		9.136	8.916
Did the victim resist crime	3.560	14.661	8.423	7.745	4.631	9.136		1.517
Did the offender overpower victim	3.276	14.464	8.166	7.874	4.198	8.916	1.517	

*This is a dissimilarity matrix

Distance Analysis Among Owner's Behavior Variables (Association of Dependency)

Table 13 shows the similarity matrix within owner's behavior variables. This analysis provides relationship within variables as well as conveys the level of dependency among them. The correlation between the variables i.e. "did crime occur in the absence of victim" and "how much time remains away from the target"; "what was victim doing that time" and "how much time remains away from the target" both the value have significant correlation at the 0.05 level.

Regression Coefficient Between Owner's Behavior Variables and Crime Category

Table 14 shows the results of regression. The value of β_0 is 6.230, which means that all the owner's behavior variables are excluded then this model predicts 6.230of crime category. The value of β_1 is 0.01664, which conveys that with every unit increase in the variable average time spent at home scale, the crime category is increased by 0.01664 units. This interpretation is true only if the effects of other owner's behavior variables are held constant. All other unstandardized value interpreted in the same way.

The value of standardized β_1 is 0.005 that means that the variable "average time spent at home" scale increases by unit standard deviation, crime category is increased per 0.005 unit standard deviation. This interpretation is true only if the effects of other owner's behavior variables are held constant. All other standardized value β is interpreted in the same way.

The t value for the distance between crime target and owner at the time of crime commission variable is -5.908 ($P<0.05$). It is a significant predictor of crime category while t value for the variable average time spent at home is 0.075 ($P > 0.05$) the non-significant predictor of crime category. The similar way all other values can be interpreted for this model.

Table 13
Correlation Matrix of Owner's Behavior Variables

→ ↓ *Independent Owners Behavior Variables*	*Average time spent at home*	*How much time remains away from the target*	*Distance between workplace and crime scene*	*Distance between crime target and owner at the time of crime commission*	*Did crime occur in the absence of victim*	*What was victim doing that time*	*Did the victim resist crime*	*Did the offender over power victim*
Average time spent at home		.321	.218	-.084	.280	.247	-.064	-.047
How much time remains away from the target	.321		.164	-.237	.678	.386	-.269	-.177
Distance between workplace and crime scene	.218	.164		-.142	.243	.299	-.229	.048
Distance between crime target and owner at the time of crime commission	-.084	-.237	-.142		-.509	-.290	.159	.068
Did crime occur in the absence of victim	.280	.678	.243	-.509		.236	-.334	-.176
What was victim doing that time	.247	.386	.299	-.290	.236		-.184	-.079
Did the victim resist crime	-.064	-.269	-.229	.159	-.334	-.184		.254
Did the offender overpower victim	-.047	-.177	.048	.068	-.176	-.079	.254	

*This is a similarity matrix

Table 14
Regression Coefficients Between Owner's Behavior Variables and Crime Category

Crime Scene Variables	*Unstandardized Coefficients B*	*Std. Error*	*Standardized Coefficients Beta*	*t*	*Sig.*
(Constant)	6.230	2.492		2.500	.013
Average time spent at home	1.664E-02	.222	.005	.075	.940
How much time remains away from the target	-.212	.048	-.381	-4.404	.000
Distance between workplace and crime scene	1.300E-02	.081	.010	.161	.872
Distance between crime target and owner at the time of crime commission	-.561	.095	-.419	-5.908	.000
Did crime occur in the absence of victim	-1.391	.407	-.325	-3.420	.001
What was victim doing that time	7.659E-02	.079	.066	.967	.335
Did the victim resist crime	-.194	.640	-.019	-.302	.763
Did the offender overpower victim	.236	1.119	.013	.211	.833

** *Dependent Variable:* Crime Category.

Analysis of Variance (ANOVA) Between Owner's Behavior Variables and Crime Category

Table 15 exhibits an analysis of variance (ANOVA) that tests whether the model is significantly better at predicting the outcome. The model examines interaction between all owner's behavior variables and crime category. This analysis shows the three values i.e. variation explained by the model [model sum of squares (SSM)], variation unexplained by the model [residual sum of squares (SSR)] and total variation of the model [total sum of square (SST)]. The result of ANOVA shows that model sum of squares (SSM) is 247.979; while residual sum of squares (SSR) is 428.176 whereas total sum of square (SST) is 676.155. The value of F-ratio is greater than 1, which means that the independent owner's behavior variables have significant contribution in dependent variable [crime category]. The F-ratio value is 13.827, which is significant [$P < .001$] in terms of affecting or causing the occurrence of crime. The exact magnitude of the F-ratio can be assessed using critical values for the corresponding degree of freedom.

Table 15
Analysis of Variance [ANOVA] Between Owner's Behavior Variables and Crime Category

Model Parameters	*Sum of Squares*	*df*	*Mean Square*	*F*	*Sig.*
Regression	247.979	8	30.997	13.827	.000
Residual	428.176	191	2.242		
Total	676.155	199			

* *Predictors:* (Constant), Did the offender overpower victim, Average time spent at home, Distance between crime target and owner at the time of crime commission, Distance between workplace and crime scene, Did the victim resist crime, What was victim doing that time, How much time remains away from the target, Did crime occur in the absence of victim

** *Dependent Variable:* Crime Category

Model Showing Summary Between Owner's Behavior Variables and Crime Category

Table 16 describes proportional association between owner's behavior variables and crime category [R = 0.606].

The co-efficient of determination (R^2) value is 0.367, if this value is converted into percentage then it suggests that owner's behavior variables account for 36.7 per cent of the variability in crime category. This contribution is remarkable and explains the extent to which the various aspects of behavior of owner are situationally responsible in causing the occurrence of crime.

Table 16
Model Summary Between Owner's Behavior Variables and Crime Category

R	*R Square*	*Adjusted R Square*	*Std. Error of the Estimate*	*Change Statistics R Square Change*	*F Change*
.606	.367	.340	1.50	.367	13.827

* *Predictors:* (Constant), Did the offender overpower victim, Average time spent at home, Distance between crime target and owner at the time of crime commission, Distance between workplace and crime scene, Did the victim resist crime, What was victim doing that time, How much time remains away from the target, Did crime occur in the absence of victim.

Regression Co-efficient Between Owner's Behavior Variables and Target Vulnerability

Table 17 shows the results of regression. The value of β_0 is 0.618 that means that the all owners' behavior variables are excluded and this model predicts 0.618 per unit of target vulnerability. The value of β_1 is -0.07.220 that means every unit increase in the scale of average time spent at home is increased by -0.07.220 units. This must be true if the effects of other owner's behavior variable are held constant. The value of standardized β_1 is -0.040, which means that average time spent at home scale can increase by unit standard deviation, target vulnerability is increased by -0.040 standard deviations. This interpretation is true only if the effects of other owner's behavior variable are held constant. All other un-standardized β values and standardized β value are interpreted in the same way.

Table 17
Regression Coefficients Between Owner's Behavior Variables and Target Vulnerability

Crime Scene Variables	*Unstandardized Coefficients B*	*Std. Error*	*Standardized Coefficients Beta*	*t*	*Sig.*
(Constant)	.618	1.497		.413	.680
Average time spent at home	-7.220E-02	.133	-.040	-.542	.588
How much time remains away from the target	-5.072E-02	.029	-.181	-1.751	.082
Distance between workplace and crime scene	3.680E-02	.049	.057	.759	.449
Distance between crime target and owner at the time of crime commission	.134	.057	.199	2.353	.020
Did crime occurs in the absence of victim	9.656E-02	.244	.045	.395	.693
What was victim doing that time	-2.657E-02	.048	-.045	-.559	.577
Did the victim resist crime	-.162	.385	-.032	-.421	.674
Did the offender overpower victim	.937	.672	.101	1.394	.165

** *Dependent Variable:* What made target lucrative

The t value for distance between crime target and owner at the time of crime commission variable is 2.353 (P > 0.05) is a significant predictor of target vulnerability, while t-value for "did crime occur in the absence of victim" is 0.395 (P < 0.05) are non-significant predictor of target vulnerability.

Analysis of Variance [ANOVA] Between Owner's Behavior Variables and Target Vulnerability

Table 18 shows the results of analysis of variance (ANOVA). The result of ANOVA shows that model sum of square (SSM) is 17.446 (explained variance) and residual sum of squares (SSR) is 154.429 (unexplained variance) where as total sum of squares (SST) is 171.875 (total variance). The F ratio value is 2.697 (Level of significance = 0.008, P > .05), which shows non-significant results. This means there is much un-explained variance than explained variance in this model.

Table 18
Analysis of Variance [ANOVA] Between Owner's Behavior Variables and Target Vulnerability

Model Parameters	*Sum of Squares*	*df*	*Mean Square*	*F*	*Sig.*
Regression	17.446	8	2.181	2.697	.008
Residual	154.429	191	.809		
Total	171.875	199			

* *Predictors:* (Constant), Did the offender overpower victim, Average time spent at home, Distance between crime target and owner at the time of crime commission, Distance between workplace and crime scene, Did the victim resist crime, What was victim doing that time, How much time remains away from the target, Did crime occur in the absence of victim.

** *Dependent Variable:* What made target lucrative.

Model Summary Between Owner's Behavior Variables and Target Vulnerability

Table 19 describes the multiple correlations co-efficient (R) that is .319 and defines the level of association between owner's behavior variables and target vulnerability. The coefficient of determination (R2) is 0.102 that means 10.2 per cent of the variability account for target vulnerability. The adjusted R2 value is .064 and the difference between R2 is (0.102 - .064 =

0.038) which means across different samples loss of predictive power is 3.8 per cent.

Table 19
Model Summary Between Owner's Behavior Variables and Target Vulnerability

R	*R Square*	*Adjusted R Square*	*Std. Error of the Estimate*	*Change Statistics R Square Change*	*F Change*
.319	.102	.064	.90	.102	2.697

* *Predictors:* (Constant), Did the offender overpower victim, Average time spent at home, Distance between crime target and owner at the time of crime commission, Distance between workplace and crime scene, Did the victim resist crime, What was victim doing that time, How much time remains away from the target, Did crime occur in the absence of victim.

Regression Coefficient Between Owner's Behavior Variables and Perceived Safety of Area

Table 20 shows the results of regression. The value of β_0 is 0.332, which means the all owners' behavior variables are excluded and the model predicts 0.332 of perceived safety of area. The value of β_1 is 0.07983 that means average time spent at home variable is 0.07983 proportional increase of perceived safety of area. The value of standardized β_1 is 0.071 that means average time spent at home variable is 0.071 proportional standard deviation increases as per perceived safety of area standard deviations.

The t value for distance between crime target and owner at the time of crime commission variable is 1.638 ($P < .005$) are the significance predictor of perceived safety of area while t value for what was victim doing that time variable is -.139 ($P > .005$) are the non significant predictor of perceived safety of area. It sums up that the absence of the owner becomes significant factor causing a vulnerable situation for crime commission.

Analysis of Variance (ANOVA) Between Owner's Behavior Variables and Perceived Safety of Area

Table 21 shows the analysis of variance (ANOVA). The result of ANOVA shows that model sum of square (SSM) is 2.392

Table 20
Regression Coefficients Between Owner's Behavior Variables and Perceived Safety of Area

Crime Scene Variables	*Unstandardized Coefficients B*	*Std. Error*	*Standardized Coefficients Beta*	*t*	*Sig.*
(Constant)	.332	.979		.339	.735
Average time spent at home	7.983E-02	.087	.071	.917	.361
How much time remains away from the target	-1.156E-02	.019	-.065	-.610	.543
Distance between workplace and crime scene	2.906E-02	.032	.072	.916	.361
Distance between crime target and owner at the time of crime commission	6.117E-02	.037	.144	1.638	.103
Did crime occur in the absence of victim	.205	.160	.150	1.280	.202
What was victim doing that time	-4.338E-03	.031	-.012	-.139	.889
Did the victim resist crime	.264	.252	.083	1.051	.295
Did the offender overpower victim	.163	.440	.028	.371	.711

** *Dependent Variable:* Do you find this area safe .

while residual sum of squares (SSR) is 66.088 where as total sum of square (SST) is 68.480. The F ratio is 0.864 which is non significant at P > 0.548, it means there is more unsystematic variance than systematic variance.

Table 21
Analysis of Variance [ANOVA] Between Owner's Behavior Variables and Perceived Area of Safety

Model Parameters	*Sum of Squares*	*df*	*Mean Square*	*F*	*Sig.*
Regression	2.392	8	.299	.864	.548
Residual	66.088	191	.346		
Total	68.480	199			

* *Predictors:* (Constant), Did the offender overpower victim, Average time spent at home, Distance between crime target and owner at the time of crime commission, Distance between workplace and crime scene, Did the victim resist crime, What was victim doing that time, How much time remains away from the target, Did crime occur in the absence of victim.

** *Dependent Variable:* Do you find this area safe.

Model Summary Between Owner's Behavior Variables and Perceived Safety of Area

Table 22 describes the multiple correlation coefficient (R) that is 0.187 which represents the multiple correlation between owner's behavior variables and perceived safety of area. The coefficient of determination (R2) is 0.035, which means 3.5 per cent of the variability in perceived safety of area is determined by owner's behavior variables. The adjusted R2 value is -0.005 and the difference between R2 is (0.035 - [-0.005] = 0.040) means across different sample the loss of prediction is 4.0 per cent. This explains that the perception of the subject about the safety of an area depends on his past behavior and attitude.

Table 22
Model Summary Between Owner's Behavior Variables and Perceived Area of Safety

R	*R Square*	*Adjusted R Square*	*Std. Error of the Estimate*	*Change Statistics R Square Change*	*F Change*
.187	.035	-.005	.59	.035	.864

* *Predictors:* (Constant), Did the offender overpower victim, Average time spent at home, Distance between crime target and owner at the time of crime commission, Distance between workplace and crime scene, Did the victim resist crime, What was victim doing that time, How much time remains away from the target, Did crime occur in the absence of victim

VICTIM RELATED VARIABLES

Distance Analysis Among Victim Related Variable (Association of Independency)

Table 23 shows the test of significance within victim related variables. This matrix gives a clear picture about the association of independency within variables. Table shows that occupation of victim and the way target were approached; age of the victim and the way target was approached as well as occupation of victim and construction quality of wall/premise variable have significant chi-square value. The matrix depicts the inter correlation within the chosen variables.

Table 23

Chi-square Matrix Among Victim Related Variables

Independent Victim Related Variables	*Age of the victim*	*Sex of the victim*	*Occupation of victim*	*How was target approached*	*The construction quality of wall/ premise*	*Was any implement used in the commission of crime*
Age of the victim		5.410	7.655	9.319	8.821	7.126
Sex of the victim	5.410		5.725	5.885	6.852	4.343
Occupation of victim	7.655	5.725		9.552	9.098	7.710
How was target approached	9.319	5.885	9.552		8.260	5.673
The construction quality of wall/premise	8.821	6.852	9.098	8.260		7.993
Was any implement used in the commission of crime	7.126	4.343	7.710	5.673	7.993	

* This is a dissimilarity matrix

Distance Analysis Among Victim Related Variable (Association of Dependency)

Table 24 shows multi-colinearity within the chosen independent variables. The variable 'sex of the victim' and 'was any implement used in the commission of crime' as well as sex of the victim and construction quality of wall/premise, both the value have significant correlation at the 0.05 levels. It exhibits from the study that the variables do not show any strong multi-colinearity among them (Conventionally for multi-colinearity the correlation value must be in between 0.60 to 0.80).

Regression Coefficient Between Victim's Related Variables and Crime Category

Table 25 shows the results of regression. The value of β_0 is 5.466, which means the all victim's related variables are excluded then model that predicts 5.466 of crime category.

The value of β_1 is -0.381 and it infers that variable of age of the victim is inversely proportional to crime category. The negative sign denotes the inverse relation between the two variables. The value of standardized β_1 is negative [-0.205] that means age of the victim is [in proportional standard deviation, terms] varies along crime category standard deviations.

The t statistic value for "implement used" in the commission of crime variable is -4.850 (Level of significance = .000, $P < .005$). It is a significance predictor of crime category while t value for the variable quality of wall/premise is 0.166 (Level of significance = 0.869, $P > .005$) and it is not a significant predictor of crime category.

Analysis of Variance (ANOVA) Between Victim's Related Variables and Crime Category

Table 26 denotes the components of analysis of variance (ANOVA). The result of ANOVA shows that model sum of square (SSM) is 150.087 while residual sum of squares (SSR) is 514.695 where as total sum of square (SST) is 664.782. The F ratio is 9.234 which are significant at $P < .001$, it means there is more systematic variance than unsystematic variance and model over all predict crime category significantly well.

Table 24
Correlation Matrix Among Victim Related Variables

Independent Victim Related Variables	*Age of the victim*	*Sex of the victim*	*Occupation of victim*	*How was target approached*	*The construction quality of wall/ premise*	*Was any implement used in the commission of crime*
Age of the victim		.068	.111	-.152	-.113	.005
Sex of the victim	.068		.208	.149	-.274	.327
Occupation of victim	.111	.208		-.113	-.054	-.026
How was target approached	-.152	.149	-.113		.211	.387
The construction quality of wall/premise	-.113	-.274	-.054	.211		.003
Was any implement used in the commission of crime	.005	.327	-.026	.387	.003	

* This is a similarity matrix

Table 25
Regression Coefficients Between Victim's Related Variables and Crime Category

Victim Related Variables	*Unstandardized Coefficients B*	*Std. Error*	*Standardized Coefficients Beta*	*t*	*Sig.*
(Constant)	5.466	1.081		5.056	.000
Age of the victim	-.381	.121	-.205	-3.144	.002
Sex of the victim	-.839	.379	-.162	-2.215	.028
Occupation of victim	-5.624E-02	.119	-.031	-.474	.636
How was target approached	.222	.114	.141	1.942	.054
The construction quality of wall/premise	1.525E-02	.092	.011	.166	.869
Was any implement used in the commission of crime	-.901	.186	-.352	-4.850	.000

** *Dependent Variable:* Crime Category

Table 26
Analysis of Variance [ANOVA] Between Victim's Related Variables and Crime Category

Model Parameters	*Sum of Squares*	*df*	*Mean Square*	*F*	*Sig.*
Regression	150.087	6	25.015	9.234	.000
Residual	514.695	190	2.709		
Total	664.782	196			

* *Predictors:* (Constant), Was any implement used in the commission of crime, the construction quality of wall/premise, Occupation of victim, Age of the victim, How was target approached, Sex of the victim.

***Dependent Variable:* Crime Category

Model Summary Between Victim's Related Variables and Crime Category

Table 27 describes the multiple correlation coefficient (R) that is 0.475 represents the multiple correlation between victim's related variables and crime category. The coefficient of determination (R2) is 0.226 which means 22.6 per cent of the variability in crime category is determined by victim's related variables. The adjusted R2 value is 0.201 and the difference between R2 is (0.226 - 0.201= 0.025) means across different sample the loss of prediction is 2.5 per cent.

Table 27
Model Summary Between Victim's Related Variables and Crime Category

R	*R Square*	*Adjusted R Square*	*Std. Error of the Estimate*	*Change Statistics R Square Change*	*F Change*
.475	.226	.201	1.65	.226	9.234

* *Predictors:* (Constant), Was any implement used in the commission of crime, the construction quality of wall/premise, Occupation of victim, Age of the victim, How was target approached, Sex of the victim.

Regression Coefficient Between Victim's Related Variables and Target Vulnerability

Table 28 shows the results of regression. The value of β_0 is 4.349, which means that all the victim's related variables are excluded and the model predicts 4.349 of the variable target vulnerability.

Table 28
Regression Coefficients Between Victim's Related Variables and Target Vulnerability

Crime Scene Variables	*Unstandardized Coefficients B*	*Std. Error*	*Standardized Coefficients Beta*	*t*	*Sig.*
(Constant)	4.349	.566		7.684	.000
Age of the victim	-2.258E-02	.063	-.024	-.356	.722
Sex of the victim	-.553	.198	-.213	-2.789	.006
Occupation of victim	3.253E-02	.062	.036	.523	.601
How was target approached	-.148	.060	-.188	-2.471	.014
The construction quality of wall/premise	-8.409E-02	.048	-.126	-1.744	.083
Was any implement used in the commission of crime	-.162	.097	-.126	-1.666	.097

** *Dependent Variable:* What made target lucrative

The value of β_1 is -2.258E-02. This means every unit change in the age of the victim variable scale results into change by - 0.02258 units in the target vulnerability variable. The value of standardized β_1 is -0.024, which means every unit standard deviation variation in the 'age of the victim' scale causes the variation of -0.024 standard deviation units in the variable of target vulnerability. This interpretation is true only if the other victim's related variables are held constant.

The t - statistic value for the Sex of thè victim variable [P < 0.05) is the significant predictor of target vulnerability while t-value for Age of the victim variable is [0.722, P < 0.05) is a non significant predictor of target vulnerability. These corresponding significance value arranging in increasing order gives that sex of the victim is a significant and age of the victim is non-significant predictor of target vulnerability.

Analysis of Variance (ANOVA) Between Victim's Related Variables and Target Vulnerability

Table 29 indicates the components of analysis of variance (ANOVA). The result of ANOVA shows that F ratio is 5.812 which is significant at P < .001, it means model overall predicts target vulnerability significantly.

Table 29
Analysis of Variance [ANOVA] Between Victim's Related Variables and Target Vulnerability

Model Parameters	*Sum of Squares*	*df*	*Mean Square*	*F*	*Sig.*
Regression	25.885	6	4.314	5.812	.000
Residual	141.039	190	.742		
Total	166.924	196			

* *Predictors:* (Constant), Was any implement used in the commission of crime, the construction quality of wall/premise, Occupation of victim, Age of the victim, How was target approached, Sex of the victim.

***Dependent Variable:* What made target lucrative.

Model Summary Between Victim's Related Variables and Target Vulnerability

Table 30 describes the multiple correlation coefficient (R) which is 0.394 while coefficient of determination (R2) is 0.155 means 15.5 per cent of the variability in target vulnerability is determined by the victim's related variables.

Table 30
Model Summary Between Victim's Related Variables and Target Vulnerability

R	*R Square*	*Adjusted R Square*	*Std. Error of the Estimate*	*Change Statistics R Square Change*	*F Change*
.394	.155	.128	.86	.155	5.812

* *Predictors:* (Constant), Was any implement used in the commission of crime, the construction quality of wall/premise, Occupation of victim, Age of the victim, How was target approached, Sex of the victim.

Regression Coefficient Between Victim's Related Variables and Perceived Area of Safety

Table 31 shows the results of regression. The value of β_0 is 1.979, which means that the entire victim's related variables are excluded then this model predicts 1.979 of perceived safety of area. The value of β_1 0.01527 implies that every unit increase in the age of the victim scale causes variation of 0.01527 units in the perceived safety of area. This interpretation is true only it the effects of other victim's related variables are held constant. All other unstandardized value could be interpreted in the same way.

Table 31
Regression Coefficients Between Victim's Related Variables and Perceived Area of Safety

Crime Scene Variables	*Unstandardized Coefficients B*	*Std. Error*	*Standardized Coefficients Beta*	*t*	*Sig.*
(Constant)	1.979	.376		5.262	.000
Age of the victim	1.527E-02	.042	.026	.362	.718
Sex of the victim	.181	.132	.109	1.372	.172
Occupation of victim	-5.815E-02	.041	-.102	-1.408	.161
How was target approached	-.120	.040	-.239	-3.012	.003
The construction quality of wall/premise	-1.286E-02	.032	-.030	-.401	.689
Was any implement used in the commission of crime	.144	.065	.177	2.231	.027

** *Dependent Variable:* Do you find this area safe.

The t-statistic value for "How was target approached" variable is [P<0.05) significant predictor of perceived safety of area while t value for the age of the victim variable [P > 0.05) are the non-significant predictor of perceived safety of area. The similar way all other t statistic value can be interpreted for this model.

Analysis of Variance (ANOVA) Between Victim's Related Variables and Perceived Area of Safety

Table 32 exhibits an analysis of variance (ANOVA) that tests whether the model is significant at predicting the outcome. In this case, the model means the interaction between entire victim's related variables and perceived safety of area. This analysis offers three values i.e. variation explained by the model [model sum of squares (SSM)], variation unexplained by the model [residual sum of squares (SSR)] and total variation of the model [total sum of square (SST)]. The result of ANOVA shows that model sum of squares (SSM) is 5.521, while residual sum of squares (SSR) is 62.266 whereas total sum of square (SST) is 67.787. The F-ratio value is significant [P < .012], which means model has significantly predicted the outcome. The exact magnitude of the F-ratio can be assessed using critical values for the corresponding degree of freedom.

Table 32
Analysis of Variance [ANOVA] Between Victim's Related Variables and Perceived Area of Safety

Model Parameters	*Sum of Squares*	*df*	*Mean Square*	*F*	*Sig.*
Regression	5.521	6	.920	2.808	.012
Residual	62.266	190	.328		
Total	67.787	196			

* *Predictors:* (Constant), Was any implement used in the commission of crime, the construction quality of wall/premise, Occupation of victim, Age of the victim, How was target approached, Sex of the victim.

** *Dependent Variable:* Do you find this area safe.

Model Summary Between Victim's Related Variables and Perceived Area of Safety

Table 33 describes the overall fit of model which value of R (multiple correlation coefficient) 0.285 and it shows the level of proportional association between victim's related variables and perceived safety of area.

The co-efficient of determination (R2) value is 0.081, if this value is converted into percentage then it implies that victim's related variables account for 8.1 per cent of the variability in perceived safety of area. The adjusted R2 value is 0.052 and the difference between R2 is (0.081-0.052 = 0.029) which means loss of predictive power is 2.9 per cent (across different samples in the same population).

Table 33
Model Summary Between Victim's Related Variables and Perceived Area of Safety

R	*R Square*	*Adjusted R Square*	*Std. Error of the Estimate*	*Change Statistics R Square Change*	*F Change*
.285	.081	.052	.57	.081	2.808

* *Predictors:* (Constant), Was any implement used in the commission of crime, the construction quality of wall/premise, Occupation of victim, Age of the victim, How was target approached, Sex of the victim.

CRIME VULNERABILITY VARIABLES

Distance Analysis Among Crime Vulnerability Variables (Association of Independency)

Table 34 shows the proximity matrix (dissimilarity) in respect of the crime vulnerability variables. The association of independency has been examined through chi square test. This analysis has been done to find out the interaction with regard to the Independent crime vulnerability variables. The chi-square is useful to test whether variables differ significantly or not, also useful to determine the extent of association between cross-tabulated variables. The result of chi-square shows that there is statistical significant difference with regard to the variables Status of Case and Value of loss due to crime; Crime scene visible to others and Value of loss due to crime; Description of crime scene and Status of Case as well as Crime scene visible to others and Status of Case. Table shows that

Table 34
Chi-square Matrix Among Crime Vulnerability Variables

Independent Crime Vulnerability Variables	*Anything available at crime scene used in the crime commission*	*Value of loss due to crime (in rupees)*	*Status of Case*	*Description of crime scene*	*Presence of security measures at crime scene*	*Crime scene visible to others*
Anything available at crime scene used in the crime commission		7.888	8.568	7.723	6.643	8.778
Value of loss due to crime (in rupees)	7.888		11.705	9.722	9.678	11.301
Status of Case	8.568	11.705		11.044	9.785	10.931
Description of crime scene	7.723	9.722	11.044		8.812	11.466
Presence of security measures at crime scene	6.643	9.678	9.785	8.812		9.781
Crime scene visible to others	8.778	11.301	10.931	11.466	9.781	

* This is a dissimilarity matrix

the chi-square value is highest in case of the variables Status of Case and Value of loss due to crime, where as it is lowest in case of Presence of security measures at crime scene and anything available at crime scene used in the crime commission variables.

Distance Analysis Among Crime Vulnerability Variables (Association of Dependency)

Table 35 shows the proximity matrix (similarity) with regard to the crime vulnerability variables. The association of dependency has been examined through correlation analysis. This analysis has been done to examined the co-linearity among the independent crime vulnerability variables. It is shown in Table that presence of security measures at crime scene and anything available at crime scene used in the crime commission variables were moderately correlated. This study also shows that the crime vulnerability variables are not correlated significantly which means there is not any significant dependency between them.

Regression Co-efficient Between Crime Vulnerability Variables and Crime Category

Table 36 shows the co-efficient of regression model within crime vulnerability variables and crime category. The value of unstandardized β_1 is -0.04992 which means "anything available at crime scene used in the crime commission" variable influences -0.04992 or -4.9 per cent of crime category while other predictors are held constant. All the un-standardized β value can be interpreted in the same way. The t-value for Presence of security measures at crime scene is ($P<0.001$) is a significant predictor of crime category, while anything available at crime scene used in the crime commission variable is ($P >0.749$) a non-significant predictor of crime category.

Analysis of Variance (ANOVA) Between Crime Vulnerability Variables and Crime Category

Table 37 depicts analysis of variance (ANOVA) to examine whether the model is significant at predicting the outcome.

Table 35
Correlation Matrix Among Crime Vulnerability Variables

Independent Crime Vulnerability Variables	*Anything available at crime scene used in the crime commission*	*Value of loss due to crime (in rupees)*	*Status of Case*	*Description of crime scene*	*Presence of security measures at crime scene*	*Crime scene visible to others*
Anything available at crime scene used in the crime commission		-.144	-.034	.067	.140	-.074
Value of loss due to crime (in rupees)	-.144		-.151	.080	-.104	-.073
Status of Case	-.034	-.151		-.025	.005	.036
Description of crime scene	.067	.080	-.025		.132	-.129
Presence of security measures at crime scene	.140	-.104	.005	.132		-.025
Crime scene visible to others	-.074	-.073	.036	-.129	-.025	

Table 36
Regression Coefficients Between Crime Vulnerability Variables and Crime Category

Crime Vulnerability Variables	*Unstandardized Coefficients B*	*Std. Error*	*Standardized Coefficients Beta*	*t*	*Sig.*
(Constant)	3.150	.698		4.511	.000
Anything available at crime scene used in the crime commission	-4.992E-02	.156	-.019	-.321	.749
Value of loss due to crime (in rupees)	.465	.083	.345	5.619	.000
Status of Case	-9.470E-02	.082	-.069	-1.154	.250
Description of crime scene	4.434E-02	.102	.026	.435	.664
Presence of security measures at crime scene	-.814	.140	-.351	-5.798	.000
Crime scene visible to others	-.281	.091	-.186	-3.098	.002

** *Dependent Variable:* Crime Category.

The model includes the interaction between crime vulnerability variables and crime category. This analysis suggests three values i.e. variation explained by the model [model sum of squares (SSM)], variation unexplained by the mode l[residual sum of squares (SSR)] and total variation of the model [total sum of square (SST)]. The results of ANOVA show that total sum of square (SST) is 672.844. The value of F-ratio is greater than 1 means that the independent crime vulnerability variables have significant contribution in

Table 37
Analysis of Variance [ANOVA] Between Crime Vulnerability Variables and Crime Category

Model Parameters	*Sum of Squares*	*df*	*Mean Square*	*F*	*Sig.*
Regression	219.257	6	36.543	15.468	.000
Residual	453.588	192	2.362		
Total	672.844	198			

* *Predictors:* (Constant), Crime scene visible to others, Presence of security measures at crime scene, Status of Case, Anything available at crime scene used in the crime commission, Description of crime scene, Value of loss due to crime (in rupees)

***Dependent Variable:* Crime Category.

dependent variable [crime category]. The F-ratio value [15.468] is significant [P < .001] which means model has significantly predicted of the outcome. The exact magnitude of the F-ratio can be assessed using critical values for the corresponding degree of freedom.

Model Summary Between Crime Vulnerability Variables and Crime Category

Table 38 describes the overall fit of model with value of R (multiple correlation coefficient) is 0.571, which means there is 0.571 level proportional association between crime vulnerability variables and crime category.

If the co-efficient of determination [0.326] is converted into per centage, it suggests that crime vulnerability variables account for 32.6 per cent of the variability in crime category. Hence this set of variable turn act to be a significant predictor to the nature of crime occurred.

Table 38
Model Summary Between Crime Vulnerability Variables and Crime Category

R	*R Square*	*Adjusted R Square*	*Std. Error of the Estimate*	*Change Statistics R Square Change*	*F Change*
.571	.326	.305	1.54	.326	15.468

* *Predictors:* (Constant), Crime scene visible to others, Presence of security measures at crime scene, Status of Case, Anything available at crime scene used in the crime commission, Description of crime scene, Value of loss due to crime (in rupees).

Regression Co-efficient Between Crime Vulnerability Variables and Target Vulnerability

Table 39 shows the results of regression. The value β_0 of [2.819] implies that all the crime vulnerability variables are excluded then this model predict 2.819 per unit of target vulnerability. The value of β_1 is -0.134 that means with every unit variation in the "anything available at crime scene used in the crime commission" variable scale the target vulnerability is varied by -0.134 units. This must be true if the effects of other crime vulnerability variables are held constant.

The t-statistic value for presence of security measures at crime scene variable [P > 0.05) is a significant predictor of target vulnerability, while t-value for description of crime scene is [P < 0.05) is a non-significant predictor of target vulnerability. All other value of t-static can be interpreted in the same way.

Table 39
Regression Coefficients Between Crime Vulnerability Variables and Target Vulnerability

Crime Scene Variables	*Unstandardized Coefficients B*	*Std. Error*	*Standardized Coefficients Beta*	*t*	*Sig.*
(Constant)	2.819	.408		6.915	.000
Anything available at crime scene used in the crime commission	-.134	.091	-.104	-1.475	.142
Value of loss due to crime (in rupees)	5.936E-02	.048	.087	1.227	.221
Status of Case	1.495E-02	.048	.022	.312	.755
Description of crime scene	4.922E-03	.060	.006	.083	.934
Presence of security measures at crime scene	-.296	.082	-.253	-3.607	.000
Crime scene visible to others	-.052	.053	-.068	-.975	.331

** *Dependent Variable:* What made target lucrative?

Analysis of Variance (ANOVA) Between Crime Vulnerability Variables and Target Vulnerability

Table 39 offers the analysis of variance (ANOVA). The result of ANOVA shows that model sum of square (SSM) is 17.138 (explained variance) and residual sum of squares (SSR) is 154.661 (unexplained variance) where as total sum of squares (SST) is 171.799 (total variance). The F ratio value is 3.546[P <0.05), which shows significant results. This means in this model there is much explained variance than unexplained variance.

Model Summary Between Crime Vulnerability Variables and Target Vulnerability

Table 40 describes the multiple correlations co-efficient [0.316], which defines the level of association between crime

Table 39
Analysis of Variance [ANOVA] Between Crime Vulnerability Variables and Target Vulnerability

Model Parameters	*Sum of Squares*	*df*	*Mean Square*	*F*	*Sig.*
Regression	17.138	6	2.856	3.546	.002 a
Residual	154.661	192	.806		
Total	171.799	198			

* *Predictors:* (Constant), Crime scene visible to others, Presence of security measures at crime scene, Status of Case, Anything available at crime scene used in the crime commission, Description of crime scene, Value of loss due to crime(in rupees).
***Dependent Variable:* What made target lucrative.

vulnerability variables and target vulnerability. The coefficient of determination (R2) is 0.100 that means 10.0 per cent of the variability account for target vulnerability. The adjusted R2 value is 0.072 and the difference between R2 is (0.100 - 0.072 = 0.028) which means across different samples loss of predictive power is 2.8 per cent.

Table 40
Model Summary Between Crime Vulnerability Variables and Target Vulnerability

R	*R Square*	*Adjusted R Square*	*Std. Error of the Estimate*	*Change Statistics R Square Change*	*F Change*
.316	.100	.072	.90	.100	3.546

* *Predictors:* (Constant), Crime scene visible to others, Presence of security measures at crime scene, Status of Case, Anything available at crime scene used in the crime commission, Description of crime scene, Value of loss due to crime (in rupees)

Regression Coefficient Between Crime Vulnerability Variables and Perceived Area of Safety

Table 41 shows the results of regression. The value β_0 of [1.611] suggests that all the crime vulnerability variables are excluded then model predicts 1.611of perceived safety of area.

The value of β is 0.117 that means 'anything available at crime scene used in the crime commission' variable is responsible for 0.117 proportional increase of perceived safety of area. The value of standardized β_1 is 0.143 that means 'anything available at crime scene used in the crime commission' variable accounts for 0.143 proportional standard deviation increase as per perceived area of safety scale standard deviation.

The t statistic value for 'anything available at crime scene used in the crime commission' variable is 1.968 (Level of significance = .050, P >.005) is a moderately significant predictor of perceived safety of area while t value for 'crime scene visible to others' variable is the non significant predictor of perceived safety of area.

Table 41
Regression Coefficients Between Crime Vulnerability Variables and Perceived Safety of Area

Crime Scene Variables	*Unstandardized Coefficients B*	*Std. Error*	*Standardized Coefficients Beta*	*t*	*Sig.*
(Constant)	1.611	.266		6.053	.000
Anything available at crime scene used in the crime commission	.117	.059	.143	1.968	.050
Value of loss due to crime (in rupees)	-.021	.032	-.048	-.657	.512
Status of Case	2.913E-02	.031	.067	.931	.353
Description of crime scene	-.036	.039	-.068	-.939	.349
Presence of security measures at crime scene	-.036	.054	-.048	-.666	.506
Crime scene visible to others	1.949E-02	.035	.040	.563	.574

** *Dependent Variable:* Do you find this area safe.

Analysis of Variance (ANOVA) Between Crime Vulnerability Variables and Perceived Area of Safety

Table 42 gives the components of analysis of variance (ANOVA). The result of ANOVA shows that model sum of square (SSM) is 2.493 while residual sum of squares (SSR) is 65.929 where as total sum of square (SST) is 68.422. The F ratio is 1.210 which is non-significant at P >.001, it means there is more unsystematic variance than systematic variance and model does not over all predict perceived safety of area significantly well.

Table 42
Analysis of Variance [ANOVA] Between Crime Vulnerability Variables and Perceived Safety of Area

Model Parameters	*Sum of Squares*	*df*	*Mean Square*	*F*	*Sig.*
Regression	2.493	6	.415	1.210	.303 a
Residual	65.929	192	.343		
Total	68.422	198			

* *Predictors:* (Constant), Crime scene visible to others, Presence of security measures at crime scene, Status of Case, Anything available at crime scene used in the crime commission, Description of crime scene, Value of loss due to crime (in rupees).
** *Dependent Variable:* Do you find this area safe?

Model Summary Between Crime Vulnerability Variables and Perceived Safety of Area

Table 43 describes the multiple correlation coefficient (R) that is 0.191 represents the multiple correlation between crime vulnerability variables and perceived area of safety. The coefficient of determination (R2) is 0.036 which means 3.6 per cent of the variability in perceived safety of area is determined by crime vulnerability variables. The adjusted R2 value is 0.006 and the difference between R2 is (0.036 - 0.006 = 0.030) means across different sample the loss of prediction is 3.0 per cent.

Table 43
Model Summary Between Crime Vulnerability Variables and Perceived Area of Safety

R	*R Square*	*Adjusted R Square*	*Std. Error of the Estimate*	*Change Statistics R Square Change*	*F Change*
.191	.036	.006	.59	.036	1.210

* *Predictors:* (Constant), Crime scene visible to others, Presence of security measures at crime scene, Status of Case, Anything available at crime scene used in the crime commission, Description of crime scene, Value of loss due to crime(in rupees)

NOTE

The F-ratio is a measure of how much the model has improved the prediction of the outcome compare to the level of inaccuracy of the model and this is a ratio of systematic variance to unsystematic variance. In simple words mean square regression is divided by mean square residual the value obtained is known is F-ratio.

5

Analysis of Situational Crime Variables—Part-II

This chapter mainly deals with the situational variables pertaining to various crime category studied in the city of Sagar. The findings reported in this chapter display the characteristics relating to crime and victims in the context of certain other variables. The data have been subjected to various statistical techniques for drawing the inferences.

CRIME SCENE VARIABLES

Distance Analysis among Crime-scenes Variables (Association of Independency)

Table 1 shows the proximity matrix (dissimilarity) with respect to the crime scene variables. The association of independency has been examined through chi square test. This analysis has been made to find out the interaction among the independent crime scene variables. The result of chi-square shows that there is statistically significant difference between week of occurrence and lighting arrangement in the premises; week of occurrence and lighting arrangement on the immediate street; week of occurrence and time of occurrence; week of occurrence and outdoor scene of crime. The chi-square value was found to be of highest independency in case of week of occurrence and lighting arrangement on the immediate street, where as it was lowest independency in case of time of occurrence and scene of crime.

Table 1
Chi-square Matrix Among Crime Scene Variables

Independent Crime Scene Variables	*Week of Occurrence*	*Time of Occurrence*	*Location of Scene of Crime*	*In case of outdoor scene of crime*	*Lighting arrangement on the immediate street*	*Lighting arrangement in the premises*	*Was it easy for offender to commit this crime*
Week of Occurrence		5.782	4.093	5.946	6.378	6.348	5.492
Time of Occurrence	5.782		1.755	4.398	4.039	4.454	3.595
Location of Scene of Crime	4.093	1.755		3.419	3.064	3.299	2.664
In case of outdoor scene of crime	5.946	4.398	3.419		5.140	5.656	4.644
Lighting arrangement on the immediate street	6.378	4.039	3.064	5.140		2.976	3.617
Lighting arrangement in the premises	6.348	4.454	3.299	5.656	2.976		3.778
Was it easy for offender to commit this crime	5.492	3.595	2.664	4.644	3.617	3.778	

* This is a dissimilarity matrix

Distance Analysis Among Crime Scene Variables (Association of Dependency)

Table 2 shows the proximity matrix (similarity) among the crime-scene variables. The association of dependency has been examined through correlation analysis. This analysis has been made to find out the co-linearity among the independent crime scene variables. It is evident from Table that lighting arrangement on the immediate street and lighting arrangement in the premises were highly correlated. The other variables were not found to be significant correlated. Table also gives hierarchy of the crime scenes variables by arranging the correlation values in descending order i.e. lighting arrangement on the immediate street, lighting arrangement in the premises, location of scene of crime, was it easy for offender to commit this crime, outdoor scene of crime, week of occurrence and time of occurrence.

Regression Co-efficient between Crime Scene Variables and Crime Category

The regression analysis is performed to find out the extent, direction and strength of relationship between several variables and a dependent variable. Table 3 shows the co-efficient of regression model within crime scene variables and crime category. Table shows the value within five parameters. These are unstandardized β, standard error, standardized â, t-value and level of significance.

The value of unstandardized β 1 is -.101, this means week of occurrence influences -.101 per cent unstandardized β of crime category variable, while other predictor is held constant. All the un-standardized value can be interpreted in the same way. The t-value for location of scene of crime [-2.427, $P < 0.01$) is a significant predictor of crime category, while week of occurrence and time of occurrence is non-significant predictor of crime category.

Analysis of Variance (ANOVA) between Crime Scene Variables and Crime Category

Table 4 conveys that the F-ratio [2.516] is significant [$P < 0.02$]. In this case, there is a probability of .02 that an F ratio of this

Table 2
Correlation Matrix Among Crime Scene Variables

Independent Crime Scene Variables	*Week of Occurrence*	*Time of Occurrence*	*Location of Scene of Crime*	*In case of outdoor scene of crime*	*Lighting arrangement on the immediate street*	*Lighting arrangement in the premises*	*Was it easy for offender to commit this crime*
Week of Occurrence		-.016	.049	.039	-.155	-.106	-.061
Time of Occurrence	-.016		.052	.021	.084	.015	-.134
Location of Scene of Crime	.049	.052		-.175	.008	.012	-.168
In case of outdoor scene of crime	.039	.021	-.175		-.053	-.193	-.119
Lighting arrangement on the immediate street	-.155	.084	.008	-.053		.634	.253
Lighting arrangement in the premises	-.106	.015	.012	-.193	.634		.266
Was it easy for offender to commit this crime	-.061	-.134	-.168	-.119	.253	.266	

* This is a similarity matrix

Table 3
Regression Coefficients between Crime Scene Variables and Crime Category

Crime Scene Variables	*Unstandardized Coefficients B*	*Std. Error*	*Standardized Coefficients Beta*	*t*	*Sig.*
(Constant)	10.523	2.174		4.840	.000
Week of Occurrence	-.101	.153	-.071	-.660	.511
Time of Occurrence	-.095	.344	-.030	-.277	.782
Location of Scene of Crime	-3.181	1.311	-.266	-2.427	.018
Outdoor scene of crime	-.411	.266	-.171	-1.546	.127
Lighting arrangement on the immediate street	-.321	.349	-.129	-.919	.361
Lighting arrangement in the premises	-.528	.323	-.230	-1.633	.107
Was it easy for offender to commit this crime?	-.415	.427	-.111	-.972	.334

** *Dependent Variable*: Crime Category

size would occur by chance (that's only a 0.1% chance) and hence the observed significant value is less than .05 it can be said that the regression model overall predicts crime category significantly. $SS_T = SS_M + SS_R$

Table 4
Analysis of Variance [ANOVA] between Crime Scene Variables and Crime Category

Model Parameters	*Sum of Squares*	*df*	*Mean Square*	*F*	*Sig.*
Regression	54.730	7	7.819	2.516	.023(a)
Residual	223.757	72	3.108		
Total	278.488	79			

* *Predictors:* (Constant), Was it easy for offender to commit this crime, Week of Occurrence, Location of Scene of Crime, Lighting arrangement in the premises, Time of Occurrence, Outdoor scene of crime, Lighting arrangement on the immediate street.
** *Dependent Variable:* Crime Category.

Model Showing Summary between Crime Scene Variables and Crime Category

Table 5 describes whether the model is effective in predicting crime category. This summary Table provides the value of R and R^2 for the model that has been derived. The model includes effect of all the crime scene variables and crime category and nature of relationship between them. The Table shows the value of multiple correlation co-efficient [R], coefficient of determination [R^2], Adjusted R^2, standard error of the estimate and F-ratio. The R value [0.443] represents the multiple correlations between crime scene variables and crime category. The value of R^2 Coefficient of determination is 0.197, which suggests that crime scene variables account for 19.7 per cent of the variation for crime category.

The difference between coefficient of determination [R^2] and adjusted R^2 shows the loss of predictive power across different samples. In fact the difference between the values is 0.197 - 0.118 = 0.079 (about 7.9 per cent). This means across different samples in the same population the loss of prediction is 7.9 per cent.

Table 5
Model Showing Summary Between Crime Scene Variables and Crime Category

R	*R Square*	*Adjusted R Square*	*Std. Error of the Estimate*	*R Square Change*	*F Change*
.443(a)	.197	.118	1.763	.197	2.516

* *Predictors:* (Constant), Was it easy for offender to commit this crime?, Week of Occurrence, Location of Scene of Crime, Lighting arrangement in the premises, Time of Occurrence, Lighting arrangement on the immediate street.

This shrinkage means that if the model were derived from the population rather than a sample it would account for approximately 2.7 per cent variance in the outcome.

Regression Coefficient between Crime Scene Variables and Target Vvulnerability

Table 6 shows the result of regression. The value of β_0 is 3.736, which means that all the variables are excluded and then this model predicts 3.736 of target vulnerability. The value β_1 of is 0.033, which can be interpreted in the way that with every unit increase in the week of occurrence scale, the target vulnerability is increased by 0.033 units. This interpretation is true only if the effects of other crime scene variable are held constant. All other unstandardized values interpreted in the same way.

The value of standardized β_1 [0.052] implies that week of occurrence scale and target vulnerability were increased per 0.052 unit standard deviation. This interpretation is true only if the effects of other crime scene variable are held constant. All other standardized β value is interpreted in the same way.

The t-statistic value for the location of scene of crime is [-2.631, $P<0.01$) is the significant predictor of target vulnerability while t value for the outdoor scene of crime variable is [-0.207, $P > 0.05$) the non-significant predictor of target vulnerability. The similar way all other t statistic value can be interpreted for this model.

Analysis of Variance (ANOVA) between Crime Scene Variables and Ttarget Vvulnerability

Table 7 exhibits analysis of variance (ANOVA) that tests whether the model is significantly better at predicting the

Table 6
Regression Coefficients Between Crime Scene Variables and Target vulnerability

Crime Scene Variables	*Unstandardized Coefficients B*	*Std. Error*	*Standardized Coefficients Beta*	*t*	*Sig.*
(Constant)	3.736	.986		3.790	.000
Week of Occurrence	.033	.069	.052	.472	.638
Time of Occurrence	-.036	.156	-.026	-.230	.819
Location of Scene of Crime	-1.564	.594	-.299	-2.631	.010
Outdoor scene of crime	-.025	.121	-.024	-.207	.836
Lighting arrangement on the immediate street	.081	.158	.074	.511	.611
Lighting arrangement in the premises	.038	.147	.038	.258	.797
Was it easy for offender to commit this crime	.206	.193	.126	1.068	.289

** *Dependent Variable:* What made target lucrative

outcome. This analysis shows three values i.e. variation explained by the model [model sum of squares (SSM)], variation unexplained by the model [residual sum of squares (SSR)] and total variation of the model [total sum of square (SST)]. The result of ANOVA shows that model sum of squares (SSM) is 16.777, while residual sum of squares (SSR) is 155.098 where as total sum of square (SST) is 171.875. The value of F-ratio is [1.612 $p<0.146$] which explains that the independent crime scene variables have significant contribution to dependent variable [target vulnerability]. The exact magnitude of the F-ratio can be assessed using critical values for the corresponding degree of freedom.

Table 7
Analysis of Variance [ANOVA] between Crime Scene Variables and Target Vulnerability

Model Parameters	*Sum of Squares*	*df*	*Mean Square*	*F*	*Sig.*
Regression	7.210	7	1.030	1.612	.146(a)
Residual	45.990	72	.639		
Total	53.200	79			

* *Predictors:* (Constant), Was it easy for offender to commit this crime, Week of Occurrence, Location of Scene of Crime, Lighting arrangement in the premises, Time of Occurrence, Outdoor scene of crime, Lighting arrangement on the immediate street.

** *Dependent Variable:* What made target lucrative.

Model Summary Between Crime Scene Variables and Target Vulnerability

Table 8 shows that the value of R (multiple correlation coefficient) is 0.368, which describes the proportional association [0.368] between crime scene variables and target vulnerability. The co-efficient of determination (R^2) value is 0.136. If this value is converted into percentage it conveys that crime scene variables account for 13.6 per cent of the variability in target vulnerability. The adjusted R2 value is 0.051 and the difference between R^2 (0.136 - 0.051 = 0.085) means loss of predictive power is 8.5 per cent (across different samples in the same population).

Table 8
Model Summary between Crime Scene Variables and Target Vulnerability

R	*R Square*	*Adjusted R Square*	*Std. Error of the Estimate*	*Change Statistics R Square Change*	*F Change*
.368(a)	.136	.051	.799	.136	1.612

* *Predictors:* (Constant), Was it easy for offender to commit this crime, Week of Occurrence, Location of Scene of Crime, Lighting arrangement in the premises, Time of Occurrence, Outdoor scene of crime, Lighting arrangement on the immediate street

Regression Co-efficient between Crime Scene Variables and Perceived Safeness of the Area

Table 9 shows the results of regression. The value of β_0 is 0.918 that conveys that all the crime scene variables are excluded and this model predicts 0.918 per unit of perceived safety of area. The value of β_1 is 0.068 that means with every unit increase in the week of occurrence variable scale the perceived safety of area variable is increased by -0.068 units. This must be true if the effects of other crime scene variable are held constant. The value of standardized β_1 is 0.0187, which means that with the increase in unit standard deviation in week of occurrence, perceived safety of area variable is increased by 0.0187 standard deviation. This interpretation is true only if the effects of other crime scene variables are held constant. All other un-standardized β values and standardized β value could be interpreted in the same way.

The t value for the variable 'Was it easy for offender to commit this crime' is 3.202 ($P > 0.05$) and is a moderately significant predictor of perceived safety of area variable, while t-value for the variable location of scene of crime is -0.558 ($P < 0.05$) is a non-significant predictor of perceived safety of area variable. All other value of t-static can be interpreted in the same way.

Analysis of Variance (ANOVA) between Crime Scene Variables and Perceived Safety of Area:

Table 10 denotes the components of analysis of variance (ANOVA). The result of ANOVA shows that model sum of square (SSM) is 4.058 (explained variance) and residual sum

Table 9

Regression Coefficients between Crime Scene Variables and Perceived Safety of Area

Crime Scene Variables	*Unstandardized Coefficients B*	*Std. Error*	*Standardized Coefficients Beta*	*t*	*Sig.*
(Constant)	.918	.542		1.695	.094
Week of Occurrence	.068	.038	.187	1.779	.079
Time of Occurrence	.142	.086	.174	1.651	.103
Location of Scene of Crime	-.182	.327	-.060	-.558	.579
In case of outdoor scene of crime	-.095	.066	-.156	-1.432	.157
Lighting arrangement on the immediate street	.125	.087	.198	1.438	.155
Lighting arrangement in the premises	-.124	.081	-.212	-1.539	.128
Was it easy for offender to commit this crime	.340	.106	.359	3.202	.002

** *Dependent Variable:* Do you find this area safe

of squares (SSR) is 13.892 (unexplained variance) where as total sum of squares (SST) is 17.950 (total variance). The F ratio value is 3.005 (Level of significance = 0.008, P < .05), which shows the significant results. This means there is much explained variance in this model than unexplained variance.

Table 10
Analysis of Variance [ANOVA] between Crime Scene Variables and Perceived Safety of Area

Model Parameters	*Sum of Squares*	*df*	*Mean Square*	*F*	*Sig.*
Regression	4.058	7	.580	3.005	.008(a)
Residual	13.892	72	.193		
Total	17.950	79			

* *Predictors:* (Constant), Was it easy for offender to commit this crime, Week of Occurrence, Location of Scene of Crime, Lighting arrangement in the premises, Time of Occurrence, In case of outdoor scene of crime, Lighting arrangement on the immediate street
** *Dependent Variable:* Do you find this area safe

Model Summary between Crime Scene Variables and Perceived Safety of Area

Table 11 describes the multiple correlation co-efficient (R) that is 0.475, defines the level of association between crime scene variables and perceived safety of area. The coefficient of determination (R^2=0.226] suggests 22.6 per cent of the variability in crime scene variables account for perceived area of safety. The adjusted R2 value is 0.151 and the difference between R^2 [0.226 - 0.151) = 0.075] means across different samples loss of predictive power is 7.5 per cent.

Table 11
Model Summary between Crime Scene Variables and Perceived Safety of Area

R	*R Square*	*Adjusted R Square*	*Std. Error of the Estimate*	*Change Statistics R Square Change*	*F Change*
.475(a)	.226	.151	.439	.226	3.005

* *Predictors:* (Constant), Was it easy for offender to commit this crime, Week of Occurrence, Location of Scene of Crime, Lighting arrangement in the premises, Time of Occurrence, In case of outdoor scene of crime, Lighting arrangement on the immediate street

OWNERS BEHAVIOR VARIABLES

Distance Analysis among Owner's Behavior Variables (Association of Independency)

Table 12 shows the dissimilarity matrix within owner's behavior variables. This analysis is to find out the relation within variables. This matrix also gives a clear picture about the independent association among them. It is seen from Table that 'distance between crime target & owner at the time of crime commission' and 'What was victim doing that time' ; 'what was victim doing that time' and 'how much time remained away from the target' had significant chi-square value.

Distance Analysis Among Owner's Behavior Variables (Association of Dependency)

Table 13 shows the similarity matrix within owner's behavior variables. This analysis gives the insight into relation within variable as well as to provide the level of dependency among them. The correlation between the variables i.e. 'how much time remains away from the target' and 'distance between crime target and owner at the time of crime commission' had significant correlation.

Regression Coefficient between Owner's Behavior Variables and Crime Category

Table 14 shows the results of regression. The value of β_0 is 5.933, which means that all the owner's behavior variables are excluded then this model predicts 5.933 of crime category. The value of β_1 is 0.235, which conveys that with every unit increase in the variable 'average time spent at home' scale the crime category is varied by 0.235 units. This interpretation is true only if the effects of other owner's behavior variables are held constant. All other unstandardized value interpreted in the same way.

The value of standardized β_1 [0.079] suggests that the variable 'average time spent at home' scale can vary by unit standard deviation and crime category is varied per 0.079 unit

Table 12
Chi-square Matrix among Owner's Behavior Variables

Independent Owners Behavior Variables	*Average time spent at home*	*How much time remains away from the target*	*Distance between workplace and crime scene*	*Distance between crime target and owner at the time of crime commission*	*Did crime occur in the absence of victim?*	*What was victim doing that time?*	*Did the victim resist crime?*	*Did the offender over power victim?*
Average time spent at home		6.464	4.821	7.759	4.164	8.057	3.817	3.747
How much time remains away from the target	6.464		6.100	4.980	6.062	8.868	5.376	5.381
Distance between workplace and crime scene	4.821	6.100		6.362	4.282	6.447	3.885	3.872
Distance between crime target and owner at the time of crime commission	7.759	4.980	6.362		7.891	9.307	5.825	5.871
Did crime occur in the absence of victim?	4.164	6.062	4.282	7.891		7.354	4.253	4.156
What was victim doing that time?	8.057	8.868	6.447	9.307	7.354		7.781	7.734
Did the victim resist crime?	3.817	5.376	3.885	5.825	4.253	7.781		.576
Did the offender overpower victim?	3.747	5.381	3.872	5.871	4.156	7.734	.576	

*This is a dissimilarity matrix

Table 13
Correlation Matrix Among Owner's Behavior Variables

Independent Owners Behavior Variables	*Average time spent at home*	*How much time remains away from the target*	*Distance between workplace and crime scene*	*Distance between crime target and owner at the time of crime commission*	*Did crime occur in the absence of victim?*	*What was victim doing that time?*	*Did the victim resist crime?*	*Did the offender over power victim?*
Average time spent at home		.003	-.014	-.120	.155	.125	-.042	-.025
How much time remains away from the target	.003		-.173	.635	-.220	.011	.134	.126
Distance between workplace and crime scene	-.014	-.173		-.006	.002	.240	.029	.020
Distance between crime target and owner at the time of crime commission	-.120	.635	-.006		-.495	.075	.259	.241
Did crime occur in the absence of victim?	.155	-.220	.002	-.495		-.047	-.445	-.410
What was victim doing that time?	.125	.011	.240	.075	-.047		-.197	-.188
Did the victim resist crime?	-.042	.134	.029	.259	-.445	-.197		.940
Did the offender overpower victim?	-.025	.126	.020	.241	-.410	-.188	.940	

*This is a similarity matrix

Table 14

Regression Coefficients between Owner's Behavior Variables and Crime Category

Crime Scene Variables	*Unstandardized Coefficients B*	*Std. Error*	*Standardized Coefficients Beta*	*t*	*Sig.*
(Constant)	5.933	1.463		4.057	.000
Average time spent at home	.235	.176	.079	1.335	.184
How much time remains away from the target	-.142	.193	-.057	-.735	.463
Distance between workplace and crime scene	.147	.258	.035	.572	.568
Distance between crime target and owner at the time of crime commission	-.948	.138	-.591	-6.890	.000
Did crime occur in the absence of victim	-2.836	.355	-.585	-7.989	.000
What was victim doing that time	.198	.098	.126	2.023	.045
Did the victim resist crime	.500	1.433	.060	.349	.727
Did the offender overpower victim	.441	1.481	.050	.298	.766

** *Dependent Variable:* Crime Category

standard deviation. This interpretation is true only if the effects of other owner's behavior variables are held constant. All other standardized β value is interpreted in the same way.

The t value for 'did crime occur in the absence of victim' variable [P<0.05) is a significant predictor of crime category while t value for the variable 'did the offender overpower victim' [P > 0.05) is the non-significant predictor of crime category. The similar way all other values can be interpreted for this model.

Analysis of Variance (ANOVA) between Owner's Behavior Variables and Crime Category

Table 15 depicts an analysis of variance (ANOVA) that tests whether the model is significantly better at predicting the outcome. The model examines the interaction between all owner's behavior variables and crime category. This analysis shows that the three values i.e. variation explained by the model [model sum of squares (SSM)], variation unexplained by the model [residual sum of squares (SSR)] and total variation of the model [total sum of square (SST)]. The result of ANOVA shows that model sum of squares (SSM) is 252.409, while residual sum of squares (SSR) is 336.470 whereas total sum of square (SST) is 588.879. The value of F-ratio is greater than 1 means that these independent owner's behavior variables have significant contribution in dependent variable.

Table 15
Analysis of Variance [ANOVA] between Owner's Behavior Variables and Crime Category

Model Parameters	*Sum of Squares*	*df*	*Mean Square*	*F*	*Sig.*
Regression	252.409	8	31.551	16.222	.000(a)
Residual	336.470	173	1.945		
Total	588.879	181			

* *Predictors*: (Constant), Did the offender overpower victim, Average time spent at home, Distance between crime target and owner at the time of crime commission, Distance between workplace and crime scene, Did the victim resist crime, What was victim doing that time, How much time remains away from the target, Did crime occurs in the absence of victim.

** *Dependent Variable:* Crime Category.

[crime category]. The F-ratio value is significant [$P < .001$] in terms of affecting the occurrence of crime. The exact magnitude of the F-ratio can be assessed using critical values for the corresponding degree of freedom.

Model Showing Summary between Owner's Behavior Variables and Crime Category

Table 16 describes proportional association between owner's behavior variables and crime category [$R^2 = 0.655$].

The co-efficient of determination (R^2) value is 0.429, if we convert this value into per centage than it can be said that owner's behavior variables account for 42.9 per cent of the variability in crime category. This contribution explains the extent to which the various aspects of behavior of owner are situationally responsible in affecting the occurrence of crime.

Table 16
Model Summary between Owner's Behavior Variables and Crime Category

R	*R Square*	*Adjusted R Square*	*Std. Error of the Estimate*	*Change Statistics R Square Change*	*F Change*
.655(a)	.429	.402	1.395	.429	16.222

* *Predictors:* (Constant), Did the offender overpower victim, Average time spent at home, Distance between crime target and owner at the time of crime commission, Distance between workplace and crime scene, Did the victim resist crime, What was victim doing that time, How much time remains away from the target, Did crime occurs in the absence of victim.

Regression Co-efficient between Owner's Behavior Variables and Target Vulnerability

Table 17 shows the results of regression. The value of β_0 [1.923] suggests that the all owner's behavior variables are excluded and this model predicts 1.923 per unit of target vulnerability. The value of β_1 [-0.191] implies that every unit increase in the scale of average time spent at home is increased by -0.191 units. This must be true if the effects of other owner's behavior variable are held constant. The value of standardized β_1 [-0.150] suggests that average time spent at home scale can increase by unit standard deviation, target vulnerability is an increased by -0.150 standard deviation. This interpretation is true only if the effects of other owner's behavior variable are held constant. All other un-standardized β values and standardized β value are interpreted in the same way.

The t value for 'did the victim resist crime' variable is 2.301 ($P > 0.05$) is a significant predictor of target vulnerability, while t-value for did crime occurs in the absence of victim is 0.360 ($P < 0.05$) are non-significant predictor of target vulnerability.

Analysis of Variance [ANOVA] between Owner's Behavior Variables and Target Vulnerability

Table 18 shows the results of analysis of variance (ANOVA). The result of ANOVA shows that model sum of square (SSM) is 8.227 (explained variance) and residual sum of squares (SSR) is 100.482 (unexplained variance) where as total sum of squares (SST) is 108.709 (total variance). The F ratio value is 1.771 (Level of significance = 0.08, $P > .05$), which shows non-significant results. This means there is much un-explained variance than explained variance in this model.

Model Summary between Owner's Behavior Variables and Target Vulnerability

Table 19 describes the multiple correlations co-efficient (R) that is 0.275 and it defines the level of association between owner's behavior variables and target vulnerability. The coefficient of determination (R^2) is 0.076 that means 7.6 per cent of the variability accounts for target vulnerability. The adjusted R^2 value is .033 and the difference between R^2 is (0.076 - 0.033 = 0.043) which means across different samples loss of predictive power is 4.3 per cent.

Regression Coefficient between Owner's Behavior Variables and Perceived Safety of Area

Table 20 shows the results of regression. The value of β_0 is 1.673, which means the all owner's behavior variables are excluded and the model predicts 1.673 of perceived safety of area.

The t value for 'distance between workplace and crime scene' variable is -1.460 ($P < .005$) are the significance predictor

Table 17

Regression Coefficients between Owner's Behavior Variables and Target Vulnerability

Crime Scene Variables	*Unstandardized Coefficients B*	*Std. Error*	*Standardized Coefficients Beta*	*t*	*Sig.*
(Constant)	1.923	.799		2.406	.017
Average time spent at home	-.191	.096	-.150	-1.986	.049
How much time remains away from the target	.095	.106	.089	.901	.369
Distance between workplace and crime scene	-.108	.141	-.060	-.768	.444
Distance between crime target and owner at the time of crime commission	-.126	.075	-.182	-1.672	.096
Did crime occur in the absence of victim	.070	.194	.033	.360	.720
What was victim doing that time	.086	.053	.127	1.606	.110
Did the victim resist crime	1.802	.783	.506	2.301	.023
Did the offender overpower victim	-1.206	.809	-.320	-1.489	.138

** *Dependent Variable:* What made target lucrative

Table 18
Analysis of Variance [ANOVA] between Owner's Behavior Variables and Target Vulnerability

Model Parameters	*Sum of Squares*	*df*	*Mean Square*	*F*	*Sig.*
Regression	8.227	8	1.028	1.771	.086(a)
Residual	100.482	173	.581		
Total	108.709	181			

* *Predictors:* (Constant), Did the offender overpower victim, Average time spent at home, Distance between crime target and owner at the time of crime commission, Distance between workplace and crime scene, Did the victim resist crime, What was victim doing that time, How much time remains away from the target, Did crime occurs in the absence of victim.

** *Dependent Variable:* What made target lucrative.

Table 19
Model Summary between Owner's Behavior Variables and Target Vulnerability

R	*R Square*	*Adjusted R Square*	*Std. Error of the Estimate*	*Change Statistics R Square Change*	*F Change*
.275(a)	.076	.033	.762	.076	1.771

* *Predictors:* (Constant), Did the offender overpower victim, Average time spent at home, Distance between crime target and owner at the time of crime commission, Distance between workplace and crime scene, Did the victim resist crime, What was victim doing that time, How much time remains away from the target, Did crime occurs in the absence of victim.

of perceived safety of area while t value for "what was victim doing that time" variable is 0.164 (P > .005) are the non significant predictor of perceived safety of area. It sums up that the absence of owner becomes significant factor causing a vulnerable situation for crime commission.

Analysis of Variance (ANOVA) between Owner's Behavior Variables and Perceived Safety of Area

Table 21 shows the analysis of variance (ANOVA). The result of ANOVA shows that model sum of square (SSM) is 1.522 while residual sum of squares (SSR) is 33.121 where as total sum of square (SST) is 34.643. The F ratio is 0.993 which is non significant at P > 0.443, it means there is more unsystematic variance than systematic variance.

Table 20

Regression Coefficients between Owner's Behavior Variables and Perceived Safety of Area

Crime Scene Variables	*Unstandardized Coefficients B*	*Std. Error*	*Standardized Coefficients Beta*	*t*	*Sig.*
(Constant)	1.673	.459		3.647	.000
Average time spent at home	-.012	.055	-.016	-.213	.831
How much time remains away from the target	.082	.061	.135	1.352	.178
Distance between workplace and crime scene	-.118	.081	-.115	-1.460	.146
Distance between crime target and owner at the time of crime commission	-.020	.043	-.051	-.455	.650
Did crime occur in the absence of victim	.147	.111	.125	1.319	.189
What was victim doing that time	.005	.031	.013	.164	.870
Did the victim resist crime	-.080	.450	-.040	-.178	.859
Did the offender overpower victim	.094	.465	.044	.203	.839

** *Dependent Variable:* Do you find this area safe

Table 21
Analysis of Variance [ANOVA] between Owner's Behavior Variables and Perceived Safety of Area

Model Parameters	*Sum of Squares*	*df*	*Mean Square*	*F*	*Sig.*
Regression	1.522	8	.190	.993	.443(a)
Residual	33.121	173	.191		
Total	34.643	181			

* *Predictors:* (Constant), Did the offender overpower victim, Average time spent at home, Distance between crime target and owner at the time of crime commission, Distance between workplace and crime scene, Did the victim resist crime, What was victim doing that time, How much time remains away from the target, Did crime occurs in the absence of victim.
** *Dependent Variable*: Do you find this area safe.

Model Summary between Owner's Behavior Variables and Perceived Safety of Area

Table 22 describes the multiple correlation coefficient (R) that is 0.210 represents the multiple correlation between owner's behavior variables and perceived safety of area. The coefficient of determination (R2) is 0.044, which means 4.4 per cent of the variability in perceived safety of area is determined by owner's behavior variables. The adjusted R2 value is zero and the difference between R2 is (0.044 – 0.0 = 0.044) means across different sample the loss of prediction is 4.4 per cent. This explains that the perception of the subject about the safety of an area depends on his past behaviour and attitude.

Table 22
Model Summary between Owner's Behavior Variables and Perceived Area of Safety

R	*R Square*	*Adjusted R Square*	*Std. Error of the Estimate*	*Change Statistics R Square Change*	*F Change*
.210(a)	.044	.000	.438	.044	.993

* *Predictors:* (Constant), Did the offender overpower victim, Average time spent at home, Distance between crime target and owner at the time of crime commission, Distance between workplace and crime scene, Did the victim resist crime, What was victim doing that time, How much time remains away from the target, Did crime occurs in the absence of victim.

VICTIM RELATED VARIABLES

Distance Analysis among Victim Related Variable (Association of Independency)

Table 23 shows test of significance within victim related variables. This matrix gives a picture about the association of independency within variables. Table shows that 'age of the victim' and 'was any implement used in the commission of crime' variable as well as 'sex of the victim' and 'was any implement used in the commission of crime' variable had significant chi-square values.

Distance Analysis among Victim Related Variable (Association of Dependency)

Table 24 shows the test of correlation within victim related variables. This matrix provides the association of dependency within variables. It is also to find out the multi-colinearity within the independent variables. The variable 'age of the victim' and 'sex of the victim' as well as 'age of the victim' and 'how was target approached' both the value have significant correlation at the 0.05 level. It is seen from the study that both the variables show strong multi-colinearity. (Conventionally for multi-colinearity the correlation value must be in between 0.60 to 0.80).

Regression Coefficient between Victim's Related Variables and Crime Category

Table 25 shows the results of regression. The value of β_0 is 1.500, which means the all victim's related variables are excluded then model predicts 1.500 of crime category.

The value of β_1 is 8.47E-018 and it infers that the variable age of the victim is 8.47E-018 proportional to crime category variable. The negative sign denotes the inverse relation between the two variables.

The t statistic value for all the variable doesn't occur because standard error for all the selected victim related variable is nil that's why t-value as well as significant value does not occur for all the variables.

Table 23
Chi-square Matrix among Victim Related Variables

Independent Crime Scene Variables	*Age of the victim*	*Sex of the victim*	*Occupation of victim*	*How was target approached*	*The construction quality of wall/premise*	*Was any implement used in the commission*
Age of the victim		.311	.834	1.222	.735	.972
Sex of the victim	.311		.512	1.051	.823	.957
Occupation of victim	.834	.512		1.177	1.009	1.224
How was target approached	1.222	1.051	1.177		1.118	.474
The construction quality of wall/premise	.735	.823	1.009	1.118		.966
Was any implement used in the commission of crime	.972	.957	1.224	.474	.966	

* This is a dissimilarity matrix

Table 24
Correlation Matrix among Victim Related Variables

Independent Crime Scene Variables	*Age of the victim*	*Sex of the victim*	*Occupation of victim*	*How was target approached*	*The construction quality of wall/premise*	*Was any implement used in the commission*
Age of the victim		.870	.302	-.853	.426	-.302
Sex of the victim	.870		.577	-.816	.000	-.577
Occupation of victim	.302	.577		-.707	.000	-1.000
How was target approached	-.853	-.816	-.707		-.500	.707
The construction quality of wall/premise	.426	.000	.000	-.500		.000
Was any implement used in the commission of crime	-.302	-.577	-1.000	.707	.000	

* This is a similarity matrix

Table 25
Regression Coefficients between Victim's Related Variables and Crime Category

Victim Related Variables	*Unstandardized CoefficientsB*	*Std. Error*	*Standardized Coefficients Beta*	*t*	*Sig.*
(Constant)	1.500	.000		.	.
Age of the victim	8.47E-018	.000	.000	.	.
Sex of the victim	.500	.000	.816	.	.
Occupation of victim	-.500	.000	-.577	.	.
How was target approached	1.500	.000		.	.
The construction quality of wall/premise	8.47E 018	.000	.000	7	Was
any implement used in the commission of crime	.500	.000	.816	.	.

** *Dependent Variable:* Crime Category.

CRIME VULNERABILITY VARIABLES

Distance Analysis Among Crime Vulnerability Variables (Association of Independency)

Table 26 shows the proximity matrix (dissimilarity) in respect of the crime vulnerability variables. The association of independency has been examined through chi square test. This analysis has been done to examine the interaction among the independent crime vulnerability variables. The result of chi-square shows that there is statistical significant difference with regard to the variables 'Crime scene visible to others' and 'value of loss due to crime' ; 'Crime scene visible to others' and 'Status of Case' ; 'Description of crime scene' and 'Status of Case'. It shows that the chi-square value is highest in case of the variables 'Crime scene visible to others' and 'Value of loss due to crime', where as it was lowest in case of, 'anything available at crime scene used in the crime commission' and 'value of loss due to crime' variables.

Distance Analysis Among Crime Vulnerability Variables (Association of Dependency):

Table 27 shows the proximity matrix (similarity) with regard to the crime vulnerability variables. The association of

Table 26

Chi-square Matrix among Crime Vulnerability Variables

Independent Crime Vulnerability Variables	*Anything available at crime scene used in the crime commission*	*Value of loss due to crime (in rupees)*	*Status of Case*	*Description of crime scene*	*Presence of security measures at crime scene*	*Crime scene visible to others*
Anything available at crime scene used in the crime commission		5.606	6.280	7.282	5.951	8.415
Value of loss due to crime (in rupees)	5.606		8.765	8.780	8.343	10.829
Status of Case	6.280	8.765		8.879	8.808	9.896
Description of crime scene	7.282	8.780	8.879		8.461	11.282
Presence of security measures at crime scene	5.951	8.343	8.808	8.461		9.513
Crime scene visible to others	8.415	10.829	9.896	11.282	9.513	

* This is a dissimilarity matrix.

Table 27
Correlation Matrix Among Crime Vulnerability Variables

Independent Crime Vulnerability Variables	*Anything available at crime scene used in the crime commission*	*Value of loss due to crime (in rupees)*	*Status of Case*	*Description of crime scene*	*Presence of security measures at crime scene*	*Crime scene visible to others*
Anything available at crime scene used in the crime commission		.088	.006	-.007	.117	-.038
Value of loss due to crime (in rupees)	.088		.015	.161	.004	-.043
Status of Case	.006	.015		.159	-.095	.126
Description of crime scene	-.007	.161	.159		.093	-.103
Presence of security measures at crime scene	.117	.004	-.095	.093		-.059
Crime scene visible to others	-.038	-.043	.126	-.103	-.059	

* This is a similarity matrix

dependency has been ascertained through correlation analysis. This analysis has been performed to find out the co-linearity among the independent crime vulnerability variables. It is shown in Table that 'description of crime scene' and 'value of loss due to crime' variables were moderately correlated. This study also shows that the crime vulnerability variables are not correlated significantly which means there is not any significant dependency between them.

Regression Co-efficient between Crime Vulnerability Variables and Crime Category

Table 28 shows the co-efficient of regression model within crime vulnerability variables and crime category. The value of unstandardized β_1 is 1.255 which means "anything available at crime scene used in the crime commission" variable influences 1.255 per cent of crime category while other predictors are held constant. All the un-standardized βvalue can be interpreted in the same way.

The t-value for Value of loss due to crime is ($P<0.001$) is a significant predictor of crime category, while status of case is a non-significant ($P >0.235$) predictor of crime category.

Analysis of Variance (ANOVA) between Crime Vulnerability Variables and Crime Category

Table 29 depicts analysis of variance (ANOVA) to examine whether the model is significant at predicting the outcome. The model includes the interaction between crime vulnerability variables and crime category. This analysis suggests the three values i.e. variation explained by the model [model sum of squares (SSM)], variation unexplained by the model [residual sum of squares (SSR)] and total variation of the model [total sum of square (SST)]. The results of ANOVA shows that total sum of square (SST) is 643.495.

The value of F-ratio is greater than 1, which means that the independent crime vulnerability variables had significant contribution to dependent variable [crime category]. The F-ratio value [16.699] is significant [$P < .001$], which means model has significantly predicted the outcome. The exact magnitude

Table 28
Regression Coefficients between Crime Vulnerability Variables and Crime Category

Crime Scene Variables	*Unstandardized Coefficients B*	*Std. Error*	*Standardized Coefficients Beta*	*t*	*Sig.*
(Constant)	-1.253	.978		-1.281	.202
Anything available at crime scene used in the crime commission	1.255	.432	.172	2.907	.004
Value of loss due to crime (in rupees)	.628	.093	.405	6.785	.000
Status of Case	.125	.105	.072	1.192	.235
Description of crime scene	.213	.104	.125	2.048	.042
Presence of security measures at crime scene	-.585	.148	-.237	-3.962	.000
Crime scene visible to others	-.326	.088	-.220	-3.682	.000

** *Dependent Variable:* Crime Category

of the F-ratio can be assessed using critical values for the corresponding degree of freedom.

Table 30
Analysis of Variance [ANOVA] between Crime Vulnerability Variables and Crime Category

Model Parameters	*Sum of Squares*	*df*	*Mean Square*	*F*	*Sig.*
Regression	221.415	6	36.902	16.699	.000(a)
Residual	422.080	191	2.210		
Total	643.495	197			

* *Predictors:* (Constant), Crime scene visible to others, Presence of security measures at crime scene, Status of Case, Anything available at crime scene used in the crime commission, Description of crime scene, Value of loss due to crime (in rupees)
** *Dependent Variable:* Crime Category.

Model Summary Between Crime Vulnerability Variables and Crime Category

Table 31 describes the overall fit of the model. The value of R (multiple correlation coefficient) is 0.587, which means there is 0.587 level proportional association between crime vulnerability variables and crime category.

If the co-efficient of determination [0.344] is converted into percentage, it suggests that socio-cultural variables account for 34.4 percent of the variability in crime category. Hence this set of variables turn out to be a significant predictor of the nature of crime occurred.

Table 31
Model Summary between Crime Vulnerability Variables and Crime Category

R	*R Square*	*Adjusted R Square*	*Std. Error of the Estimate*	*Change Statistics R Square Change*	*F Change*
.587(a)	.344	.323	1.487	.344	16.699

* *Predictors:* (Constant), Crime scene visible to others, Presence of security measures at crime scene, Status of Case, Anything available at crime scene used in the crime commission, Description of crime scene, Value of loss due to crime (in rupees).

Regression Co-efficient between Crime Vulnerability Variables and Target Vulnerability

Table 32 shows the results of regression. The value of β_0 [2.274] implies that all the crime vulnerability variables are excluded then this model predict 2.274 per unit of target vulnerability. The value of β_1 is -0.433 that means with every unit variation in the "anything available at crime scene used in the crime commission" variable scale, the target vulnerability is varied by -0.433 units. This must be true if the effects of other crime vulnerability variables are held constant.

The t statistic value for " crime scene variable" [$P > 0.001$) is a significant predictor of target vulnerability, while t-value for "presence of security measures at crime scene" variable [$P < 0.05$) is a non-significant predictor of target vulnerability. All other value of t-static can be interpreted in the same way.

Analysis of Variance (ANOVA) between Crime Vulnerability Variables and Target Vulnerability

Table 33 offers the analysis of variance (ANOVA). The result of ANOVA shows that model sum of square (SSM) is 19.569 (explained variance) and residual sum of squares (SSR) is 115.204 (unexplained variance) whereas total sum of squares (SST) is 134.773 (total variance). The F ratio value is 5.407 ($P < .05$), which shows significant results. This means this model has much explained variance than unexplained variance.

Model Summary between Crime Vulnerability Variables and Target Vulnerability

Table 34 describes the multiple correlations co-efficient (R) [0.381] which defines the level of association between crime vulnerability variables and target vulnerability. The coefficient of determination (R^2) is 0.145 means 14.5 per cent of the variability account for target vulnerability. The adjusted R2 value is 0.118 and the difference between R^2 is (0.145 - 0.118 = 0.027) which means across different samples loss of predictive power is 2.7 per cent.

Table 32
Regression Coefficients between Crime Vulnerability Variables and Target Vulnerability

Crime Scene Variables	*Unstandardized Coefficients B*	*Std. Error*	*Standardized Coefficients Beta*	*t*	*Sig.*
(Constant)	2.274	.511		4.451	.000
Anything available at crime scene used in the crime commission	-.433	.226	-.130	-1.922	.056
Value of loss due to crime(in rupees)	.117	.048	.165	2.419	.016
Status of Case	-.037	.055	-.046	-.667	.505
Description of crime scene	.225	.054	.288	4.136	.000
Presence of security measures at crime scene	.057	.077	.050	.737	.462
Crime scene visible to others	.080	.046	.118	1.738	.084

** *Dependent Variable:* What made target lucrative

Table 33
Analysis of Variance [ANOVA] between Crime Vulnerability Variables and Target Vulnerability:

Model Parameters	*Sum of Squares*	*df*	*Mean Square*	*F*	*Sig.*
Regression	19.569	6	3.261	5.407	.000(a)
Residual	115.204	191	.603		
Total	134.773	197			

* *Predictors:* (Constant), Crime scene visible to others, Presence of security measures at crime scene, Status of Case, Anything available at crime scene used in the crime commission, Description of crime scene, Value of loss due to crime(in rupees).

***Dependent Variable:* What made target lucrative

Table 34
Model Summary between Crime Vulnerability Variables and Target Vulnerability

R	*R Square*	*Adjusted R Square*	*Std. Error of the Estimate*	*Change Statistics R Square Change*	*F Change*
.381(a)	.145	.118	.777	.145	5.407

* *Predictors:* (Constant), Crime scene visible to others, Presence of security measures at crime scene, Status of Case, Anything available at crime scene used in the crime commission, Description of crime scene, Value of loss due to crime(in rupees).

Regression Coefficient between Crime Vulnerability Variables and Perceived Safety of Area

Table 35 shows the results of regression. The value of β_0 [1.893] suggests that all the crime vulnerability variables are excluded then model predicts 1.893 of perceived safety of area.

The value of β_1 [0.025] suggests that 'anything available at crime scene used in the crime commission' variable is responsible for 0.025 proportional increase of perceived safety of area. The value of standardized β_1 [0.14] conveys 'anything available at crime scene used in the crime commission' variable accounts for 0.14 proportional standard deviation increase as per perceived safety of area scale standard deviation.

The t statistic value for "presence of security measures at crime scene" variable -1.144 (P >.005) is a moderately

Table 35

Regression Coefficients between Crime Vulnerability Variables and Perceived Safety of Area

Crime Scene Variables	*Unstandardized Coefficients B*	*Std. Error*	*Standardized Coefficients Beta*	*t*	*Sig.*
(Constant)	1.893	.300		6.316	.000
Anything available at crime scene used in the crime commission	.025	.132	.014	.187	.852
Value of loss due to crime(in rupees)	.009	.028	.023	.320	.749
Status of Case	-.041	.032	-.095	-1.281	.202
Description of crime scene	-9.10E-005	.032	.000	-.003	.998
Presence of security measures at crime scene	-.052	.045	-.084	-1.144	.254
Crime scene visible to others	.002	.027	.006	.089	.930

** *Dependent Variable:* Do you find this area safe

significant predictor of perceived safety of area, while t value for "crime scene visible to others" variable is 0.089 (P > .005) are the non significant predictor of perceived safety of area.

Analysis of Variance (ANOVA) between Crime Vulnerability Variables and Perceived Safety of Area

Table 36 gives the components of analysis of variance (ANOVA). The result of ANOVA shows that model sum of square (SSM) is 0.597 while residual sum of squares (SSR) is 39.626 where as total sum of square (SST) is 40.222. The F ratio [0.479] is a non-significant, which means there is more unsystematic variance than systematic variance and model does not over all predict perceived safety of area significantly.

Table 36
Analysis of Variance [ANOVA] between Crime Vulnerability Variables and Perceived Safety of Area

Model Parameters	*Sum of Squares*	*df*	*Mean Square*	*F*	*Sig.*
Regression	.597	6	.099	.479	.823(a)
Residual	39.626	191	.207		
Total	40.222	197			

* *Predictors:* (Constant), Crime scene visible to others, Presence of security measures at crime scene, Status of Case, Anything available at crime scene used in the crime commission, Description of crime scene, Value of loss due to crime (in rupees).

** *Dependent Variable:* Do you find this area safe

Model summary between crime vulnerability variables and perceived safety of area:

Table 37 describes the multiple correlation coefficient (R = 0.122] that represents the multiple correlation between crime vulnerability variables and perceived safety of area. The coefficient of determination (R^2 =0.015] implies that 1.5 per cent of the variability in perceived safety of area is determined by crime vulnerability variables. The adjusted R^2 value is -0.016 and the difference between R^2 [0.015 - (-0.006] = 0.021) means across different sample the loss of prediction is 2.1 per cent.

Table 37
Model Summary between Crime Vulnerability Variables and Perceived Safety of Area

R	*R Square*	*Adjusted R Square*	*Std. Error of the Estimate*	*Change Statistics R Square Change*	*F Change*
.122(a)	.015	-.016	.455	.015	.479

*** *Predictors:* (Constant), Crime scene visible to others, Presence of security measures at crime scene, Status of Case, Anything available at crime scene used in the crime commission, Description of crime scene, Value of loss due to crime (in rupees)**

6

Advanced Analysis of Situational Correlates of Crime

In the preceding chapter, situational variables were examined independently or in cross-tabulation format. In order to provide a more interacting and comprehensive picture of the variable under study, the selected variables have been subjected to advanced statistical analysis in the present chapter. It is mentionable that the nature of data in the present study was mostly on nominal and ordinal levels. Therefore certain non-parametric tests have been used to study the differences between the two samples. The Mann-Whitney U test has been used in the exercise for measuring the significance of difference, if any. To calculate the ANOVA [Analysis of Variance] in the present study, the Kruskal-Wallis test a non-parametric alternative to the one-way ANOVA, has been used.

It may be pertinent to study as to whether there is any significant statistical difference between the groups of victims in Bhopal and Sagar so far as crime category is concerned. The U and KW ANOVA tests were performed for this purpose. The null hypothesis for the analysis suggests that there is no significant difference in the groups of victims belonging to Bhopal and Sagar on the subject of crime category. The output of this test, as shown in Table 1, suggests that the two groups vary significantly ($U=18190.5$, $W=38290.5$, $Z=-1.681$ $p<0.093$, KW ANOVA $\chi^2 = 2.824$, $p<0.093$). Hence the null hypothesis is rejected.

Table 1

Crime Category	*Place of study*	*N*	*Mean Rank*	*Sum of Ranks*
	Bhopal	200	191.45	38290.50
	Sagar	200	209.55	41909.50
	Total	400		

Test Statistics (a)

	Crime Category
Mann-Whitney U	18190.500
Wilcoxon W	38290.500
Z	-1.681
Asymp. Sig. (2-tailed)	.093
Kruskal-Wallis Test	
Chi-Square	2.824
df	1
Asymp. Sig.	.093

a Kruskal Wallis Test.
b Grouping Variable: Place of study.

Table 2

Week of Occurrence	*Place of study*	*N*	*Mean Rank*	*Sum of Ranks*
	Bhopal	200	200.62	40123.50
	Sagar	200	200.38	40076.50
	Total	400		

Test Statistics (a)

	Week of Occurrence
Mann-Whitney U	19976.500
Wilcoxon W	40076.500
Z	-.021
Asymp. Sig. (2-tailed)	.983
Kruskal-Wallis Test	
Chi-Square	.001
df	1
Asymp. Sig.	.983

a Kruskal Wallis Test.
b Grouping Variable: Place of study.

The study also attempted to look at the differences in the groups of victims in Bhopal and Sagar regarding the week of occurrence of incidence. The null hypothesis for the analysis has been that there were no significant differences in the groups of victims from Bhopal and Sagar with respect to the week of occurrence. The output of the application of U test and KW ANOVA as shown in Table 2 suggests that there was no statistically significant differences (U=19976.5, W =40076.5, Z= -.021p< 0.983, KW ANOVA χ^2 = .001, p< 0.983) between the two groups. The null hypothesis is therefore accepted.

Table 3

Time of Occurrence	*Place of study*	N	*Mean Rank*	*Sum of Ranks*
	Bhopal	200	197.66	39531.00
	Sagar	200	203.35	40669.00
	Total	400		

Test Statistics (a)

	Time of Occurrence
Mann-Whitney U	19431.000
Wilcoxon W	39531.000
Z	-.518
Asymp. Sig. (2-tailed)	.604
Kruskal-Wallis Test	
Chi-Square	.268
df	1
Asymp. Sig.	.604

a Kruskal Wallis Test.
b Grouping Variable: Place of study.

The present exercise intended to measure the differences in the time of occurrence amongst Bhopal and Sagar cities. The null hypothesis is that there were no significant differences in the two groups of victims belonging to Bhopal and Sagar. The output of the Table 3 suggests that the two groups had no significant differences (U=19431.0, W =39531.0, Z= -.518 p< 0 .604, KW ANOVA χ^2 = .268, p< 0. 604). The null hypothesis therefore accepted.

The application of U test and KW ANOVA confirms the presence of statistically significant difference between the victims belonging to Bhopal and Sagar regarding location of scene of crime. The results shown in Table 4 indicate that null hypothesis is rejected. The two group of victims varied Significantly (U=18744.5, W =38844.5, Z= -1.325 p< 0 .185, KW ANOVA χ^2 = 1.756, p< 0.185). The mean difference in these groups confirms that Sagar is more vulnerable for location of scene of crime than Bhopal.

Table 4

Location of Scene of Crime	*Place of study*	*N*	*Mean Rank*	*Sum of Ranks*
	Bhopal	200	194.22	38844.50
	Sagar	200	206.78	41355.50
	Total	400		

Test Statistics(a)

	Location of Scene of Crime
Mann-Whitney U	18744.500
Wilcoxon W	38844.500
Z	-1.325
Asymp. Sig. (2-tailed)	.185
Kruskal-Wallis Test	
Chi-Square	1.756
df	1
Asymp. Sig.	.185

a Kruskal Wallis Test.
b Grouping Variable: Place of study.

Table 5

In case of outdoor scene of crime	*Place of study*	*N*	*Mean Rank*	*Sum of Ranks*
	Bhopal	200	179.43	35885.50
	Sagar	200	221.57	44314.50
	Total	400		

Test Statistics(a)

	In case of outdoor scene of crime
Mann-Whitney U	15785.500
Wilcoxon W	35885.500
Z	-3.818
Asymp. Sig. (2-tailed)	.001
Kruskal-Wallis Test	
Chi-Square	14.579
df	1
Asymp. Sig.	.001

a Kruskal Wallis Test.
b Grouping Variable: Place of study.

The present study looked in to the differences in the groups of victims from Bhopal and Sagar regarding outdoor scene of crime. The application of U test and KW ANOVA confirms [Table 5] the presence of statistically significance differences (U=15785.5, W =35885.5, Z= -3.818 p< 0 .001, KW ANOVA χ^2 = 14.579, p< 0.001) in the two groups. The null hypothesis is rejected. The mean rank on the subject confirms the fact that the victim from Sagar relatively had greater incidents of outdoor scene of crime. There is need to search some possible explanations to this finding.

Table 6

The Lighting arrangement on immediate street	*Place of study*	*N*	*Mean Rank*	*Sum of Ranks*
	Bhopal	200	191.93	38385.50
	Sagar	200	209.07	41814.50
	Total	400		

Test Statistics(a)

	In case of outdoor scene of crime
Mann-Whitney U	18285.500
Wilcoxon W	38385.500
Z	-1.555
Asymp. Sig. (2-tailed)	.120
Kruskal-Wallis Test	
Chi-Square	2.418
df	1
Asymp. Sig.	.120

a Kruskal Wallis Test.
b Grouping Variable: Place of study.

To examine the significance of difference in lighting arrangement on the immediate street in case of two groups of victims, the null hypothesis is that there is no significant difference amongst the two groups. The output of this test as shown in Table 6 suggests that the two groups of victims from Bhopal and Sagar had significant differences (U=18285.5, W =38385.5, Z= -1.555 p< 0 .120, KW ANOVA χ^2 = 2.418, p< 0.120). The null hypothesis is therefore rejected.

Table 7

Lighting arrangement in the premises	*Place of study*	*N*	*Mean Rank*	*Sum of Ranks*
	Bhopal	200	194.05	38810.50
	Sagar	200	206.95	41389.50
	Total	400		

Test Statistics(a)

	Lighting arrangement in the premises
Mann-Whitney U	18710.500
Wilcoxon W	38810.500
Z	-1.155
Asymp. Sig. (2-tailed)	.248
Kruskal-Wallis Test	
Chi-Square	1.334
df	1
Asymp. Sig.	.248

a Kruskal Wallis Test.
b Grouping Variable: Place of study.

The above Table shows differences in the victims from Bhopal and Sagar with respect to lighting arrangement in the premises. The output of the test as shown in Table 7 confirms that there is not any significant differences between the two groups (U=18710.5, W =38810.5, Z= -1.155 $p< 0.248$, KW ANOVA $\chi^2 = 1.334$, $p< 0.248$). The null hypothesis is therefore rejected.

It has been attempted to study as to whether there is any statistically significant difference between the group of victims belonging to Bhopal and Sagar so far as the easiness to commit crime by the offender was concerned. The U Test and KW ANOVA have been performed for this purpose. The null hypothesis for the analysis is that there was no significant difference between the two groups regarding "was it easy for offender to commit this crime"? The results of this test show [Table 8] that two group varied significantly (U =19124.0, W = 39224.0, Z = -0.888 $p< 0.375$, KW ANOVA $\chi^2 = 0.788$, $p< 0.375$). Hence the null hypothesis is accepted.

Table 8

Was it easy for offender to commit this crime?	*Place of study*	*N*	*Mean Rank*	*Sum of Ranks*
	Bhopal	200	204.88	40976.00
	Sagar	200	196.12	39224.00
	Total	400		

Test Statistics(a)

	Was it easy for offender to commit this crime
Mann-Whitney U	19124.000
Wilcoxon W	39224.000
Z	-.888
Asymp. Sig. (2-tailed)	.375
Kruskal-Wallis Test	
Chi-Square	.788
df	1
Asymp. Sig.	.375

a Kruskal Wallis Test
b Grouping Variable: Place of study

Table 9

Average time spent at home	*Place of study*	*N*	*Mean Rank*	*Sum of Ranks*
	Bhopal	200	173.84	34768.00
	Sagar	200	227.16	45432.00
	Total	400		

Test Statistics(a)

	Average time spent at home
Mann-Whitney U	14668.000
Wilcoxon W	34768.000
Z	-5.424
Asymp. Sig. (2-tailed)	.001
Kruskal Wallis Test	
Chi-Square	29.418
df	1
Asymp. Sig.	.001

a Kruskal Wallis Test
b Grouping Variable: Place of study

The study shows that there is any significant difference between the two groups of victims with respect to average time spent by the victim at home. It has been observed in the study [Table 9] that there was significant difference between the two groups on this variable (U=14668.0, W =34768.0, Z= -5.424 $p < 0.001$, KW ANOVA $\chi^2 = 29.418$, $p < 0.001$). The null hypothesis is therefore rejected.

Table 10

How much time remains away from the target?	*Place of study*	*N*	*Mean Rank*	*Sum of Ranks*
	Bhopal	200	215.09	43017.00
	Sagar	198	183.76	36384.00
	Total	398		

Test Statistics(a)

	How much time remains away from the target
Mann-Whitney U	16683.000
Wilcoxon W	36384.000
Z	-3.040
Asymp. Sig. (2-tailed)	.002
Kruskal-Wallis Test	
Chi-Square	9.242
df	1
Asymp. Sig.	.002

a Kruskal Wallis Test
b Grouping Variable: Place of study.

An attempt has been made in this study to find out if there are the statistically significant differences between the two groups of victims belonging to Bhopal and Sagar with respect to the duration the victim was away from the target. The findings show that the two groups had significant differences (U=16683.0, W =36384.0, Z= -3.040 $p < 0.002$, KW ANOVA $\chi^2 = 9.242$, $p < 0.002$). Thus, the null hypothesis is rejected.

It may be relevant to study as to whether there are any significant differences between the groups of victims so far as distance between work place of victim and crime scene is concerned. The output shows [Table 11] that there is a significant difference between the two groups (U=15242.5, W =35342.5, Z= -5.285 $p < 0.001$, KW ANOVA $\chi^2 = 27.930$, $p < 0.001$). The null hypothesis is therefore rejected.

Table 11

Distance between workplace and crime scene?	*Place of study*	*N*	*Mean Rank*	*Sum of Ranks*
	Bhopal	200	224.29	44857.50
	Sagar	200	176.71	35342.50
	Total	400		

Test Statistics(a)

	Distance between workplace and crime scene
Mann-Whitney U	15242.500
Wilcoxon W	35342.500
Z	-5.285
Asymp. Sig. (2-tailed)	.001
Kruskal-Wallis Test	
Chi-Square	27.930
df	1
Asymp. Sig.	.001

a Kruskal Wallis Test.
b Grouping Variable: Place of study.

Table 12

Distance between Crime Target and Owner at the Time of Crime commission?	*Place of study*	*N*	*Mean Rank*	*Sum of Ranks*
	Bhopal	200	200.29	40057.00
	Sagar	200	200.72	40143.00
	Total	400		

Test Statistics(a)

	Distance between crime target and owner at the time of crime commission
Mann-Whitney U	19957.000
Wilcoxon W	40057.000
Z	-.040
Asymp. Sig. (2-tailed)	.968
Kruskal-Wallis Test	
Chi-Square	.002
df	1
Asymp. Sig.	.968

a Kruskal Wallis Test
b Grouping Variable: Place of study

The study attempted to look at the differences in the groups of victims belonging to Bhopal and Sagar regarding 'distance between crime target and owner at the time of crime commission'. The null hypothesis for the analysis has been that there are no significant differences in the groups of victims with respect to 'distance between crime target and owner at the time of crime commission'. The output of the application of U test and KW ANOVA, as shown in Table 12, conveys the presence of no statistically significant differences (U=19957.0, W =40057.0, Z= -.040 p< 0.968, KW ANOVA χ^2 = .002, p< 0. 968) between the two groups. The null hypothesis is therefore accepted.

Table 13

Did crime occur in the absence of victim?	*Place of study*	*N*	*Mean Rank*	*Sum of Ranks*
	Bhopal	200	203.00	40600.00
	Sagar	200	198.00	39600.00
	Total	400		

Test Statistics(a)

	Distance between crime target and owner
Mann-Whitney U	19500.000
Wilcoxon W	39600.000
Z	-.591
Asymp. Sig. (2-tailed)	.554
Kruskal-Wallis Test	
Chi-Square	.349
df	1
Asymp. Sig.	.554

a Kruskal Wallis Test.
b Grouping Variable: Place of study.

Crime of theft occurs in the absence of victim. The differences between the two groups of victims in the selected cities were examined. The null hypothesis is stated that there were no differences between the groups. The outcome also shows [Table 13] that there was no statistically significant difference (U=19500.0, W =39600.0, Z= -.591 p< 0.554, KW ANOVA χ^2 = .349, p< 0.554) between two groups. Thus null hypothesis is accepted.

Table 14

What was victim doing that time?	*Place of study*	N	*Mean Rank*	*Sum of Ranks*
	Bhopal	200	219.12	43823.00
	Sagar	200	181.89	36377.00
	Total	400		

Test Statistics(a)

	What was victim doing that time
Mann-Whitney U	16277.000
Wilcoxon W	36377.000
Z	-3.367
Asymp. Sig. (2-tailed)	.001
Kruskal-Wallis Test	
Chi-Square	11.339
df	1
Asymp. Sig.	.001

a Kruskal Wallis Test.
b Grouping Variable: Place of study.

Victim's engagement at the time of crime commission is a crucial factor for vulnerability. The study of the two groups of victims of Bhopal and Sagar shows [Table 14] significant differences in respect of this variable. The value of Mann-Whitney U test, Kruskal Wallis test as well as other tests confirms that there were significant differences between the two groups (U=16277.0, W =36377.0, Z= -3.367 p< 0.001, KW ANOVA $\chi^2 = 11.339$, p< 0.001) and thus, the null hypothesis is rejected.

Table 15 shows the differences between the two groups of victims regarding if the victim resisted crime or not. It has been observed from the study that there were statistically significant differences between the two groups (U=19196.5, W =39296.5, Z= -1.689 p< 0.091, KW ANOVA $\chi^2 = 2.854$, p< 0.091). The null hypothesis is rejected.

The age of victim is a significant factor in the occurrence of crime. A study has been made if the two groups of victim's varied significantly in respect of age. The null hypothesis states that there were no significant differences between the two groups. Table 16 shows that there were no statistically

Table 15

Did the victim resist crime?	*Place of study*	*N*	*Mean Rank*	*Sum of Ranks*
	Bhopal	200	204.52	40903.50
	Sagar	200	196.48	39296.50
	Total	400		

Test Statistics(a)

	Did the victim resist crime
Mann-Whitney U	19196.500
Wilcoxon W	39296.500
Z	-1.689
Asymp. Sig. (2-tailed)	.091
Kruskal-Wallis Test	
Chi-Square	2.854
df	1
Asymp. Sig.	.091

a Kruskal Wallis Test
b Grouping Variable: Place of study.

Table 16

Age of the victim	*Place of study*	*N*	*Mean Rank*	*Sum of Ranks*
	Bhopal	200	200.66	40131.50
	Sagar	200	200.34	40068.50
	Total	400		

Test Statistics(a)

	Age of the victim
Mann-Whitney U	19968.500
Wilcoxon W	40068.500
Z	-.028
Asymp. Sig. (2-tailed)	.977
Kruskal-Wallis Test	
Chi-Square	.001
df	1
Asymp. Sig.	.977

a Kruskal Wallis Test.
b Grouping Variable: Place of study.

significant differences (U=19968.5, W =40068.5, Z= -.028 p< 0.977, KW ANOVA χ^2 = .001, p< 0.977) between the two groups. Thus, the null hypothesis is accepted.

Table 17 examines the differences, if any, in the two groups of samples regarding the sex of victim. The null hypothesis states that there were no significant differences between the two groups of victims. The output shows the statistically significant (U=18500.0, W =38600.0, Z= -2.371p< 0.018, KW ANOVA χ^2 = 5.620, p< 0.018) differences between the two groups. Thus null hypothesis is rejected.

Table 17

Sex of the victim	*Place of study*	*N*	*Mean Rank*	*Sum of Ranks*
	Bhopal	200	208.00	41600.00
	Sagar	200	193.00	38600.00
	Total	400		

Test Statistics(a)

	Sex of the victim
Mann-Whitney U	18500.000
Wilcoxon W	38600.000
Z	-2.371
Asymp. Sig. (2-tailed)	.018
Kruskal-Wallis Test	
Chi-Square	5.620
df	1
Asymp. Sig.	.018

a Kruskal Wallis Test.

b Grouping Variable: Place of study.

Table 18

Occupation of victim	*Place of study*	*N*	*Mean Rank*	*Sum of Ranks*
	Bhopal	199	205.25	40844.50
	Sagar	200	194.78	38955.50
	Total	399		

Test Statistics(a)

	Occupation of victim
Mann-Whitney U	18855.500
Wilcoxon W	38955.500
Z	-.953
Asymp. Sig. (2-tailed)	.341
Kruskal-Wallis Test	
Chi-Square	.908
df	1
Asymp. Sig.	.341

a Kruskal Wallis Test.

b Grouping Variable: Place of study.

The data shown in Table 18 examines if there was any statistically difference between the two groups of victims regarding the occupation of victim. The null hypothesis states that there were no significant differences between the two groups of victims. The output shows [Table 18] that there were no statistically significant differences (U=18855.5, W =38955.5, Z= -.953 p< 0.341, KW ANOVA χ^2 = .908, p< 0.341) between the two groups. Thus the null hypothesis is accepted.

Table 19

How was target approached?	*Place of study*	*N*	*Mean Rank*	*Sum of Ranks*
	Bhopal	200	215.40	43079.00
	Sagar	200	185.61	37121.00
	Total	400		

Test Statistics(a)

	How was target approached
Mann-Whitney U	17021.000
Wilcoxon W	37121.000
Z	-2.820
Asymp. Sig. (2-tailed)	.005
Kruskal-Wallis Test	
Chi-Square	7.954
df	1
Asymp. Sig.	.005

a Kruskal Wallis Test.
b Grouping Variable: Place of study.

It become quite crucial in the manner the target was approached by the offender. The study shows [Table 19] that there is statistically significant difference between the groups of victims regarding this variable. The value of U, W, Z and KW test shows (U=17021.0, W =37121.0, Z= -2.820 p< 0.005, KW ANOVA χ^2 = 7.954, p< 0.005) that there was a significant difference between both the groups of Bhopal and Sagar victims. Thus the null hypothesis is rejected.

Table 20 shows the difference in the two groups with respect of construction quality of wall/premise of victim's house or shop. The KW test shows that there were significant differences between these groups regarding the variable examined. The statistical figures are (U=19505.0, W =39605.0, Z= -1.394 p< 0.163, KW ANOVA $\chi 2$ = 1.943, p< 0.163). The null hypothesis is rejected.

Table 20

The construction quality of wall/premise	*Place of study*	*N*	*Mean Rank*	*Sum of Ranks*
	Bhopal	200	198.03	39605.00
	Sagar	200	202.98	40595.00
	Total	400		

Test Statistics(a)

	The construction quality of wall/premise
Mann-Whitney U	19505.000
Wilcoxon W	39605.000
Z	-1.394
Asymp. Sig. (2-tailed)	.163
Kruskal-Wallis Test	
Chi-Square	1.943
df	1
Asymp. Sig.	.163

a Kruskal Wallis Test.
b Grouping Variable: Place of study.

Table 21

Was any implement used in the commission of crime?	*Place of study*	*N*	*Mean Rank*	*Sum of Ranks*
	Bhopal	198	205.80	40748.00
	Sagar	200	193.27	38653.00
	Total	398		

Test Statistics(a)

	Was any implement used in the commission of crime
Mann-Whitney U	18553.000
Wilcoxon W	38653.000
Z	-1.372
Asymp. Sig. (2-tailed)	.170
Kruskal-Wallis Test	
Chi-Square	1.883
df	1
Asymp. Sig.	.170

a Kruskal Wallis Test
b Grouping Variable: Place of study

Generally, the offenders use any implement available in the premises of victim in the commission of theft or burglary from houses/shop. It has been observed [Table 21] that there was a significant difference in the groups of victims regarding this variable. There is a statistically significant difference between both the groups (U=18553.0, W =38653.0, Z= -1.372 p< 0.170, KW ANOVA $\chi 2$ = 1.883, p< 0.170). The null hypothesis is rejected.

Table 22

Anything available at crime scene used in the crime commission?	*Place of study*	*N*	*Mean Rank*	*Sum of Ranks*
	Bhopal	200	204.95	40989.50
	Sagar	200	196.05	39210.50
	Total	400		

Test Statistics(a)

	Anything available at crime scene used in the crime commission
Mann-Whitney U	19110.500
Wilcoxon W	39210.500
Z	-1.991
Asymp. Sig. (2-tailed)	.046
Kruskal-Wallis Test	
Chi-Square	3.965
df	1
Asymp. Sig.	.046

a Kruskal Wallis Test.
b Grouping Variable: Place of study.

It may be important to study as to whether there is any significant statistical difference between the groups of victims so far as "anything available at crime scene used in the crime commission" is concerned. The U and KW ANOVA tests were performed for this purpose. The null hypothesis states that there was no significant difference in the two groups regarding this variable. The output of this test, as shown in Table 22, suggests that the two groups vary significantly (U=19110.5, W =39210.5, Z= -1.991 p< 0.046, KW ANOVA χ^2 = 3.965, p< 0.046). Hence, the null hypothesis is rejected.

Table 23

What made target lucrative?	*Place of study*	*N*	*Mean Rank*	*Sum of Ranks*
	Bhopal	200	183.64	36727.50
	Sagar	200	217.36	43472.50
	Total	400		

Test Statistics(a)

	What made target lucrative
Mann-Whitney U	16627.500
Wilcoxon W	36727.500
Z	-3.196
Asymp. Sig. (2-tailed)	.001
Kruskal-Wallis Test	
Chi-Square	10.213
df	1
Asymp. Sig.	.001

a Kruskal Wallis Test.
b Grouping Variable: Place of study.

The study examined the differences in the selected groups of victims regarding "What made target lucrative"? The null hypothesis for the analysis has been that there were no significant differences in the groups of victims with respect to target lucrativity. The output of the application of U test and KW ANOVA, as shown in Table 23, confirm the presence of statistically significant differences (U=16627.5, W =36727.5, Z= -3.196 $p < 0.001$, KW ANOVA $\chi 2$ = 10.213, $p < 0.001$) between two groups. The null hypothesis is therefore rejected.

The value of loss due to crime is a key factor in the occurrence of crime. The value of loss due to theft/burglary was studied in case of the selected groups of victims in the two cities. The null hypothesis states that there were no significant differences between the two groups. Table 24 shows that there were no statistically significant differences (U=19274.5, W =39374.5, Z= -.667 $p < 0.505$, KW ANOVA χ^2 = 0.445, $p < 0.505$) in these groups. Thus, the null hypothesis is accepted.

Table 24

Value of loss due to crime (in rupees)	*Place of study*	*N*	*Mean Rank*	*Sum of Ranks*
	Bhopal	200	204.13	40825.50
	Sagar	200	196.87	39374.50
	Total	400		

Test Statistics(a)

	Value of loss due to crime (in rupees)
Mann-Whitney U	19274.500
Wilcoxon W	39374.500
Z	-.667
Asymp. Sig. (2-tailed)	.505
Kruskal-Wallis Test	
Chi-Square	.445
df	1
Asymp. Sig.	.505

a Kruskal Wallis Test. ·
b Grouping Variable: Place of study.

Table 25

Status of Case	*Place of study*	*N*	*Mean Rank*	*Sum of Ranks*
	Bhopal	200	185.39	37077.00
	Sagar	200	215.62	43123.00
	Total	400		

Test Statistics(a)

	Status of Case
Mann-Whitney U	16977.000
Wilcoxon W	37077.000
Z	-2.818
Asymp. Sig. (2-tailed)	.005
Kruskal-Wallis Test	
Chi-Square	7.943
df	1
Asymp. Sig.	.005

a Kruskal Wallis Test.
b Grouping Variable: Place of study.

It may be pertinent to study as to whether there are any statistical significant differences between the groups of victims so far as status of case is concerned. The output shows [Table 25] that there is a significant difference between the two groups (U=16977.0, W = 37077.0, Z= -2.818 p< 0.005, KW ANOVA $\chi^2 = 7.943$, p< 0.005). Because of significant differences in the groups under study, the null hypothesis has been rejected.

Table 26

Presence of security measures at crime scene	*Place of study*	*N*	*Mean Rank*	*Sum of Ranks*
	Bhopal	199	207.98	41389.00
	Sagar	199	191.02	38012.00
	Total	398		

Test Statistics(a)

	Presence of security measures at crime scene
Mann-Whitney U	18112.000
Wilcoxon W	38012.000
Z	-2.046
Asymp. Sig. (2-tailed)	.041
Kruskal-Wallis Test	
Chi-Square	4.185
df	1
Asymp. Sig.	.041

a Kruskal Wallis Test.
b Grouping Variable: Place of study.

This study shows [Table 26] that there is statistically significant difference between the groups of victims so far as "presence of security measures at crime scene" variable is concerned. The value of U, W, Z and KW test shows (U=18112.0, W =38012.0, Z= -2.046 p< 0.041, KW ANOVA χ^2 = 4.185, p< 0.041) that there was a significant difference between both the groups of victims. Thus, the null hypothesis is rejected.

It may be relevant to study as to whether there were any significant differences between the groups of victims in Bhopal and Sagar so far as crime scene visibility is concerned. The output shows [Table 27] that there is a significant difference between the two groups (U=17297.5, W = 37197.5, Z= -2.412 p< 0.016, KW ANOVA χ^2 = 5.816, p< 0.016). Thus, the null hypothesis is rejected.

Table 27

Crime scene visible to others?	*Place of study*	*N*	*Mean Rank*	*Sum of Ranks*
	Bhopal	200	213.01	42602.50
	Sagar	199	186.92	37197.50
	Total	399		

Test Statistics(a)

	Crime scene visible to others
Mann-Whitney U	17297.500
Wilcoxon W	37197.500
Z	-2.412
Asymp. Sig. (2-tailed)	.016
Kruskal-Wallis Test	
Chi-Square	5.816
df	1
Asymp. Sig.	.016

a Kruskal Wallis Test
b Grouping Variable: Place of study

Table 28

Locking arrangement	*Pluce of study*	*N*	*Mean Rank*	*Sum of Ranks*
	Bhopal	142	163.40	23202.50
	Sagar	163	143.94	23462.50
	Total	305		

Test Statistics(a)

	Locking arrangement
Mann-Whitney U	10096.500
Wilcoxon W	23462.500
Z	-2.098
Asymp. Sig. (2-tailed)	.036
Kruskal-Wallis Test	
Chi-Square	4.402
df	1
Asymp. Sig.	.036

a Kruskal Wallis Test
b Grouping Variable: Place of study.

It may be appropriate to study as to whether there were any significant differences between the groups of victims so far as 'locking arrangement' is concerned. The output shows [Table 28] that there is a significant difference between the two groups (U=10096.5, W =23462.5, Z= -2.098 p< 0.036, KW ANOVA $\chi^2 = 4.402$, p< 0.036). The null hypothesis is therefore rejected.

Table 29

Was there police patrolling?	*Place of study*	*N*	*Mean Rank*	*Sum of Ranks*
	Bhopal	197	149.54	29459.00
	Sagar	200	247.72	49544.00
	Total	397		

Test Statistics(a)

	Was there police patrolling
Mann-Whitney U	9956.000
Wilcoxon W	29459.000
Z	-9.528
Asymp. Sig. (2-tailed)	.001
Kruskal-Wallis Test	
Chi-Square	90.782
df	1
Asymp. Sig.	.001

a Kruskal Wallis Test
b Grouping Variable: Place of study.

There are studies to suggest that police patrolling may have a controlling effect on likely crime in the community. It is in this context the present exercise intended to measure the differences experienced by the two groups regarding this variable. The null hypothesis is that there were no significant differences amongst the two groups. The output of the Table 29 suggests that the two groups had highly significant differences (U=9956.0, W =29459.0, Z= -9.528 p< 0.001, KW ANOVA χ^2 = 90.782, p< 0.001). The null hypothesis is therefore rejected.

It has been attempted to find out if there was any significant difference between the groups of victims so far as the "presence of any one capable to prevent crime on the scene of crime" is concerned. The null hypothesis states that there were no significant differences between the groups of victims. The output shows [Table 33] that there was no statistically significant difference (U=19610.0, W =39710.0, Z= -.192 p< 0.848, KW ANOVA χ^2 = 0.037, p< 0.848) between the two groups. Thus null hypothesis is accepted.

Table 30

Was there anybody on the scene capable of preventing crime?	*Place of study*	*N*	*Mean Rank*	*Sum of Ranks*
	Bhopal	198	200.46	39691.00
	Sagar	200	198.55	39710.00
	Total	398		

Test Statistics(a)

	Was there anybody on the scene capable of preventing crime
Mann-Whitney U	19610.000
Wilcoxon W	39710.000
Z	-.192
Asymp. Sig. (2-tailed)	.848
Kruskal-Wallis Test	
Chi-Square	.037
df	1
Asymp. Sig.	.848

a Kruskal Wallis Test
b Grouping Variable: Place of study.

Table 31

Presence of people around, when crime occurred?	*Place of study*	*N*	*Mean Rank*	*Sum of Ranks*
	Bhopal	200	208.94	41787.50
	Sagar	200	192.06	38412.50
	Total	400		

Test Statistics(a)

	Presence of people around, when crime occurred
Mann-Whitney U	18312.500
Wilcoxon W	38412.500
Z	-1.579
Asymp. Sig. (2-tailed)	.114
Kruskal-Wallis Test	
Chi-Square	2.494
df	1
Asymp. Sig.	.114

a Kruskal Wallis Test
b Grouping Variable: Place of study

The present study examined as to whether there were any statistical significant differences between the groups of victims so far as 'Presence of people around, when crime occurred' is concerned. The output shows [Table 31] that there is a significant difference between the two groups (U=18312.5, W = 38412.5, Z= -1.579 p< 0.114, KW ANOVA $\chi^2 = 2.494$, p< 0.114). Thus, the null hypothesis has been rejected.

Table 32

History of earlier attempts?	*Place of study*	*N*	*Mean Rank*	*Sum of Ranks*
	Bhopal	199	203.50	40496.50
	Sagar	199	195.50	38904.50
	Total	398		

Test Statistics(a)

	History of earlier attempts
Mann-Whitney U	19004.500
Wilcoxon W	38904.500
Z	-1.396
Asymp. Sig. (2-tailed)	.163
Kruskal-Wallis Test	
Chi-Square	1.950
df	1
Asymp. Sig.	.163

a Kruskal Wallis Test.
b Grouping Variable: Place of study.

This study shows [Table 32] that there is statistically significant difference between the groups of victims so far as "History of earlier attempts of theft with the victim" variable is concerned. The value of U, W, Z and KW test shows (U=19004.5, W =38904.5, Z= -1.396 p< 0.163, KW ANOVA χ^2 = 1.950, p< 0.163) that there was a significant difference between both the groups of victims. Thus, the null hypothesis is rejected.

This study shows [Table 33] that there is statistically significant difference between the groups of victims so far as "Location of crime scene" variable is concerned. The value of U, W, Z and KW test shows (U= 0.001, W =20100.0, Z= -17.867 p< 0.001, KW ANOVA $\chi^2 = 319.216$, p< 0.001) that there was a significant difference between both the groups. Thus, the null hypothesis is rejected.

Table 33

Location of crime scene	*Place of study*	*N*	*Mean Rank*	*Sum of Ranks*
	Bhopal	200	100.50	20100.00
	Sagar	200	300.50	60100.00
	Total	400		

Test Statistics(a)

	Location of crime scene
Mann-Whitney U	.001
Wilcoxon W	20100.000
Z	-17.867
Asymp. Sig. (2-tailed)	.001
Kruskal-Wallis Test	
Chi-Square	319.216
df	1
Asymp. Sig.	.001

a Kruskal Wallis Test
b Grouping Variable: Place of study

Table 34

Profile of resident	*Place of study*	*N*	*Mean Rank*	*Sum of Ranks*
	Bhopal	199	201.54	40106.00
	Sagar	200	198.47	39694.00
	Total	399		

Test Statistics(a)

	Profile of resident
Mann-Whitney U	19594.000
Wilcoxon W	39694.000
Z	-1.033
Asymp. Sig. (2-tailed)	.302
Kruskal-Wallis Test	
Chi-Square	1.067
df	1
Asymp. Sig.	.302

a Kruskal Wallis Test.
b Grouping Variable: Place of study.

The application of U test and KW ANOVA confirms the presence of statistically significant difference between the groups of victims regarding profile of residents living in the area. The results shown in Table 34 indicate that null hypothesis is rejected. The two group of victims varied significantly (U=19594.0, W = 39694.0, Z = -1.033 p< 0.302, KW ANOVA χ^2 = 1.067, p< 0.302).

Table 35

Predominant characteristic of locality	*Place of study*	*N*	*Mean Rank*	*Sum of Ranks*
	Bhopal	199	205.98	40991.00
	Sagar	200	194.05	38809.00
	Total	399		

Test Statistics(a)

	Predominant characteristic of locality
Mann-Whitney U	18709.000
Wilcoxon W	38809.000
Z	-1.087
Asymp. Sig. (2-tailed)	.277
Kruskal-Wallis Test	
Chi-Square	1.182
df	1
Asymp. Sig.	.277

a Kruskal Wallis Test.
b Grouping Variable: Place of study.

This study depicts that 'predominant characteristics of locality' in the two cities varied significantly. The output of the non-parametric test confirms that there is statistically significant (U=18709.0, W =38809.0, Z= -1.087 p< 0.277, KW ANOVA χ^2 = 1.182, p< 0.277) differences in the two groups. Thus, the null hypothesis is rejected.

There are studies to suggest that there was a reduction in crime due to surveillance/security arrangements. It is in this context the present exercise intended to measure the differences in respect surveillance/security arrangements in the selected cities. The null hypothesis is that there were no significant differences in the two groups of victims. The output of test [Table 36] suggests that the two groups had highly significant differences (U= 14910.0, W =34810.0, Z= -5.027 p< 0.001, KW ANOVA χ^2 = 25.274, p< 0.001). The null hypothesis is therefore rejected.

Table 36

Surveillance/Security arrangements	*Place of study*	*N*	*Mean Rank*	*Sum of Ranks*
	Bhopal	199	174.92	34810.00
	Sagar	200	224.95	44990.00
	Total	399		

Test Statistics(a)

	Surveillance/Security arrangements
Mann-Whitney U	14910.000
Wilcoxon W	34810.000
Z	-5.027
Asymp. Sig. (2-tailed)	.001
Kruskal-Wallis Test	
Chi-Square	25.274
df	1
Asymp. Sig.	.001

a Kruskal Wallis Test.
b Grouping Variable: Place of study.

Table 37

Do you find this area safe?	*Place of study*	*N*	*Mean Rank*	*Sum of Ranks*
	Bhopal	200	197.10	39420.00
	Sagar	200	203.90	40780.00
	Total	400		

Test Statistics(a)

	Do you find this area safe
Mann-Whitney U	19320.000
Wilcoxon W	39420.000
Z	-.718
Asymp. Sig. (2-tailed)	.473
Kruskal-Wallis Test	
Chi-Square	.516
df	1
Asymp. Sig.	.473

a Kruskal Wallis Test.
b Grouping Variable: Place of study.

This study attempted to examine the differences in the two groups of victims regarding perceived safety of area. The null hypothesis for the analysis has been that there were no significant differences in the groups of victims with respect to perceived safety of area. The output of the application of U test and KW ANOVA as shown in Table 37 suggests no statistically significant differences (U=19320.0, W =39420.0, Z= -.718 p< 0.473, KW ANOVA χ^2 = 0.516, p< 0.473) between the two groups. The null hypothesis is therefore accepted.

Table 38

Do you feel that opportunities to commit this crime in this locality are in abundance?	*Place of study*	*N*	*Mean Rank*	*Sum of Ranks*
	Bhopal	200	213.06	42612.50
	Sagar	200	187.94	37587.50
	Total	400		

Test Statistics(a)

	Do you feel that opportunities to commit this crime in this locality are in abundance
Mann-Whitney U	17487.500
Wilcoxon W	37587.500
Z	-2.684
Asymp. Sig. (2-tailed)	.007
Kruskal-Wallis Test	
Chi-Square	7.201
df	1
Asymp. Sig.	.007

a Kruskal Wallis Test.
b Grouping Variable: Place of study.

It may be imperative to study as to whether there was any significant statistical difference between the two groups of victims regarding "feeling of opportunities to commit this crime in this locality are in abundance". The U and KW ANOVA tests were performed for this purpose. The null hypothesis for the analysis has been that there is no significant difference in the groups of victims. The output of this test, as shown in Table 38, suggests that the two groups varied significantly (U=17487.5, W =37587.5, Z= -2.684 p< 0.007, KW ANOVA χ^2 = 7.201, p< 0.007). Hence, the null hypothesis is rejected.

Table 39

Do you consider that there is crime problem in your neighbourhood?	*Place of study*	*N*	*Mean Rank*	*Sum of Ranks*
	Bhopal	199	217.74	43330.00
	Sagar	200	182.35	36470.00
	Total	399		

Test Statistics(a)

	Do you consider that there is crime problem in your neighbourhood
Mann-Whitney U	16370.000
Wilcoxon W	36470.000
Z	-3.667
Asymp. Sig. (2-tailed)	.001
Kruskal-Wallis Test	
Chi-Square	13.447
df	1
Asymp. Sig.	.001

a Kruskal Wallis Test.
b Grouping Variable: Place of study.

An attempt has been made to find out the difference between the two groups of victims with respect to opinion about that "there is crime problem in your neighborhood". The findings show that the two groups had significant differences on this context (U=16370.0, W =36470.0, Z= -3.667 p< 0.001, KW ANOVA χ^2 = 13.447, p< 0.001). Thus, the null hypothesis is rejected.

This exercise measured the differences of opinions regarding the reason of crime proneness in neighborhood with victims from the two cities. The null hypothesis is that there were no significant differences in the two groups of victims. The output of the Table 40 suggests that the two groups had no significant differences on this experience (U=12892.0, W =27257.0, Z= -.958 p< 0.338, KW ANOVA χ^2 = 0.917, p< 0.338). The null hypothesis therefore accepted.

Table 40

What makes the neighbourhood crime prone?	*Place of study*	*N*	*Mean Rank*	*Sum of Ranks*
	Bhopal	169	161.28	27257.00
	Sagar	162	170.92	27689.00
	Total	331		

Test Statistics(a)

	What makes the neighbourhood crime prone
Mann-Whitney U	12892.000
Wilcoxon W	27257.000
Z	-.958
Asymp. Sig. (2-tailed)	.338
Kruskal-Wallis Test	
Chi-Square	.917
df	1
Asymp. Sig.	.338

a Kruskal Wallis Test.
b Grouping Variable: Place of study.

Table 41

Do You feel opportunities for crime can be reduced by?	*Place of study*	*N*	*Mean Rank*	*Sum of Ranks*
	Bhopal	200	199.18	39835.50
	Sagar	199	200.83	39964.50
	Total	399		

Test Statistics(a)

	Do You feel opportunities for crime can be reduced by
Mann-Whitney U	19735.500
Wilcoxon W	39835.500
Z	-.155
Asymp. Sig. (2-tailed)	.877
Kruskal-Wallis Test	
Chi-Square	.024
df	1
Asymp. Sig.	.877

a Kruskal Wallis Test.
b Grouping Variable: Place of study.

The study explored as to whether there was any significant difference between the groups of victims so far as the degree of "feeling opportunities for crime reduction" is concerned. The U Test and KW ANOVA have been performed for this purpose. The null hypothesis for the analysis has been shows that there was no significant difference between both the groups on this count. The results of this test show [Table 41] that two group varied significantly (U =19735.5, W = 39835.5, Z = -.155 p< 0.877, KW ANOVA χ^2 = 0.024, p< 0.877). Hence, the null hypothesis is accepted.

Table 42

Do you think most of the crime of theft/burglary take because of the negligence part of the victim?	*Place of study*	*N*	*Mean Rank*	*Sum of Ranks*
	Bhopal	199	212.59	42306.00
	Sagar	200	187.47	37494.00
	Total	399		

Test Statistics(a)

	Do you think most of the crime of theft/burglary take because of the negligence part of the victim
Mann-Whitney U	17394.000
Wilcoxon W	37494.000
Z	-2.642
Asymp. Sig. (2-tailed)	.008
Kruskal-Wallis Test	
Chi-Square	6.979
df	1
Asymp. Sig.	.008

a Kruskal Wallis Test.
b Grouping Variable: Place of study.

It may be appropriate to study as to whether there are any statistical significant differences between the groups of victims so far as negligence of victim is concerned. The output shows [Table 42] that there is a significant difference between the two groups (U= 17394.0, W = 37494.0, Z= -2.642 p< 0.008, KW ANOVA χ^2 = 6.979, p< 0.008). The null hypothesis is rejected.

Table 43

Do you think victim create opportunity for crimes by?	*Place of study*	*N*	*Mean Rank*	*Sum of Ranks*
	Bhopal	197	197.95	38996.00
	Sagar	199	199.05	39610.00
	Total	396		

Test Statistics(a)

	Do you think victim create opportunity for crimes by
Mann-Whitney U	19493.000
Wilcoxon W	38996.000
Z	-.118
Asymp. Sig. (2-tailed)	.906
Kruskal-Wallis Test	
Chi-Square	.014
df	1
Asymp. Sig.	.906

a Kruskal Wallis Test.
b Grouping Variable: Place of study.

The opinions of victims studied in the two cities were examined regarding "victim create opportunity for crimes". The null hypothesis states that there were no significant differences between the two groups. The observations made in Table 43 shows that there were no statistically significant differences (U=19493.0, W =38996.0, Z= -.118 p< 0.906, KW ANOVA χ^2 = 0.014, p< 0.906) between the two groups. Thus, the null hypothesis is accepted.

The victim's opinions in the two cities regarding "Opportunity makes the thief" have been examined to know the differences. The output of the non-parametric test confirms that there is statistically significant (U=16178.0, W =36278.0, Z= -5.409 p< 0.001, KW ANOVA χ^2 = 29.258, p< 0.001) differences between the two groups. Thus, the null hypothesis is rejected.

It may be essential to study as to whether there was any significant statistical difference between the groups of victims so far as "avoidance of traveling in late nights by public transport" is concerned. The U and KW ANOVA tests were

Table 44

Opportunity makes the thief	*Place of study*	*N*	*Mean Rank*	*Sum of Ranks*
	Bhopal	200	219.61	43922.00
	Sagar	200	181.39	36278.00
	Total	400		

Test Statistics(a)

	Opportunity makes the thief
Mann-Whitney U	16178.000
Wilcoxon W	36278.000
Z	-5.409
Asymp. Sig. (2-tailed)	.001
Kruskal-Wallis Test	
Chi-Square	29.258
df	1
Asymp. Sig.	.001

a Kruskal Wallis Test
b Grouping Variable: Place of study.

Table 45

Do you generally avoid traveling alone in a public transport in late evening or night?	*Place of study*	*N*	*Mean Rank*	*Sum of Ranks*
	Bhopal	199	186.00	37014.00
	Sagar	199	213.00	42387.00
	Total	398		

Test Statistics(a)

	Do you generally avoid traveling alone in a public transport in late evening or night
Mann-Whitney U	17114.000
Wilcoxon W	37014.000
Z	-2.912
Asymp. Sig. (2-tailed)	.004
Kruskal-Wallis Test	
Chi-Square	8.481
df	1
Asymp. Sig.	.004

a Kruskal Wallis Test
b Grouping Variable: Place of study.

performed for this purpose. The null hypothesis states that there is no significant difference in the groups of victims. The output of this test, as shown in Table 45, suggests that the two groups varied significantly (U=17114.0, W =37014.0, Z= -2.912 p< 0.004, KW ANOVA χ^2 = 8.481, p< 0.004). Hence, the null hypothesis is rejected.

Table 46

If yes, it is because of?	*Place of study*	*N*	*Mean Rank*	*Sum of Ranks*
	Bhopal	87	71.97	6261.00
	Sagar	51	65.29	3330.00
	Total	138		

Test Statistics(a)

	If yes, it is because of
Mann-Whitney U	2004.000
Wilcoxon W	3330.000
Z	-.975
Asymp. Sig. (2-tailed)	.329
Kruskal-Wallis Test	
Chi-Square	.952
df	1
Asymp. Sig.	.329

a Kruskal Wallis Test.
b Grouping Variable: Place of study.

The present exercise intended to measure the differences in the groups of victims regarding their opinion on "reason of avoidance of traveling in late nights by public transport". The null hypothesis is that there were no significant differences in the two groups of victims. The output of the Table 50 suggests that the two groups had no significant differences (U= 2004.0, W = 3330.0, Z= -.975 p< 0.329, KW ANOVA χ^2 = 0.952, p< 0.329). The null hypothesis therefore accepted.

The avoidance of visiting certain places and areas in the city because of possibility of crime or violence is generally present in the crime situation. It has been observed [Table 47] that there was a significant difference between the two groups of victims for this particular variable. There is a statistically significant difference between both the groups (U=16533.0,

W =36633.0, Z= -3.426 p< 0.001, KW ANOVA χ^2 = 11.739, p< 0.001). The null hypothesis is therefore rejected.

Table 47

Do you avoid visiting certain places and areas of the city because of possibility of crime or violence?	*Place of study*	*N*	*Mean Rank*	*Sum of Ranks*
	Bhopal	200	183.17	36633.00
	Sagar	199	216.92	43167.00
	Total	399		

Test Statistics(a)

	Do you avoid visiting certain places and areas of the city because of possibility of crime or violence
Mann-Whitney U	16533.000
Wilcoxon W	36633.000
Z	-3.426
Asymp. Sig. (2-tailed)	.001
Kruskal-Wallis Test	
Chi-Square	11.739
df	1
Asymp. Sig.	.001

a Kruskal Wallis Test
b Grouping Variable: Place of study

Table 48

If yes, specify the possibility of crime in that area?	*Place of study*	*N*	*Mean Rank*	*Sum of Ranks*
	Bhopal	96	76.70	7363.50
	Sagar	55	74.77	4112.50
	Total	151		

Test Statistics(a)

	If yes, specify the possibility of crime in that area
Mann-Whitney U	2572.500
Wilcoxon W	4112.500
Z	-.295
Asymp. Sig. (2-tailed)	.768
Kruskal-Wallis Test	
Chi-Square	.087
df	1
Asymp. Sig.	.768

a Kruskal Wallis Test
b Grouping Variable: Place of study

The differences in the groups of victims were also measured regarding "reason of possibility of crime in that area" in the two cities. The null hypothesis is that there were no significant differences between the two groups of victims. The output of the Table 48 suggests that the two groups had no significant differences (U= 2572.5, W = 4112.5, Z= -.295 p< 0.768, KW ANOVA χ^2 = 0.087, p< 0.768). The null hypothesis is therefore accepted.

Table 49

"No one is safe in this city", please give your opinion by putting sign	*Place of study*	*N*	*Mean Rank*	*Sum of Ranks*
	Bhopal	200	192.02	38404.50
	Sagar	196	205.11	40201.50
	Total	396		

Test Statistics(a)

	"No one is safe in this city", please give your opinion by putting sign
Mann-Whitney U	18304.500
Wilcoxon W	38404.500
Z	-1.190
Asymp. Sig. (2-tailed)	.234
Kruskal-Wallis Test	
Chi-Square	1.417
df	1
Asymp. Sig.	.234

a Kruskal Wallis Test
b Grouping Variable: Place of study.

The application of U test and KW ANOVA confirms the presence of statistically significant difference in the victims from Bhopal and Sagar regarding their opinions on "No one is safe in this city". The results shown in Table 49 indicate that the null hypothesis is rejected. The two groups of victims varied significantly (U=18304.5, W =38404.5, Z= -1.190 p< 0.234, KW ANOVA χ^2 = 1.417, p< 0.234).

Table 50

Have you ever been harassed or assaulted by anybody because of your caste, class, religion or sexual status?	*Place of study*	*N*	*Mean Rank*	*Sum of Ranks*
	Bhopal	200	196.00	39200.00
	Sagar	200	205.00	41000.00
	Total	400		

Test Statistics(a)

	Have you ever been harassed or assaulted by anybody because of your caste, class, religion or sexual status
Mann-Whitney U	19100.000
Wilcoxon W	39200.000
Z	-1.348
Asymp. Sig. (2-tailed)	.178
Kruskal-Wallis Test	
Chi-Square	1.816
df	1
Asymp. Sig.	.178

a Kruskal Wallis Test
b Grouping Variable: Place of study.

The effort has been made in this study to find out if there is any significant difference in the two groups of victims with respect to harassment or assault by anybody because of caste, class, religion or sexual status. The finding shows that the two groups had significant differences (U=19100.0, W =39200.0, Z= -1.348 p< 0.178, KW ANOVA χ^2 = 1.816, p< 0.178). Thus, the null hypothesis is rejected.

This study shows [Table 51] that there was significant difference between the groups of victims so far as "basis on which victim have been assaulted or harassed" has been concerned. The value of U, W, Z and KW test shows (U= 236.5, W =467.5, Z= -2.181 p< 0.029, KW ANOVA χ^2 = 4.758, p< 0.029) that there was a significant difference between the two groups of victims. Thus, the null hypothesis is rejected.

Table 51

If yes, explain the basis on which you have been assaulted or harassed?	*Place of study*	*N*	*Mean Rank*	*Sum of Ranks*
	Bhopal	34	31.54	1072.50
	Sagar	21	22.26	467.50
	Total	55		

Test Statistics(a)

	If yes, explain the basis on which you have been assaulted or harassed
Mann-Whitney U	236.500
Wilcoxon W	467.500
Z	-2.181
Asymp. Sig. (2-tailed)	.029
Kruskal-Wallis Test	
Chi-Square	4.758
df	1
Asymp. Sig.	.029

a Kruskal Wallis Test
b Grouping Variable: Place of study

Table 52

Do you think that during the last five years, the crime in the neighborhood has?	*Place of study*	*N*	*Mean Rank*	*Sum of Ranks*
	Bhopal	200	217.72	43543.50
	Sagar	197	180.00	35459.50
	Total	397		

Test Statistics(a)

	Do you think that during the last five years, the crime in the neighborhood has
Mann-Whitney U	15956.500
Wilcoxon W	35459.500
Z	-4.425
Asymp. Sig. (2-tailed)	.001
Kruskal-Wallis Test	
Chi-Square	19.578
df	1
Asymp. Sig.	.001

a Kruskal Wallis Test
b Grouping Variable: Place of study

To examine the differences in perception of victims about "status of the crime in the neighborhood in the last five years"? The null hypothesis is that there is no significant difference between the two groups. The output of this test [Table 52] suggests that the two groups of victims had significant difference (U=15956.5, W =35459.5, Z= -4.425 p< 0.001, KW ANOVA $\chi^2 = 19.578$, p< 0.001). The null hypothesis is therefore rejected.

Table 53

In case, crime has increased, please specify the crimes	*Place of study*	*N*	*Mean Rank*	*Sum of Ranks*
	Bhopal	150	162.60	24390.00
	Sagar	175	163.34	28585.00
	Total	325		

Test Statistics(a)

	In case, crime has increased, please specify the crimes
Mann-Whitney U	13065.000
Wilcoxon W	24390.000
Z	-.076
Asymp. Sig. (2-tailed)	.939
Kruskal-Wallis Test	
Chi-Square	.006
df	1
Asymp. Sig.	.939

a Kruskal Wallis Test
b Grouping Variable: Place of study.

This present exercise intended to measure the differences in the two groups of victims regarding their views on the type of crime registered increase in the locality. The null hypothesis is that there were no significant differences amongst the two groups of Bhopal and Sagar victims. The output of the Table 53 suggests that the two groups had no significant differences (U= 13065.0, W = 24390.0, Z= -.076 p< 0.939, KW ANOVA $\chi^2 = 0.006$, p< 0.939). The null hypothesis is therefore accepted.

Table 54

Could you indicate which one or two of the following crimes occur mostly in your area?	*Place of study*	*N*	*Mean Rank*	*Sum of Ranks*
	Bhopal	194	193.42	37523.00
	Sagar	191	192.58	36782.00
	Total	385		

Test Statistics(a)

	Could you indicate which one or two of the following crimes occur mostly in your area
Mann-Whitney U	18446.000
Wilcoxon W	36782.000
Z	-.090
Asymp. Sig. (2-tailed)	.928
Kruskal-Wallis Test	
Chi-Square	.008
df	1
Asymp. Sig.	.928

a Kruskal Wallis Test
b Grouping Variable: Place of study.

The two groups of victims opinioned about the crime which occur most in the locality. The null hypothesis states that there were no significant differences between the two groups. Table 54 shows that there was no statistically significant differences (U=18446.0, W =36782.0, Z= -.090 $p<$ 0.928, KW ANOVA $\chi2$ = 0.008, $p<$ 0.928) occur between the two groups. Thus, the null hypothesis is accepted.

7

Opinions of Victims on Situational Crime Factors

The study of perceptions and opinions of direct victims of various crimes could be quite significant to explore the situational factors responsible for making the target and sites vulnerable to crime occurrence. The present chapter focuses on the victim experiences and opinions in relation to certain independent variables examined in this study.

Table 1 shows that the most victims had the opinion that the places they were living were not safe [67.5 percent]. Only a few victims had the opinion that places they were living were safe [27.8 per cent]. The value of χ^2 suggests that two parameters are related. The likelihood ratio is also significant while linear-by-linear association is non-significant.

Table 2 depicts that the most victims had the opinion that the opportunities to commit this crime in this locality were in abundance [68.8 per cent] while some [26.8 per cent] victims had the opinion that opportunities to commit this crime in this locality were not frequent. The Chi-Square value is significant [χ^2 = 49.59, P< 0.001]. The likelihood ratio is significant while linear-by-linear association is also significant.

Table 3 shows that the most of the victims [64.9 per cent] consider that there was crime problem in the neighbourhood and a few victims had the opinion that there was no crime

Table 1
Showing Responses on "Do You Find this Area Safe?"

Police Station	Percentile Count	Do you find this area safe? Yes	No	Can't Say	Total
Bhopal Kotwali	Count	23	34	3	60
	% within Police Station	38.3%	56.7%	5.0%	100.0%
	% within Do you find this area safe	20.7%	12.6%	15.8%	15.0%
Mangalwara Bhopal	Count	13	25	2	40
	% within Police Station	32.5%	62.5%	5.0%	100.0%
	% within Do you find this area safe	11.7%	9.3%	10.5%	10.0%
T.T. Nagar Bhopal	Count	15	34	7	56
	% within Police Station	26.8%	60.7%	12.5%	100.0%
	% within Do you find this area safe	13.5%	12.6%	36.8%	14.0%
Jahangirabad Bhopal	Count	13	27	4	44
	% within Police Station	29.5%	61.4%	9.1%	100.0%
	% within Do you find this area safe	11.7%	10.0%	21.1%	11.0%
Civil Lines Sagar	Count	8	11	2	21
	% within Police Station	38.1%	52.4%	9.5%	100.0%
	% within Do you find this area safe	7.2%	4.1%	10.5%	5.3%
Gopal Ganj Sagar	Count	16	42	0	58
	% within Police Station	27.6%	72.4%	.0%	100.0%
	% within Do you find this area safe	14.4%	15.6%	.0%	14.5%
Kotwali Sagar	Count	9	50	1	60
	% within Police Station	15.0%	83.3%	1.7%	100.0%
	% within Do you find this area safe	8.1%	18.5%	5.3%	15.0%

Contd...

Police Station	*Percentile Count*	*Do you find this area safe?* *Yes*	*No*	*Can't Say*	*Total*
Motinagar Sagar	Count	8	32	0	40
	% within Police Station	20.0%	80.0%	.0%	100.0%
	% within Do you find this area safe	7.2%	11.9%	.0%	10.0%
Cant Sagar	Count	6	15	0	21
	% within Police Station	28.6%	71.4%	.0%	100.0%
	% within Do you find this area safe	5.4%	5.6%	.0%	5.3%
Total	Count	111	270	19	400
	% within Police Station	27.8%	67.5%	4.8%	100.0%
	% within Do you find this area safe	100.0%	100.0%	100.0%	100.0%

Chi-Square Test

	Value	*df*	*Asymp. Sig. (2-sided)*
Pearson Chi-Square	30.653(a)	16	.015
Likelihood Ratio	34.267	16	.005
Linear-by-Linear Association	1.067	1	.302
N of Valid Cases	400		

a 9 cells (33.3%) have expected count less than 5. The minimum expected count is 1.00

Table 2

Showing Responses on "do you Feel that Opportunities to Commit this Crime in this Locality are in Abundance?"

Police Station	*Percentile Count*	*Do you feel that opportunities to commit this crime in this locality are in abundance?* Yes	No	Can't Say	*Total*
Bhopal Kotwali	Count	34	24	2	60
	% within Police Station	56.7%	40.0%	3.3%	100.0%
	% within Do you feel that opportunities to commit this crime in this locality are in abundance	12.4%	22.4%	11.1%	15.0%
Mangalwara Bhopal	Count	25	12	3	40
	% within Police Station	62.5%	30.0%	7.5%	100.0%
	% within Do you feel that opportunities to commit this crime in this locality are in abundance	9.1%	11.2%	16.7%	10.0%
T. T. Nagar Bhopal	Count	36	17	3	56
	% within Police Station	64.3%	30.4%	5.4%	100.0%
	% within Do you feel that opportunities to commit this crime in this locality are in abundance	13.1%	15.9%	16.7%	14.0%
Jahangirabad Bhopal	Count	30	11	3	44
	% within Police Station	68.2%	25.0%	6.8%	100.0%
	% within Do you feel that opportunities to commit this crime in this locality are in abundance	10.9%	10.3%	16.7%	11.0%

Contd...

Police Station	Percentile Count	Do you feel that opportunities to commit this crime in this locality are in abundance? Yes	No	Can't Say	Total
Civil Lines Sagar	Count	10	5	6	21
	% within Police Station	47.6%	23.8%	28.6%	100.0%
	% within Do you feel that opportunities to commit this crime in this locality are in abundance	3.6%	4.7%	33.3%	5.3%
Gopal Ganj Sagar	Count	42	15	1	58
	% within Police Station	72.4%	25.9%	1.7%	100.0%
	% within Do you feel that opportunities to commit this crime in this locality are in abundance	15.3%	14.0%	5.6%	14.5%
Kotwali Sagar	Count	51	9	0	60
	% within Police Station	85.0%	15.0%	.0%	100.0%
	% within Do you feel that opportunities to commit this crime in this locality are in abundance	18.5%	8.4%	.0%	15.0%
Motinagar Sagar	Count	32	8	0	40
	% within Police Station	80.0%	20.0%	.0%	100.0%
	% within Do you feel that opportunities to commit this crime in this locality are in abundance	11.6%	7.5%	.0%	10.0%

Contd...

Police Station	Percentile Count	Do you feel that opportunities to commit this crime in this locality are in abundance?			
		Yes	No	Can't Say	Total
Cant Sagar	Count	15	6	0	21
	% within Police Station	71.4%	28.6%	.0%	100.0%
	% within Do you feel that opportunities to commit this crime in this locality are in abundance	5.5%	5.6%	.0%	5.3%
Total	Count	275	107	18	400
	% within Police Station	68.8%	26.8%	4.5%	100.0%
	% within Do you feel that opportunities to commit this crime in this locality are in abundance	100.0%	100.0%	100.0%	100.0%

Chi-Square Test

	Value	df	Asymp. Sig. (2-sided)
Pearson Chi-Square	49.590(a)	16	.000
Likelihood Ratio	40.352	16	.001
Linear-by-Linear Association	11.834	1	.001
N of Valid Cases	400		

9 cells (33.3%) have expected count less than 5. The minimum expected count is .95.

Table 3
Showing Responses on "Do You Consider that there is Crime Problem in Your Neighbourhood?"

		Do you consider that there is crime problem in your neighbourhood?			
Police Station	*Percentile Count*	*Yes*	*No*	*Can't Say*	*Total*
Bhopal Kotwali	Count	31	24	5	60
	% within Police Station	51.7%	40.0%	8.3%	100.0%
	% within Do you consider that there is crime problem in your neighbourhood	12.0%	19.8%	26.3%	15.0%
Mangalwara Bhopal	Count	25	13	2	40
	% within Police Station	62.5%	32.5%	5.0%	100.0%
	% within Do you consider that there is crime problem in your neighbourhood	9.7%	10.7%	10.5%	10.0%
T. T. Nagar Bhopal	Count	35	17	3	55
	% within Police Station	63.6%	30.9%	5.5%	100.0%
	% within Do you consider that there is crime problem in your neighbourhood	13.5%	14.0%	15.8%	13.8%
Jahangirabad Bhopal	Count	22	16	6	44
	% within Police Station	50.0%	36.4%	13.6%	100.0%
	% within Do you consider that there is crime problem in your neighbourhood	8.5%	13.2%	31.6%	11.0%

Contd...

Police Station	Percentile Count	Do you consider that there is crime problem in your neighbourhood?			
		Yes	No	Can't Say	Total
Civil Lines Sagar	Count	9	10	2	21
	% within Police Station	42.9%	47.6%	9.5%	100.0%
	% within Do you consider that there is crime problem in your neighbourhood	3.5%	8.3%	10.5%	5.3%
Gopal Ganj Sagar	Count	42	15	1	58
	% within Police Station	72.4%	25.9%	1.7%	100.0%
	% within Do you consider that there is crime problem in your neighbourhood	16.2%	12.4%	5.3%	14.5%
Kotwali Sagar	Count	49	11	0	60
	% within Police Station	81.7%	18.3%	.0%	100.0%
	% within Do you consider that there is crime problem in your neighbourhood	18.9%	9.1%	.0%	15.0%
Motinagar Sagar	Count	31	9	0	40
	% within Police Station	77.5%	22.5%	.0%	100.0%
	% within Do you consider that there is crime problem in your neighbourhood	12.0%	7.4%	.0%	10.0%
Cant Sagar	Count	15	6	0	21
	% within Police Station	71.4%	28.6%	.0%	100.0%
	% within Do you consider that there is crime problem in your neighbourhood	5.8%	5.0%	.0%	5.3%

Contd...

Police Station	Percentile Count	Do you consider that there is crime problem in your neighbourhood? Yes	No	Can't Say	Total
Total	Count	259	121	19	399
	% within Police Station	64.9%	30.3%	4.8%	100.0%
	% within Do you consider that there is crime problem in your neighbourhood	100.0%	100.0%	100.0%	100.0%

Chi-Square Test

	Value	df	Asymp. Sig. (2-sided)
Pearson Chi-Square	34.370(a)	16	.005
Likelihood Ratio	37.765	16	.002
Linear-by-Linear Association	16.473	1	.001
N of Valid Cases	399		

a 9 cells (33.3%) have expected count less than 5. The minimum expected count is 1.00.

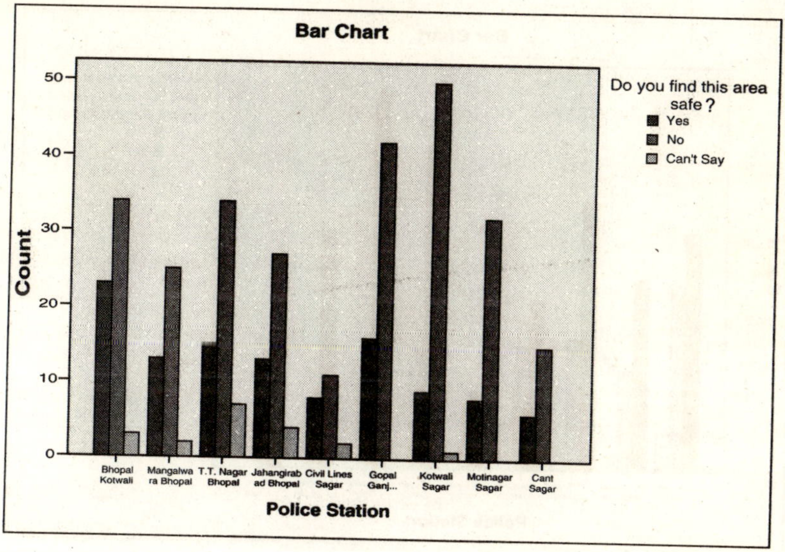

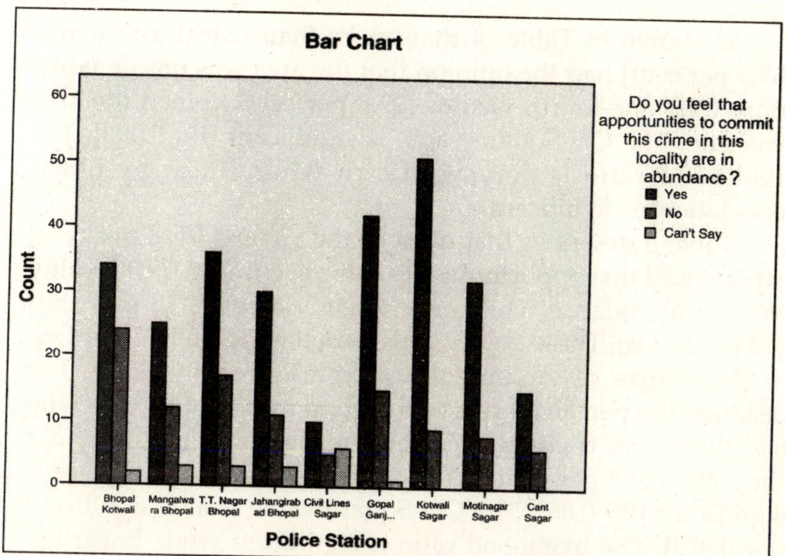

problem in your neighbourhood [30.3 per cent]. The two variables found to be related [$\chi^2 = 34.37$, $P < 0.005$]. The likelihood ratio is significant while linear-by-linear association is also significant.

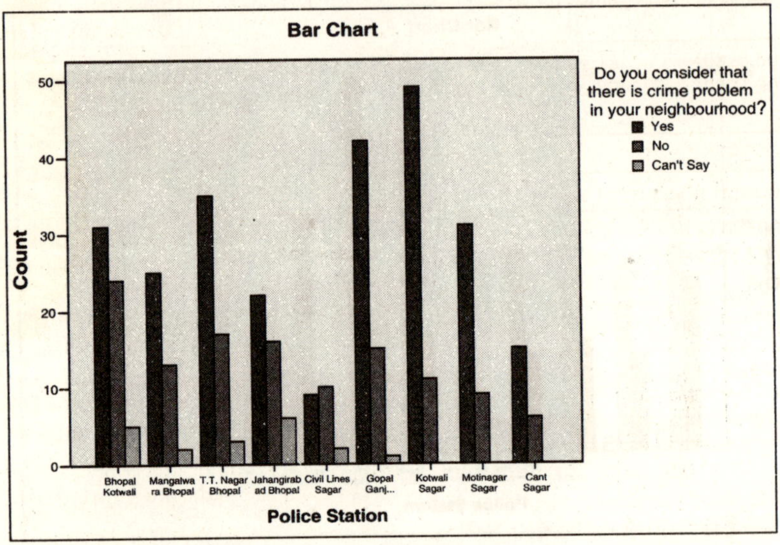

As shown in Table 4 that, more than two-third victims [67.5 per cent] had the opinion that the area was unsafe while more than one-fourth victims [27.8 per cent] opined the area was safe. The Chi-Square value is significant [P< 0.099]. The likelihood ratio is non-significant while linear-by-linear association is significant.

Table 5 describes that most of the victims [68.8 per cent] experienced that opportunities to commit crime in their locality were in abundance while only a few victims [26.8 per cent] did not feel so. These perceptions varied marginally according to the nature of victimization experienced by them. For instance, the perceived risk was highest in case of victims who had theft from residence [77 per cent] followed by theft from shop etc. [69.3 per cent]. The value of Pearson Chi-Square is Significant [P> 0.05]. The Chi-Square value is also significant [P< 0.072]. The likelihood ratio is significant while linear-by-linear association is non-significant.

As shown in Table 6 that most victims [64.9 per cent] considered the crime problem in their neighbourhood while the victims not considering it significant were 30.3 per cent. The value of Pearson Chi-Square is [P<0.05] significant. The

Table 4
Showing Crime Category wise Data Regarding Opinion on "Do you Find this Area Ssafe?"

Crime Category	*Percentile Count*	*Do you find this area safe?* Yes	No	Can't Say	*Total*
Theft from shop/ Business Place	Count	36	98	6	140
	% within Crime Category	25.7%	70.0%	4.3%	100.0%
	% within Do you find this area safe	32.4%	36.3%	31.6%	35.0%
Theft from residence	Count	17	62	8	87
	% within Crime Category	19.5%	71.3%	9.2%	100.0%
	% within Do you find this area safe	15.3%	23.0%	42.1%	21.8%
Burglary from shop	Count	0	1	0	1
	% within Crime Category	.0%	100.0%	.0%	100.0%
	% within Do you find this area safe	.0%	.4%	.0%	.3%
Vehicle theft	Count	58	109	5	172
	% within Crime Category	33.7%	63.4%	2.9%	100.0%
	% within Do you find this area safe	52.3%	40.4%	26.3%	43.0%
Total	Count	111	270	19	400
	% within Crime Category	27.8%	67.5%	4.8%	100.0%
	% within Do you find this area safe	100.0%	100.0%	100.0%	100.0%

Chi-Square Test

	Value	*df*	*Asymp. Sig. (2-sided)*
Pearson Chi-Square	10.673(a)	6	.099
Likelihood Ratio	10.506	6	.105
Linear-by-Linear Association	4.916	1	.027
N of Valid Cases	400		

a 4 cells (33.3%) have expected count less than 5. The minimum expected count is .05.

Table 5
Showing Crime Category wise Data Regarding Opinion on "Do you Feel that Opportunities to Commit this Crime in this Locality are in Abundance?"

		Do you feel that opportunities to commit this crime in this locality are in abundance?			
Crime Category	*Percentile Count*	*Yes*	*No*	*Can't Say*	*Total*
Theft from shop/ Business Place	Count	97	39	4	140
	% within Crime Category	69.3%	27.9%	2.9%	100.0%
	% within Do you feel that opportunities to commit this crime in this locality are in abundance	35.3%	36.4%	22.2%	35.0%
Theft from residence	Count	67	13	7	87
	% within Crime Category	77.0%	14.9%	8.0%	100.0%
	% within Do you feel that opportunities to commit this crime in this locality are in abundance	24.4%	12.1%	38.9%	21.8%
Burglary from shop	Count	1	0	0	1
	% within Crime Category	100.0%	.0%	.0%	100.0%
	% within Do you feel that opportunities to commit this crime in this locality are in abundance	.4%	.0%	.0%	.3%
Vehicle theft	Count	110	55	7	172
	% within Crime Category	64.0%	32.0%	4.1%	100.0%
	% within Do you feel that opportunities to commit this crime in this locality are in abundance	40.0%	51.4%	38.9%	43.0%

Contd...

		Do you feel that opportunities to commit this crime in this locality are in abundance?			
Crime Category	*Percentile Count*	*Yes*	*No*	*Can't Say*	*Total*
Total	Count	275	107	18	400
	% within Crime Category	68.8%	26.8%	4.5%	100.0%
	% within Do you feel that opportunities to commit this crime in this locality are in abundance	100.0%	100.0%	100.0%	100.0%

Chi-Square Test

	Value	*df*	*Asymp. Sig. (2-sided)*
Pearson Chi-Square	11.596(a)	6	.072
Likelihood Ratio	12.300	6	.056
Linear-by-Linear Association	1.488	1	.222
N of Valid Cases	400		

a 4 cells (33.3%) have expected count less than 5. The minimum expected count is .05.

Table 6

Showing Crime Category wise Data Regarding Opinion on "Do you Consider that there is Crime Problem in your Neighbourhood?"

		Do you consider that there is crime problem in your neighbourhood?			
Crime Category	*Percentile Count*	*Yes*	*No*	*Can't Say*	*Total*
Theft from shop/ Business Place	Count	88	46	6	140
	% within Crime Category	62.9%	32.9%	4.3%	100.0%
	% within Do you consider that there is crime problem in your neighbourhood	34.0%	38.0%	31.6%	35.1%
Theft from residence	Count	65	14	7	86
	% within Crime Category	75.6%	16.3%	8.1%	100.0%
	% within Do you consider that there is crime problem in your neighbourhood	25.1%	11.6%	36.8%	21.6%
Burglary from shop	Count	1	0	0	1
	% within Crime Category	100.0%	.0%	.0%	100.0%
	% within Do you consider that there is crime problem in your neighbourhood	.4%	.0%	.0%	.3%
Vehicle theft	Count	105	61	6	172
	% within Crime Category	61.0%	35.5%	3.5%	100.0%
	% within Do you consider that there is crime problem in your neighbourhood	40.5%	50.4%	31.6%	43.1%

Contd...

		Do you consider that there is crime problem in your neighbourhood?			
Crime Category	*Percentile Count*	*Yes*	*No*	*Can't Say*	*Total*
Total	Count	259	121	19	399
	% within Crime Category	64.9%	30.3%	4.8%	100.0%
	% within Do you consider that there is crime problem in your neighbourhood	100.0%	100.0%	100.0%	100.0%

Chi-Square Test

	Value	*df*	*Asymp. Sig. (2-sided)*
Pearson Chi-Square	12.638(a)	6	.049
Likelihood Ratio	13.652	6	.034
Linear-by-Linear Association	.259	1	.611
N of Valid Cases	399		

a 4 cells (33.3%) have expected count less than 5. The minimum expected count is .05.

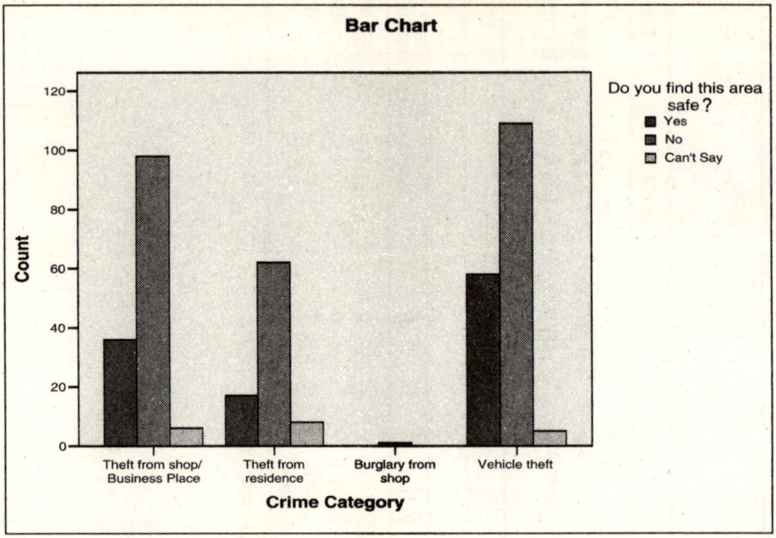

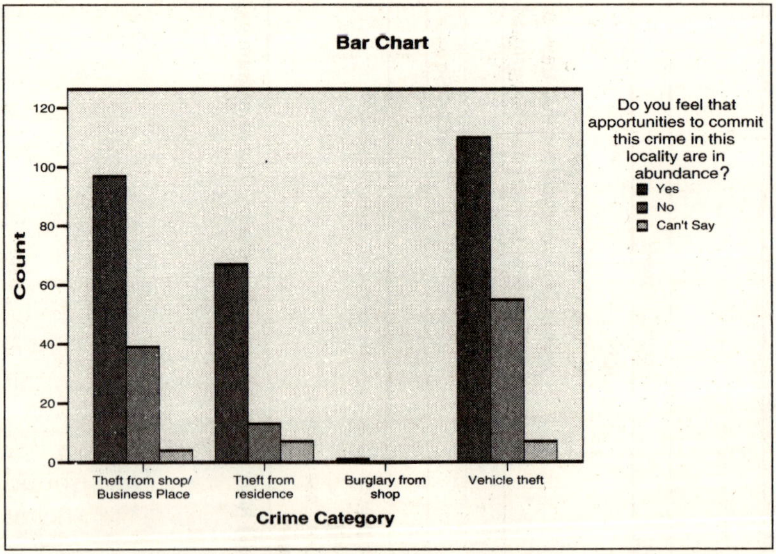

Chi-Square value is also significant [P< 0.049]. The likelihood ratio is significant while linear-by-linear association is non-significant.

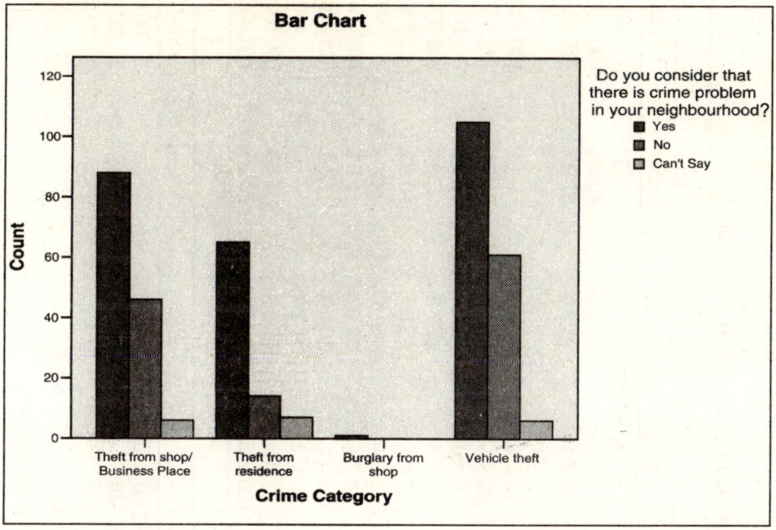

Do the victims' opinions vary according to the area to which they belong? The survey of victims in the hot and cool spots of the cities of Sagar and Bhopal show [Table 7] that in all 67.5 per cent respondents found the areas of their living as unsafe. These victims, in most cases, were living in hot spot areas. The association therefore belonging to hot spot crime area and perceived unsafeness is fairly clear. The test of association also supports it [χ^2 =25.561, p<0.001].

Respondent's perceived sense of availability of opportunity to commit crime indicates various matters giving rise to the actual crime incidence. The data provided in Table 8 shows that the two-third victims felt that the opportunities to commit this crime in their locality were utterly pronounced [68.8 Per cent] while only one-fourth victims felt otherwise [26.8 per cent]. The association between these two variables was found to be significant [p<0.006]. The likelihood ratio is significant while linear-by-linear association is also significant.

Table 9 describes that most victims [64.9 Per cent] considered that there was crime problem in their neighbourhood while only a few victims considered that there was no crime problem in their neighbourhood [30.3 per cent].

Table 7
Showing Crime Scene wise Data Regarding Opinion on "Do you Find this Area Safe" ?

Location of crime scene	*Percentile Count*	*Do you find this area safe?* Yes	No	Can't Say	*Total*
Hot Spot Bhopal	Count	28	63	11	102
	% within Location of crime scene	27.5%	61.8%	10.8%	100.0%
	% within Do you find this area safe	25.2%	23.3%	57.9%	25.5%
Cool Spot Bhopal	Count	36	57	5	98
	% within Location of crime scene	36.7%	58.2%	5.1%	100.0%
	% within Do you find this area safe	32.4%	21.1%	26.3%	24.5%
Hot Spot Sagar	Count	31	68	2	101
	% within Location of crime scene	30.7%	67.3%	2.0%	100.0%
	% within Do you find this area safe	27.9%	25.2%	10.5%	25.3%
Cool Spot Sagar	Count	16	82	1	99
	% within Location of crime scene	16.2%	82.8%	1.0%	100.0%
	% within Do you find this area safe	14.4%	30.4%	5.3%	24.8%
Total	Count	111	270	19	400
	% within Location of crime scene	27.8%	67.5%	4.8%	100.0%
	% within Do you find this area safe	100.0%	100.0%	100.0%	100.0%

Chi-Square Test

	Value	*df*	*Asymp. Sig. (2-sided)*
Pearson Chi-Square	25.561(a)	6	.001
Likelihood Ratio	25.749	6	.001
Linear-by-Linear Association	.103	1	.748
N of Valid Cases	400		

a 4 cells (33.3%) have expected count less than 5. The minimum expected count is 4.66.

Table 8

Showing Crime Scene wise Data Regarding Opinion on "Do you Feel that Opportunities to Commit this Crime in this Locality are in Abundance" ?

		Do you feel that opportunities to commit this crime in this locality are in abundance?			
Location of crime scene	*Percentile Count*	*Yes*	*No*	*Can't Say*	*Total*
Hot Spot Bhopal	Count	67	29	6	102
	% within Location of crime scene	65.7%	28.4%	5.9%	100.0%
	% within Do you feel that opportunities to commit this crime in this locality are in abundance	24.4%	27.1%	33.3%	25.5%
Cool Spot Bhopal	Count	58	35	5	98
	% within Location of crime scene	59.2%	35.7%	5.1%	100.0%
	% within Do you feel that opportunities to commit this crime in this locality are in abundance	21.1%	32.7%	27.8%	24.5%
Hot Spot Sagar	Count	67	27	7	101
	% within Location of crime scene	66.3%	26.7%	6.9%	100.0%
	% within Do you feel that opportunities to commit this crime in this locality are in abundance	24.4%	25.2%	38.9%	25.3%

Contd...

		Do you feel that opportunities to commit this crime in this locality are in abundance?			
Location of crime scene	*Percentile Count*	*Yes*	*No*	*Can't Say*	*Total*
Cool Spot Sagar	Count	83	16	0	99
	% within Location of crime scene	83.8%	16.2%	.0%	100.0%
	% within Do you feel that opportunities to commit this crime in this locality are in abundance	30.2%	15.0%	.0%	24.8%
Total	Count	275	107	18	400
	% within Location of crime scene	68.8%	26.8%	4.5%	100.0%
	% within Do you feel that opportunities to commit this crime in this locality are in abundance	100.0%	100.0%	100.0%	100.0%

Chi-Square Tests

	Value	*df*	*Asymp. Sig. (2-sided)*
Pearson Chi-Square	18.302(a)	6	.006
Likelihood Ratio	22.783	6	.001
Linear-by-Linear Association	8.715	1	.003
N of Valid Cases	400		

a 4 cells (33.3%) have expected count less than 5. The minimum expected count is 4.41.

Table 9
Showing Crime Scene wise Data Regarding Opinion on "Do you Consider that there is Crime Problem in your Neighbourhood"?

Location of crime scene	*Percentile Count*	*Do you consider that there is crime problem in your neighbourhood ?*			
		Yes	*No*	*Can't Say*	*Total*
Hot Spot Bhopal	Count	58	34	9	101
	% within Location of crime scene	57.4%	33.7%	8.9%	100.0%
	% within Do you consider that there is crime problem in your neighbourhood	22.4%	28.1%	47.4%	25.3%
Cool Spot Bhopal	Count	55	36	7	98
	% within Location of crime scene	56.1%	36.7%	7.1%	100.0%
	% within Do you consider that there is crime problem in your neighbourhood	21.2%	29.8%	36.8%	24.6%
Hot Spot Sagar	Count	67	31	3	101
	% within Location of crime scene	66.3%	30.7%	3.0%	100.0%
	% within Do you consider that there is crime problem in your neighbourhood	25.9%	25.6%	15.8%	25.3%
Cool Spot Sagar	Count	79	20	0	99
	% within Location of crime scene	79.8%	20.2%	.0%	100.0%
	% within Do you consider that there is crime problem in your neighbourhood	30.5%	16.5%	.0%	24.8%

Contd...

Location of crime scene	*Percentile Count*	*Do you consider that there is crime problem in your neighbourhood ?*			
		Yes	*No*	*Can't Say*	*Total*
Total	Count	259	121	19	399
	% within Location of crime scene	64.9%	30.3%	4.8%	100.0%
	% within Do you consider that there is crime problem in your neighbourhood	100.0%	100.0%	100.0%	100.0%

Chi-Square Test

	Value	*df*	*Asymp. Sig. (2-sided)*
Pearson Chi-Square	20.711(a)	6	.002
Likelihood Ratio	24.835	6	.000
Linear-by-Linear Association	17.493	1	.000
N of Valid Cases	399		

a 4 cells (33.3%) have expected count less than 5. The minimum expected count is 4.67.

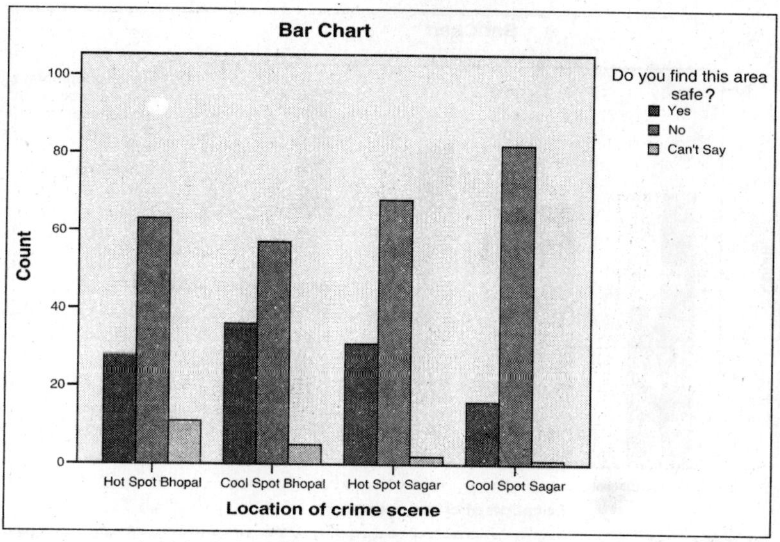

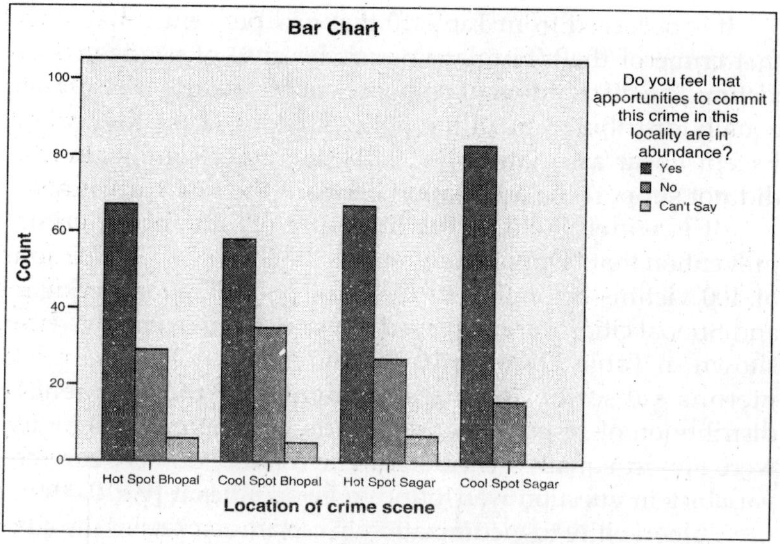

The value of Pearson Chi-Square is less than 0.05 level of significance that means the hypothesis stands rejected and the variable were not some way related. The likelihood ratio is significant while linear-by-linear association is also significant.

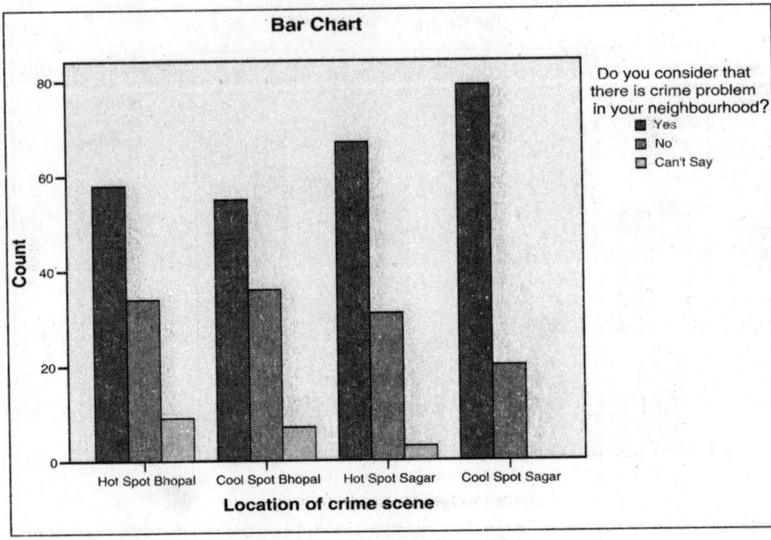

It is observed from Table 10 that 67.4 per cent victims felt that crime of theft/burglary occurs because of negligence of victim. The distribution of responses of this nature was almost equally distributed in all the police stations of the two cities. Except linear association [P< 0.01], the other significant test did not support the association between the two variables.

It is widely held in the literature on situational crime prevention that "Opportunity makes the thieves". The opinion of 400 victims belonging to different police station of Sagar and Bhopal cities were surveyed to verify the maxim. The data shown in Table 11 confirms that as many as 85.5 per cent victims subscribe to this statement and the frequency distribution of responses of victims in all nine police stations were almost equally distributed. The association between the variables in question was found to be significant [P < 0.001]

Vulnerability to victimization in certain pockets of the city is invariably perceived to be higher by the residents and it restricts their movement too. On surveying this kind of perception in this study, it has been observed [Table 12] the victim did not avoid visiting certain places because of possibility of crime in these regions [61.4 per cent]. However

Table 10

Showing Police Station wise Data Regarding Opinion on "Do You Think most of the Crime of Theft/burglary Occur Because of the Negligence of the Victim"?

Police Station	*Percentile Count*	*Do you think most of the crime of theft/burglary take because of the negligence part of the victim?*			
		Yes	*No*	*Can't Say*	*Total*
Bhopal Kotwali	Count	39	16	5	60
	% within Police Station	65.0%	26.7%	8.3%	100.0%
	% within Do you think most of the crime of theft/burglary take because of the negligence part of the victim	14.5%	16.3%	15.6%	15.0%
Mangalwara Bhopal	Count	27	10	3	40
	% within Police Station	67.5%	25.0%	7.5%	100.0%
	% within Do you think most of the crime of theft/burglary take because of the negligence part of the victim	10.0%	10.2%	9.4%	10.0%
T.T. Nagar Bhopal	Count	33	15	7	55
	% within Police Station	60.0%	27.3%	12.7%	100.0%
	% within Do you think most of the crime of theft/burglary take because of the negligence part of the victim	12.3%	15.3%	21.9%	13.8%
Jahangirabad Bhopal	Count	24	12	8	44
	% within Police Station	54.5%	27.3%	18.2%	100.0%
	% within Do you think most of the crime of theft/burglary take because of the negligence part of the victim	8.9%	12.2%	25.0%	11.0%

Contd...

Police Station	Percentile Count	Do you think most of the crime of theft/burglary take because of the negligence part of the victim? Yes	No	Can't Say	Total
Civil Lines Sagar	Count	12	8	1	21
	% within Police Station	57.1%	38.1%	4.8%	100.0%
	% within Do you think most of the crime of theft/burglary take because of the negligence part of the victim	4.5%	8.2%	3.1%	5.3%
Gopal Ganj Sagar	Count	42	13	3	58
	% within Police Station	72.4%	22.4%	5.2%	100.0%
	% within Do you think most of the crime of theft/burglary take because of the negligence part of the victim	15.6%	13.3%	9.4%	14.5%
Kotwali Sagar	Count	45	14	1	60
	% within Police Station	75.0%	23.3%	1.7%	100.0%
	% within Do you think most of the crime of theft/burglary take because of the negligence part of the victim	16.7%	14.3%	3.1%	15.0%
Motinagar Sagar	Count	29	7	4	40
	% within Police Station	72.5%	17.5%	10.0%	100.0%
	% within Do you think most of the crime of theft/burglary take because of the negligence part of the victim	10.8%	7.1%	12.5%	10.0%

Contd...

		Do you think most of the crime of theft/burglary take because of the negligence part of the victim?			
Police Station	*Percentile Count*	*Yes*	*No*	*Can't Say*	*Total*
Cant Sagar	Count	18	3	0	21
	% within Police Station	85.7%	14.3%	.0%	100.0%
	% within Do you think most of the crime of theft/burglary take because of the negligence part of the victim	6.7%	3.1%	.0%	5.3%
Total	Count	269	98	32	399
	% within Police Station	67.4%	24.6%	8.0%	100.0%
	% within Do you think most of the crime of theft/burglary take because of the negligence part of the victim	100.0%	100.0%	100.0%	100.0%

Chi-Square Test

	Value	*df*	*Asymp. Sig. (2-sided)*
Pearson Chi-Square	20.637(a)	16	.193
Likelihood Ratio	22.176	16	.138
Linear-by-Linear Association	5.722	1	.017
N of Valid Cases	399		

a 9 cells (33.3%) have expected count less than 5. The minimum expected count is 1.68.

Table 11
Showing Police Station wise Data Regarding Opinion on "Opportunity Makes the Thieve"

		Opportunity makes the thieve			
Police Station	*Percentile Count*	*Yes*	*No*	*Can't Say*	*Total*
Bhopal Kotwali	Count	44	4	12	60
	% within Police Station	73.3%	6.7%	20.0%	100.0%
	% within Opportunity makes the thieve	12.9%	30.8%	26.7%	15.0%
Mangalwara Bhopal	Count	34	2	4	40
	% within Police Station	85.0%	5.0%	10.0%	100.0%
	% within Opportunity makes the thieve	9.9%	15.4%	8.9%	10.0%
T.T. Nagar Bhopal	Count	42	1	13	56
	% within Police Station	75.0%	1.8%	23.2%	100.0%
	% within Opportunity makes the thieve	12.3%	7.7%	28.9%	14.0%
Jahangirabad Bhopal	Count	32	3	9	44
	% within Police Station	72.7%	6.8%	20.5%	100.0%
	% within Opportunity makes the thieve	9.4%	23.1%	20.0%	11.0%
Civil Lines Sagar	Count	19	1	1	21
	% within Police Station	90.5%	4.8%	4.8%	100.0%
	% within Opportunity makes the thieve	5.6%	7.7%	2.2%	5.3%
Gopal Ganj Sagar	Count	55	1	2	58
	% within Police Station	94.8%	1.7%	3.4%	100.0%
	% within Opportunity makes the thieve	16.1%	7.7%	4.4%	14.5%
Kotwali Sagar	Count	56	1	3	60
	% within Police Station	93.3%	1.7%	5.0%	100.0%
	% within Opportunity makes the theft	16.4%	7.7%	6.7%	15.0%

Contd...

Police Station	*Percentile Count*	*Opportunity makes the thieve* Yes	No	Can't Say	*Total*
Motinagar Sagar	Count	39	0	1	40
	% within Police Station	97.5%	.0%	2.5%	100.0%
	% within Opportunity makes the thieve	11.4%	.0%	2.2%	10.0%
Cant Sagar	Count	21	0	0	21
	% within Police Station	100.0%	.0%	.0%	100.0%
	% within Opportunity makes the thieve	6.1%	.0%	.0%	5.3%
Total	Count	342	13	45	400
	% within Police Station	85.5%	3.3%	11.3%	100.0%
	% within Opportunity makes the thieve	100.0%	100.0%	100.0%	100.0%

Chi-Square Test

	Value	*df*	*Asymp. Sig. (2-sided)*
Pearson Chi-Square	38.177(a)	16	.001
Likelihood Ratio	41.931	16	.000
Linear-by-Linear Association	23.432	1	.000
N of Valid Cases	400		

a 14 cells (51.9%) have expected count less than 5. The minimum expected count is .68.

Table 12

Showing Police Station wise Data Regarding Opinion on "Do You Avoid Visiting Certain Places and areas of the City Because of Possibility of Crime or Violence"?

		Do you avoid visiting certain places and areas of the city because of possibility of crime or violence?			
Police Station	*Percentile Count*	*Yes*	*No*	*Can't Say*	*Total*
Bhopal Kotwali	Count	27	28	5	60
	% within Police Station	45.0%	46.7%	8.3%	100.0%
	% within Do you avoid visiting certain places and areas of the city because of possibility of crime or violence	19.7%	11.4%	29.4%	15.0%
Mangalwara Bhopal	Count	10	29	1	40
	% within Police Station	25.0%	72.5%	2.5%	100.0%
	% within Do you avoid visiting certain places and areas of the city because of possibility of crime or violence	7.3%	11.8%	5.9%	10.0%
T.T. Nagar Bhopal	Count	28	24	4	56
	% within Police Station	50.0%	42.9%	7.1%	100.0%
	% within Do you avoid visiting certain places and areas of the city because of possibility of crime or violence	20.4%	9.8%	23.5%	14.0%
Jahangirabad Bhopal	Count	23	20	1	44
	% within Police Station	52.3%	45.5%	2.3%	100.0%
	% within Do you avoid visiting certain places and areas of the city because of possibility of crime or violence	16.8%	8.2%	5.9%	11.0%

Contd...

		Do you avoid visiting certain places and areas of the city because of possibility of crime or violence?			
Police Station	*Percentile Count*	*Yes*	*No*	*Can't Say*	*Total*
Civil Lines Sagar	Count	8	9	3	20
	% within Police Station	40.0%	45.0%	15.0%	100.0%
	% within Do you avoid visiting certain places and areas of the city because of possibility of crime or violence	5.8%	3.7%	17.6%	5.0%
Gopal Ganj Sagar	Count	12	45	1	58
	% within Police Station	20.7%	77.6%	1.7%	100.0%
	% within Do you avoid visiting certain places and areas of the city because of possibility of crime or violence	8.8%	18.4%	5.9%	14.5%
Kotwali Sagar	Count	15	43	2	60
	% within Police Station	25.0%	71.7%	3.3%	100.0%
	% within Do you avoid visiting certain places and areas of the city because of possibility of crime or violence	10.9%	17.6%	11.8%	15.0%
Motinagar Sagar	Count	9	31	0	40
	% within Police Station	22.5%	77.5%	.0%	100.0%
	% within Do you avoid visiting certain places and areas of the city because of possibility of crime or violence	6.6%	12.7%	.0%	10.0%

Contd...

Police Station	Percentile Count	*Do you avoid visiting certain places and areas of the city because of possibility of crime or violence?* Yes	No	Can't Say	Total
Cant Sagar	Count	5	16	0	21
	% within Police Station	23.8%	76.2%	.0%	100.0%
	% within Do you avoid visiting certain places and areas of the city because of possibility of crime or violence	3.6%	6.5%	.0%	5.3%
Total	Count	137	245	17	399
	% within Police Station	34.3%	61.4%	4.3%	100.0%
	% within Do you avoid visiting certain places and areas of the city because of possibility of crime or violence	100.0%	100.0%	100.0%	100.0%

Chi-Square Test

	Value	*df*	*Asymp. Sig. (2-sided)*
Pearson Chi-Square	46.128(a)	16	.000
Likelihood Ratio	46.481	16	.000
Linear-by-Linear Association	4.902	1	.027
N of Valid Cases	399		

a 9 cells (33.3%) have expected count less than 5. The minimum expected count is .85.

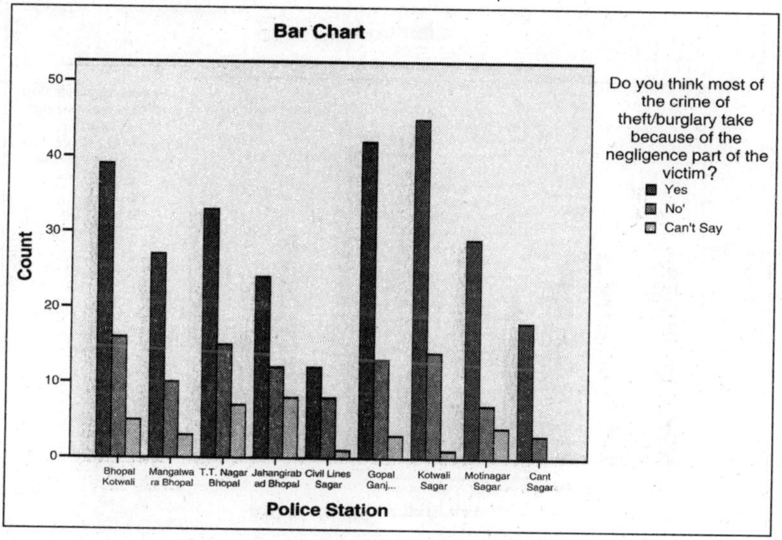

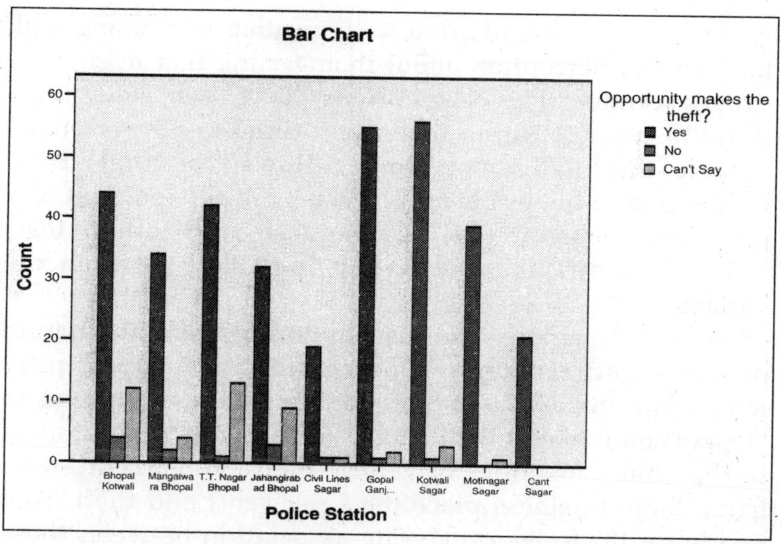

34.3 per cent respondent admitted to this fact and their distribution was concentrating in some police stations. The association of the variables was Significant [χ^2 =46.128, p<0.001].

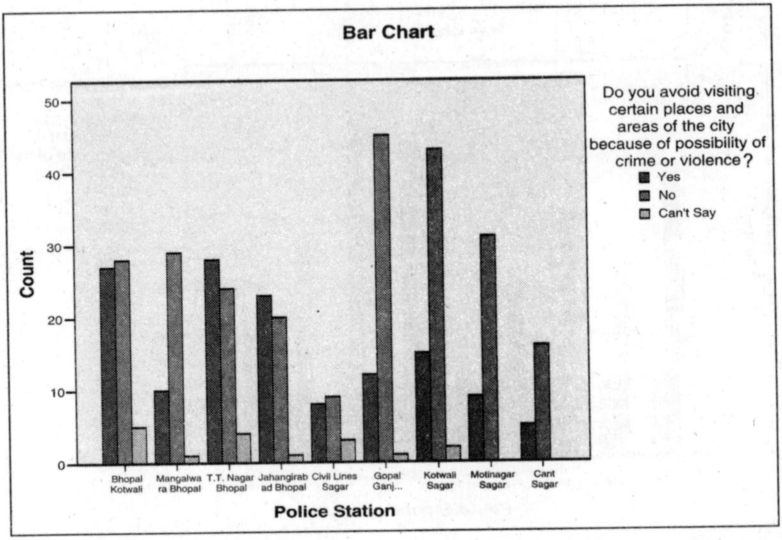

Does the nature of crime victimization vary along with the victims' perception about their feeling that negligence causes crime? The respondent [67.4 per cent] who thought negligence as factor to crime has experienced vehicle theft [78.5 per cent] followed by theft from residence and Shop/Business place [61.1 per cent and 57.9 per cent respectively]. Chi-square and other tests indicate significant association [$p<0.003$] between the variables.

Table 14 explores the distribution between the nature of crime and respondent perception on "Opportunity makes the thieves". Of 85.5 per cent who subscribed to "Opportunity makes the thieves" were mainly concentrating in the crime categories of vehicle theft [86 per cent], theft from Shop/Business place [86.4 per cent] and theft from residence [82.8 per cent]. The association between these variables however, was not supported by the tests of association.

Table 15 offers the distribution of crime category cross tabulated by respondents' perceptions about their avoiding of visiting crime prone locations. The data indicates that 61.4

Table 13

Showing Crime Category wise Data Regarding Opinion on "Do You Think Most of the Crime of Theft/Burglary Occur Because of the Negligence of the Victim"?

		Do you think most of the crime of theft/burglary take because of the negligence part of the victim?			
Crime Category	*Percentile Count*	*Yes*	*No*	*Can't Say*	*Total*
Theft from shop/ Business Place	Count	81	45	14	140
	% within Crime Category	57.9%	32.1%	10.0%	100.0%
	% within Do you think most of the crime of theft/burglary take because of the negligence part of the victim	30.1%	45.9%	43.8%	35.1%
Theft from residence	Count	53	24	9	86
	% within Crime Category	61.6%	27.9%	10.5%	100.0%
	% within Do you think most of the crime of theft/burglary take because of the negligence part of the victim	19.7%	24.5%	28.1%	21.6%
Burglary from shop	Count	0	1	0	1
	% within Crime Category	.0%	100.0%	.0%	100.0%
	% within Do you think most of the crime of theft/burglary take because of the negligence part of the victim	.0%	1.0%	.0%	.3%

Contd...

Crime Category	Percentile Count	Do you think most of the crime of theft/burglary take because of the negligence part of the victim? Yes	No	Can't Say	Total
Vehicle theft	Count	135	28	9	172
	% within Crime Category	78.5%	16.3%	5.2%	100.0%
	% within Do you think most of the crime of theft/burglary take because of the negligence part of the victim	50.2%	28.6%	28.1%	43.1%
Total	Count	269	98	32	399
	% within Crime Category	67.4%	24.6%	8.0%	100.0%
	% within Do you think most of the crime of theft/burglary take because of the negligence part of the victim	100.0%	100.0%	100.0%	100.0%

Chi-Square Test

	Value	*df*	*Asymp. Sig. (2-sided)*
Pearson Chi-Square	19.988(a)	6	.003
Likelihood Ratio	20.149	6	.003
Linear-by-Linear Association	14.129	1	.000
N of Valid Cases	399		

a 3 cells (25.0%) have expected count less than 5. The minimum expected count is .08.

Table 14
Showing Crime Category wise Data Regarding Opinion on "Opportunity Makes the Thieves"

		Opportunity makes the theft			
Crime Category	*Percentile Count*	*Yes*	*No*	*Can't Say*	*Total*
Theft from shop/	Count	121	4	15	140
Business Place	% within Crime Category	86.4%	2.9%	10.7%	100.0%
	% within Opportunity makes the thieve	35.4%	30.8%	33.3%	35.0%
Theft from residence	Count	72	1	14	87
	% within Crime Category	82.8%	1.1%	16.1%	100.0%
	% within Opportunity makes the thieve	21.1%	7.7%	31.1%	21.8%
Burglary from shop	Count	1	0	0	1
	% within Crime Category	100.0%	.0%	.0%	100.0%
	% within Opportunity makes the thieve	.3%	.0%	.0%	.3%
Vehicle theft	Count	148	8	16	172
	% within Crime Category	86.0%	4.7%	9.3%	100.0%
	% within Opportunity makes the thieve	43.3%	61.5%	35.6%	43.0%
Total	Count	342	13	45	400
	% within Crime Category	85.5%	3.3%	11.3%	100.0%
	% within Opportunity makes the thieve	100.0%	100.0%	100.0%	100.0%

Chi-Square Test

	Value	*df*	*Asymp. Sig. (2-sided)*
Pearson Chi-Square	4.982(a)	6	.546
Likelihood Ratio	5.222	6	.516
Linear-by-Linear Association	.221	1	.639
N of Valid Cases	400		

a 5 cells (41.7%) have expected count less than 5. The minimum expected count is .03.

Table 15

Showing Crime Category wise Data Regarding Opinion on "Do you Avoid Visiting Certain Places and Areas of the City Because of Possibility of Crime or Violence"?

		Do you avoid visiting certain places and areas of the city because of possibility of crime or violence?			
Crime Category	*Percentile Count*	*Yes*	*No*	*Can't Say*	*Total*
Theft from shop/ Business Place	Count	55	80	5	140
	% within Crime Category	39.3%	57.1%	3.6%	100.0%
	% within Do you avoid visiting certain places and areas of the city because of possibility of crime or violence	40.1%	32.7%	29.4%	35.1%
Theft from residence	Count	33	49	5	87
	% within Crime Category	37.9%	56.3%	5.7%	100.0%
	% within Do you avoid visiting certain places and areas of the city because of possibility of crime or violence	24.1%	20.0%	29.4%	21.8%
Burglary from shop	Count	0	1	0	1
	% within Crime Category	.0%	100.0%	.0%	100.0%
	% within Do you avoid visiting certain places and areas of the city because of possibility of crime or violence	.0%	.4%	.0%	.3%

Contd...

		Do you avoid visiting certain places and areas of the city because of possibility of crime or violence?			
Crime Category	*Percentile Count*	*Yes*	*No*	*Can't Say*	*Total*
Vehicle theft	Count	49	115	7	171
	% within Crime Category	28.7%	67.3%	4.1%	100.0%
	% within Do you avoid visiting certain places and areas of the city because of possibility of crime or violence	35.8%	46.9%	41.2%	42.9%
Total	Count	137	245	17	399
	% within Crime Category	34.3%	61.4%	4.3%	100.0%
	% within Do you avoid visiting certain places and areas of the city because of possibility of crime or violence	100.0%	100.0%	100.0%	100.0%

Chi-Square Test

	Value	*df*	*Asymp. Sig. (2-sided)*
Pearson Chi-Square	5.913(a)	6	.433
Likelihood Ratio	6.257	6	.395
Linear-by-Linear Association	3.379	1	.066
N of Valid Cases	399		

a 4 cells (33.3%) have expected count less than 5. The minimum expected count is .04.

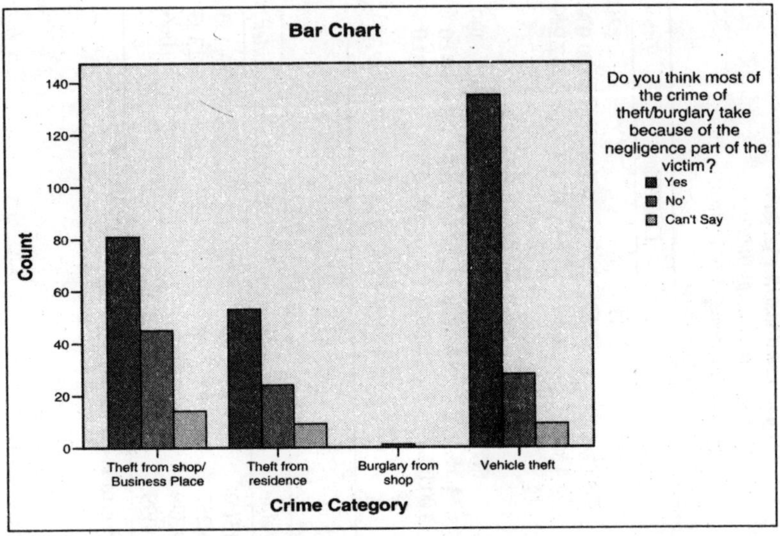

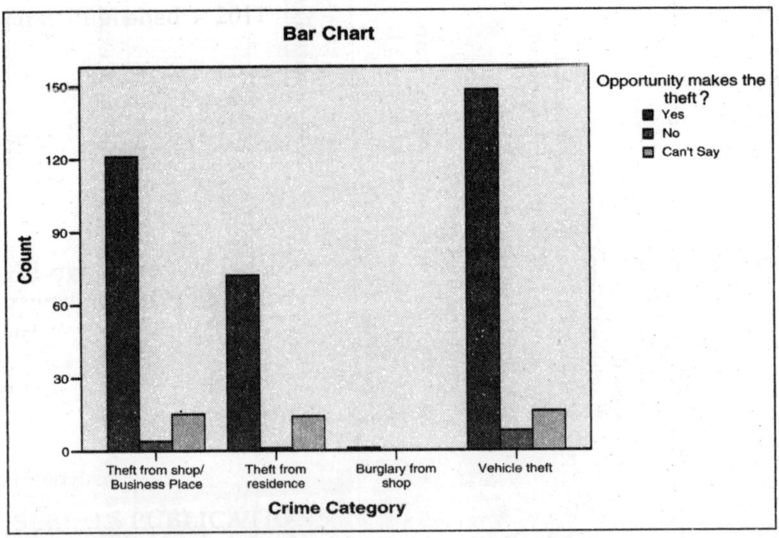

per cent victims did not avoid visiting crime prone locations and these victims were sufficiently distributed in almost in all categories of crime. The variables did not have significant association.

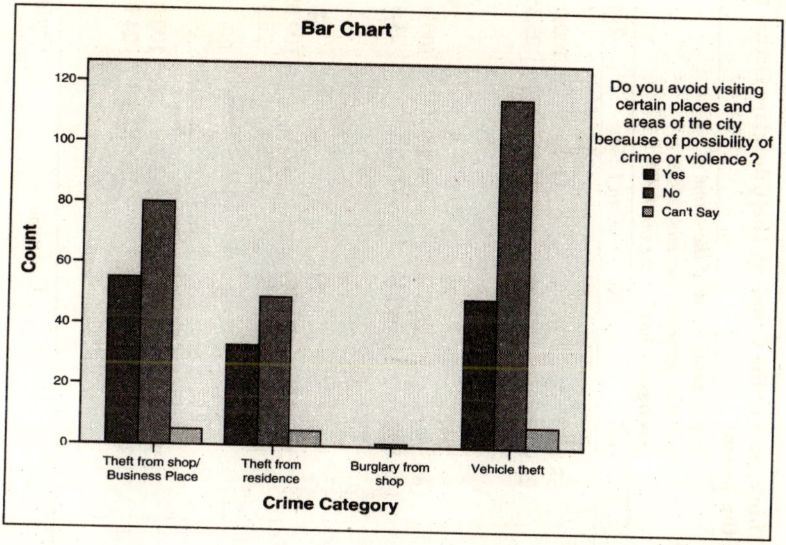

An attempt has been made to know the belongingness of the victims to hot and cool spot locations and their perceptions about negligence as a factor to crime. A perusal of Table 16 makes it clear that 67.4 per cent victims adhering to view point that negligence causes crime were predominantly belonging to cool spot and hot spot [27.1 per cent each] of Sagar city. There was only little variation about these locations in Bhopal. Chi-square test landed support to the association between these variables [χ^2 =12.090, p<0.060].

Does the perception of victims "Opportunity makes the thieves" vary in accordance with the cool and hot spot location in the cities of Bhopal and Sagar locations? Data indicated in Table 17 depict that 85.5 per cent victims with this perception were coming from hot and cool spot locations [28.1 per cent and 27.5 per cent respectively] of Sagar City. The corresponding percentage in case of Bhopal was 21.6 per cent and 22.8 per cent respectively. There was a significant association between the two variables [χ^2 = 32.169, p<0.001]

Table 18 provides the data on victims' avoiding of visiting crime prone places and their belongingness to hot and cool spot locations in the selected cities. The victims subscribing to

Table 16

Showing Crime Scene wise Data Regarding Opinion on "Do You Think Most of the Crime of Theft/Burglary Occur Because of the Negligence of the Victim"

		Do you think most of the crime of theft/burglary take because of the negligence part of the victim?			
Location of crime scene	*Percentile Count*	*Yes*	*No*	*Can't Say*	*Total*
Hot Spot Bhopal	Count	59	27	15	101
	% within Location of crime scene	58.4%	26.7%	14.9%	100.0%
	% within Do you think most of the crime of theft/burglary take because of the negligence part of the victim	21.9%	27.6%	46.9%	25.3%
Cool Spot Bhopal	Count	64	26	8	98
	% within Location of crime scene	65.3%	26.5%	8.2%	100.0%
	% within Do you think most of the crime of theft/burglary take because of the negligence part of the victim	23.8%	26.5%	25.0%	24.6%
Hot Spot Sagar	Count	73	24	4	101
	% within Location of crime scene	72.3%	23.8%	4.0%	100.0%
	% within Do you think most of the crime of theft/burglary take because of the negligence part of the victim	27.1%	24.5%	12.5%	25.3%
Cool Spot Sagar	Count	73	21	5	99
	% within Location of crime scene	73.7%	21.2%	5.1%	100.0%
	% within Do you think most of the crime of theft/burglary take because of the negligence part of the victim	27.1%	21.4%	15.6%	24.8%

Contd...

Location of crime scene	*Percentile Count*	*Do you think most of the crime of theft/burglary take because of the negligence part of the victim?*			
		Yes	*No*	*Can't Say*	*Total*
Total	Count	269	98	32	399
	% within Location of crime scene	67.4%	24.6%	8.0%	100.0%
	% within Do you think most of the crime of theft/burglary take because of the negligence part of the victim	100.0%	100.0%	100.0%	100.0%

Chi-Square Test

	Value	*df*	*Asymp. Sig. (2-sided)*
Pearson Chi-Square	12.090(a)	6	.060
Likelihood Ratio	11.590	6	.072
Linear-by-Linear Association	9.433	1	.002
N of Valid Cases	399		

a 0 cells (.0%) have expected count less than 5. The minimum expected count is 7.86.

Table 17
Showing Crime Scene wise Data Regarding Opinion on "Opportunity Makes the Thieves"

		Opportunity makes the theft			
Location of crime scene	*Percentile Count*	*Yes*	*No*	*Can't Say*	*Total*
Hot Spot Bhopal	Count	74	5	23	102
	% within Location of crime scene	72.5%	4.9%	22.5%	100.0%
	% within Opportunity makes the theft	21.6%	38.5%	51.1%	25.5%
Cool Spot Bhopal	Count	78	5	15	98
	% within Location of crime scene	79.6%	5.1%	15.3%	100.0%
	% within Opportunity makes the theft	22.8%	38.5%	33.3%	24.5%
Hot Spot Sagar	Count	96	2	3	101
	% within Location of crime scene	95.0%	2.0%	3.0%	100.0%
	% within Opportunity makes the theft	28.1%	15.4%	6.7%	25.3%
Cool Spot Sagar	Count	94	1	4	99
	% within Location of crime scene	94.9%	1.0%	4.0%	100.0%
	% within Opportunity makes the theft	27.5%	7.7%	8.9%	24.8%
Total	Count	342	13	45	400
	% within Location of crime scene	85.5%	3.3%	11.3%	100.0%
	% within Opportunity makes the theft	100.0%	100.0%	100.0%	100.0%

Chi-Square Tests

	Value	*df*	*Asymp. Sig. (2-sided)*
Pearson Chi-Square	32.169(a)	6	.000
Likelihood Ratio	33.897	6	.000
Linear-by-Linear Association	29.034	1	.000
N of Valid Cases	400		

a 4 cells (33.3%) have expected count less than 5. The minimum expected count is 3.19.

Table 18

Showing Crime Scene wise Data Regarding Opinion on "Do You Avoid Visiting Certain Places and Areas of the City Because of Possibility of Crime or Violence"

		Do you avoid visiting certain places and areas of the city because of possibility of crime or violence?			
Location of crime scene	*Percentile Count*	*Yes*	*No*	*Can't Say*	*Total*
Hot Spot Bhopal	Count	51	44	7	102
	% within Location of crime scene	50.0%	43.1%	6.9%	100.0%
	% within Do you avoid visiting certain places and areas of the city because of possibility of crime or violence	37.2%	18.0%	41.2%	25.6%
Cool Spot Bhopal	Count	37	57	4	98
	% within Location of crime scene	37.8%	58.2%	4.1%	100.0%
	% within Do you avoid visiting certain places and areas of the city because of possibility of crime or violence	27.0%	23.3%	23.5%	24.6%
Hot Spot Sagar	Count	26	70	4	100
	% within Location of crime scene	26.0%	70.0%	4.0%	100.0%
	% within Do you avoid visiting certain places and areas of the city because of possibility of crime or violence	19.0%	28.6%	23.5%	25.1%
Cool Spot Sagar	Count	23	74	2	99
	% within Location of crime scene	23.2%	74.7%	2.0%	100.0%
	% within Do you avoid visiting certain places and areas of the city because of possibility of crime or violence	16.8%	30.2%	11.8%	24.8%

Contd...

		Do you avoid visiting certain places and areas of the city because of possibility of crime or violence?			
Location of crime scene	*Percentile Count*	*Yes*	*No*	*Can't Say*	*Total*
Total	Count	137	245	17	399
	% within Location of crime scene	34.3%	61.4%	4.3%	100.0%
	% within Do you avoid visiting certain places and areas of the city because of possibility of crime or violence	100.0%	100.0%	100.0%	100.0%

Chi-Square Test

	Value	*df*	*Asymp. Sig. (2-sided)*
Pearson Chi-Square	25.796(a)	6	.000
Likelihood Ratio	25.966	6	.000
Linear-by-Linear Association	10.488	1	.001
N of Valid Cases	399		

a 4 cells (33.3%) have expected count less than 5. The minimum expected count is 4.18

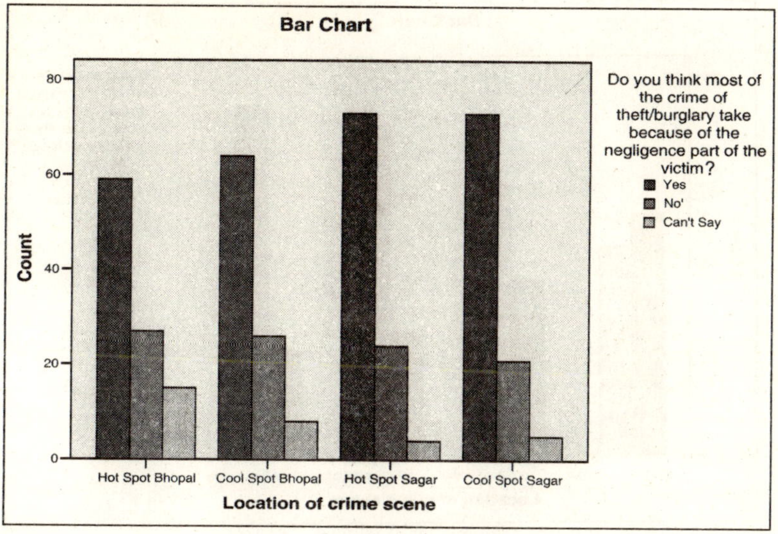

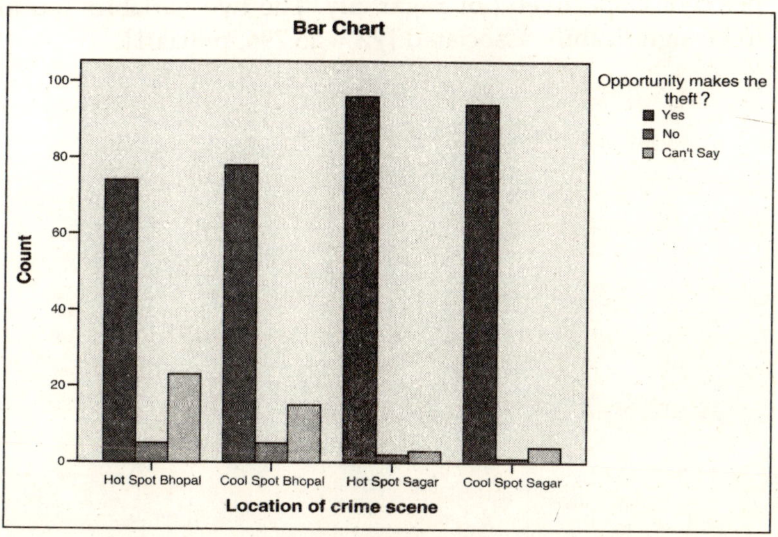

the notion [34.3 per cent] were mainly hailing from hot and cool spot areas [37.2 per cent and 27.0 per cent respectively] of Bhopal cities. The victim feeling otherwise [61.4 per cent] hailed from cool spot and hot spot locations [30.2 per cent and 28.6

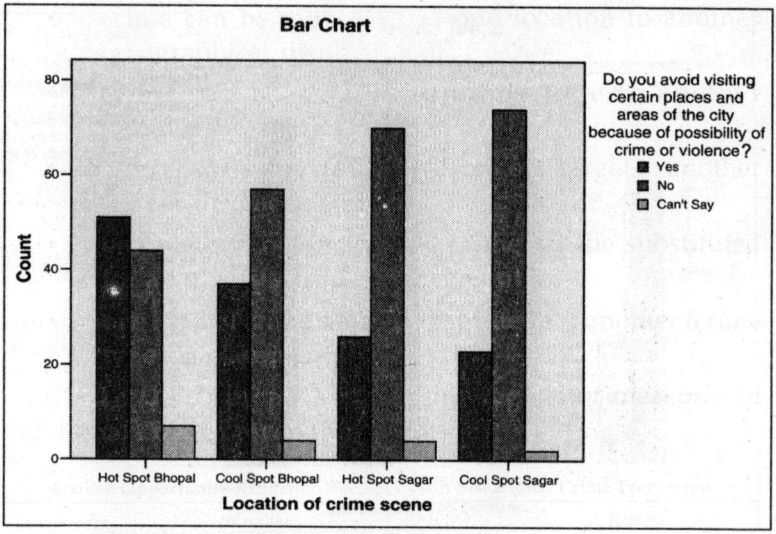

per cent respectively] of Sagar city. The two variables found to be significantly associated [$\chi 2 = 25.796$, $p<0.001$].

8

Summary and Conclusions

The present study was undertaken to look into the use and applications of situational crime prevention in the Indian context. Situational crime prevention is a relatively modern technique to reduce the incidence of crime by applying a host of managerial and tactical methods to discourage crime incidence. The main thrust in this approach is to effectively exploit the situational instigators for crime. In many parts of the world, situational crime prevention has contributed to reduce incidence of theft, burglary, vandalism, vehicle crime etc. The main proponents of situational crime prevention have carried out empirical studies showing the efficacy of this approach. Target hardening, access control, deflecting of offender, controlling facilitators, formal and natural surveillance and rule setting have been certain situational crime prevention measures used world wide in crime reduction. Crime reduction has also been considered immensely cost effective as it immediately alleviates the rising rate of crime and the economic cost of criminal justice system.

There is hardly any empirical study conducted on this subject in India. In view of the mounting arrears and consistently declining conviction rate in Indian courts, rising cost of law enforcement, trial and prison administration in India, the need to have a crime reduction strategy is more than obvious.

In view of the above, the present study has been conducted to make a critical analysis of situational crime prevention and the related opportunity theory. The main focus of the study was to examine the theoretical understanding of situational crime prevention in the Indian context. Accordingly, the study has been geared to examine the scope, efficacy and feasibility of situational crime prevention measures for indigenous setting.

The major objectives of this study were as follows:

1. To assess the extent and type of crimes that could be attributed to the ten principles of opportunity developed by R V Clarke.
2. To explore the situational dimensions attributable to the occurrence of crime in the selected sites.
3. To consider the opportunity theory model in case of selected types of crimes.
4. To assess the situational attributes in crime occurrence with the help of the perceptions of crime victims

A sample of 400 victims of various property crime occurred in the hot and cool spot locations of Bhopal and Sagar cities of Madhya Pradesh has been focused in this study. The data collection exercise was mainly carried out with the help of interview schedule specially framed for this purpose. The collected data was analyzed with the help of Statistical Package for Social Sciences [SPSS] and as many as 225 tables have been generated.

Some major findings emerged in the various sections of the study are being documented in the subsequent paragraphs.

1. The distribution of crime pattern shows that in both the cities i.e., Bhopal and Sagar, maximum crime was of theft from shop and business places i.e. 40 and 30 per cent respectively while theft from residence was lowest [19.5 and 24 per cent] respectively.
2. The most of the crime took place in second and fourth week of the month [26 per cent] in Bhopal while in Sagar most of the crime occurred in second week [27 per cent].

3. The study shows that the most crime incidence in both the cities occurred during 12 to 6 AM i.e. 35 and 40 per cent respectively. Between 6 to 12 AM the crime incidence was lowest in both the cities.
4. Mosts crime scene location was open i.e. 69.5 per cent in Bhopal and 63.5 per cent in Sagar.
5. The outdoor scene of crime was located in densely populated area [44.5 per cent in Bhopal and 28.5 per cent in Sagar]. Only in a few cases, crime occurred in thinly populated [7 per cent in Bhopal and 13 per cent in Sagar].
6. The lighting arrangements close to the crime locations of both the cites did not affect the occurrence.
7. Most of the time, victim spent (6 to 10 hours) at home, which is 75.5 per cent in Bhopal and 49.5 per cent in Sagar. There were only few victims who spent 1 to 5 hours and 16 to 20 hours at home.
8. The absence of capable guardian makes a target vulnerable for crime. In most of the cases, crime occurred in the absence of victim, which is 75.5 per cent in Bhopal and 78 per cent in Sagar. In rest of the cases, the victim was present during the occurrence of crime.
9. Most of the victims were of age group of 21 to 40 years (Bhopal 70.5 per cent and Sagar 62 per cent). There were only few cases in which victims were of age group up to 20 years or above 50 years.
10. The distribution of the sex of victims shows the preponderance of male over females. The data shows that in Bhopal 85 per cent victims were male while in Sagar 92.5 per cent victims were males. A very few victims were females in both the cities.
11. Most of the victims had service and business as their occupation while a few victims were student and wage earners in both the cities.
12. The study shows that in 66.5 cases in Bhopal and 73.5 cases in Sagar there was a use of implement in the

commission of crime while in the rest of cases there was no implement used in the commission of crime.

13. The study shows that the maximum victims were of view that the target was easily accessible [48.5 per cent in Bhopal and 57.5 per cent in Sagar]. The second main reason behind target lucratively was easy accessibility as well as cost or value of the goods.
14. The description of crime scene shows that in most of the cases, crime scene was unguarded or easily approachable.
15. The presences of security measures at the crime scene was inadequate in both the cities [73 per cent in Bhopal and 82.5 per cent in Sagar]. The rest of crime scenes were having moderate or adequate security measures.
16. The visibility of crime scene to others did not show any specific trend.
17. The locking arrangement at crime scene was inadequate in most of the cases [26.5 per cent in Bhopal and 47.5 per cent in Sagar]. There were very few cases in which adequate locking arrangement at crime scene was found.
18. In most of the cases, quality of lock was of average and poor [49.5 per cent in Bhopal and 77 per cent in Sagar]. There were few cases in which quality of lock was good.
19. In Bhopal, the police patrolling was mostly occasional [47 per cent] and in Sagar, in majority of instances, there was no police patrolling at all [76 per cent]. The regular police patrolling was found to be in 21 per cent cases in Bhopal and 1 per cent cases in Sagar.
20. The profile of respondents shows that most of the victims belonged to urban area [96.5 per cent in Bhopal and 98.5 per cent in Sagar].
21. Most of the localities covered in this study were residential and commercial [58.5 per cent in Bhopal and 58.5 per cent in Sagar].

22. The surveillance/security arrangements were perceived to be unsatisfactory by a large number of subjects [48 per cent in Bhopal and 71 per cent in Sagar].
23. Majority of the respondents, [60 per cent in Bhopal and 75 per cent in Sagar] felt their neighborhood to be unsafe.
24. A sizeable number of victims [62.5 per cent in Bhopal and 75 per cent in Sagar] found that there was easy availability of opportunity to commit crime in their localities.
25. As many as 56.5 per cent subjects in Bhopal and 73 per cent in Sagar confirmed the existence of crime problem in their localities.
26. The study on perceived nature of crime problem in the locality shows that the most respondents [57 per cent in Bhopal and 72 per cent in Sagar] found instances of petty theft to be utmost recurrent followed by burglary.
27. The factors that may be perceived by the victims to be responsible for crime are quite crucial in the situational explanation of crime. The study conveys that the movement of strangers in the area [31.5 per cent in the city of Bhopal] was the prime factor perceived by the respondents making the neighborhood crime prone. The correspondence per centage in case of Sagar city was 21 per cent. The respondents in the two cities equally felt the presence of bad character in the locality as crucial.
28. As many as 40.5 per cent respondents in Bhopal and 43 per cent in Sagar felt that crime can be reduced by increasing the police patrolling whereas 47 per cent in Bhopal and 38.5 in Sagar were of opinion that crime can be reduced by greater surveillance.
29. Majority of the respondents felt that crimes of theft/ burglary take because of the negligence of the victim.

30. The respondents in this study also expressed their opinions about the creation of opportunity by the victims. The data shows that negligence was rated to be the main way of causing opportunity [63 and 74 per cent respectively].
31. The perception "Opportunity makes the thief" as advocated by Clark was examined in this study. The study found that the respondents [76 per cent in Bhopal and 95 per cent in Sagar cities] attributed to this.
32. As many as 20 per cent and 18 per cent respondents in Bhopal and Sagar avoided traveling alone in public transport because possibility of theft.
33. The victims avoided visiting certain places because of various factors. In the areas of Bhopal and Sagar [28 and 16 per cent respondents respectively opted not to visit certain places in the cities due to hooliganism] in those areas.
34. Most of the respondents [66.5 per cent in Bhopal and 84.5 per cent in Sagar] were of the opinion that crime had increased in the last five years in their neighborhood.
35. The study clearly shows that robbery, theft or petty thefts were increasingly regarded to have increased significantly in all the locations of selected cities. Though, the respondent didn't find dacoity or sexual assault to have risen significantly.

SITUATIONAL EXPLANATIONS OF CRIME

1. The study of crime category and time of occurrence shows that most of crime incidences took place between 12 to 5.59 AM [37.5 %] and 6 to 11.59PM [30.5 %]. Theft from shop or business place mostly occurred during this time interval [25.1 %] and similarly the vehicle theft also took place during the same time frame [26.8 %]. [$\chi^2 = 50.674$, $P< 0.001$].
2. The study shows that the all types of crime were significantly higher [23 %] where lighting arrangement on

the premises was inadequate and 19 % cases of crime also took place where such arrangement was only moderate. This significantly depicts the situational role played by this factor in the crime categories covered in this study.

3. The study concludes that longer the absence of owner from home, greater the chances of crime commission. All categories of crime were most likely to occur when the owner's average time spent at home was up to 10 hours as 28.5 per cent theft from business place, 11.3 per cent theft from residence and most importantly 30.5 per cent vehicle theft took place when the owner was not close to the target of crime.
4. It has been observed from the study that most [72.8 per cent] crime occurred when the distance between workplace of victim and crime scene was within 5 Km, only 0.5 per cent crime occurred when the distance between workplace and crime scene was more than 16 Km. While considering the distance, the size of city is also found relevant.
5. The study suggests that in 76.8 per cent of crime cases, the victim was absent while in 23.3 per cent cases the victim was present. Almost 35 per cent cases of theft from shop, business places and residence occurred in the absence of victim. In case of vehicle theft 40.5 per cent occurred in the absence of victim while in 2.5 per cent cases victim was present.
6. The relation between age of the victim and nature of crime shows that most victims [33.5 per cent] were in the age group of 21 to 40 years while only 3.8 per cent victims were of age below 20 years. Almost one-fifth victims in case of theft from shop, business place and residence were within age group of 21 to 40 years. [$\chi^2 = 58.13$, $P < 0.001$]
7. The study on the sex of victim with regard to nature of crime shows that 88.8 per cent victims were male while 11.3 per cent victims were female. The theft from shop, business place and residence occurred where male victim [46.6 per cent] were involved where as in this category, only 10.3 per cent female victims were involved. In case of

vehicle theft there were 42 per cent male victims and only 1 per cent female victims were found among all. [$\chi^2 = 24.41$, $P< 0.001$].

8. The study finds the relationship between crime category and occupation of victim. It is observed from the study that most [41.1%] of the victims were of business class, while 27.8 per cent victims were of service class and only 8.8 per cent victims were wage earners. In one-fifth of the cases of theft from shop, business place and residence the victims were businessman. Most [19.3 %] of the vehicle thefts occurred with businessmen. [$\chi^2 = 27.34$, $P<0.007$]
9. The study also examined the adequacy of locking arrangement and chances of crime occurrence. It is clear from the study that in case of inadequate locking arrangement the chances of crime were higher [48.5 per cent] while in case of moderate locking arrangement had higher rate of [34.8 per cent] crime where as adequate locking arrangement had as16.7 per cent crime occurrence. In case of vehicle theft more or less similar trend was observed. [$\chi^2 = 13.24$, $P< 0.010$]
10. The study shows that more than half of the crimes occurred in the places where there was no police patrolling [53.7 %]. Areas with regular police patrolling had lower crime occurrence [11.1 %] [$\chi^2 = 24.07$, $P< 0.001$].
11. The study shows that maximum crime [59.6 %] was reported from the locations devoid of satisfactory arrangements of surveillance /security whereas the incidents were lowest [4.3 %] where these were satisfactory. [$\chi^2 = 9$, $P< 0.001$]

ADVANCED ANALYSIS OF SITUATIONAL CRIME

1. The characteristic of crime scene like open or close, guarded or unguarded, visible to others, presences of surveillance measures etc. have significantly emerged as major situational detriments of almost all categories of crime covered in this study. The statistical examinations like F ratio, multiple correlation and ANOVA confirmed this trend.

2. The vulnerability of target was also significantly determined by the location of crime occurrence.
3. Apart from being factual, the vulnerability to crime was largely a matter of victims' perception. It has been noted through out this study that perhaps having undergone the victimization experience, the victims tended to feel either crime in general in their localities has increased or the locality they live in has become unsafe. [$F=3.005$, $P< 0.05$]
4. Various tests of significance including the ANOVA etc. have clearly indicated the presence of a host of factors, which made crime happening situationally facilitating. The absence of capable guardian manifesting in terms of absence of the victim/owner from the target of theft or the length of distance between their work place and scene of crime or the victims inattentiveness or withdrawal at the time of crime occurrence were specially noted to be significant situational predictors of crime.
5. Victim's characteristics, [demographic, personal and behavioral] have also predicted significantly the nature of victimization suffered by him.

OPINIONS OF VICTIMS ON SITUATIONAL CRIME VARIABLES

1. The study shows that most victims had the opinion that the places they were living were not safe [67.5 per cent] only a few victims had the opinion that places they were living were safe [27.8 per cent].
2. The study shows that most victims [68.8 per cent] had the opinion that the opportunities to commit this crime in the locality were in abundance while a few [26.8 per cent] victims had the opinion that opportunities to commit this crime in this locality were not frequent.
3. The victims [64.9 per cent] also considered that there was crime problem in the neighbourhood and a few victims had the opinion that there was no crime problem in the neighbourhood [30.3 per cent].
4. It is observed from the study that more than two-third victims [67.5 per cent] had the opinion that the area was

unsafe while more than one-fourth victims [27.8 per cent] opined that the area was safe.

5. The study shows that most of the victims [68.8 per cent] experienced that opportunities to commit crime in their locality were in abundance only a few victims [26.8 per cent] did not feel so. These perceptions varied marginally according to the nature of victimization experienced by them. For instance, the perceived risk was highest in case of victims who had theft from residence [77 per cent] followed by theft from shop etc. [69.3 per cent].
6. The survey of victim in the hot and cool spots of the cities of Sagar and Bhopal shows that in all 67.5 per cent respondents found the areas of their living as unsafe. These victims, in most cases, were living in hot spot areas. The association therefore belonging to hot spot crime area and perceived unsafeness is fairly clear.
7. Respondent's perceived sense of availability of opportunity to commit crime indicates various matters giving rise to the actual crime incidences. The data available in the study shows that two-third of victims felt that opportunities to commit crime in their locality were utterly pronounced [68.8 Per cent] while only one-fourth victims felt otherwise [26.8 per cent].
8. It is observed from the data that 67.4 per cent victim felt that crime of theft /Burglary occur because of negligence of victim. The distribution of responses of this nature was almost equally distributed in all the police stations of the two cities.
9. The data indicate that the victim did not avoid visiting certain places because of possibility of crime in these regions [61.4 per cent]. However 34.3 per cent respondent admitted to this fact and their distribution was concentrating in some police stations.
10. The respondents [67.4 per cent] who thought negligence as factor to crime has experienced vehicle theft [78.5 per cent] followed by theft from residence and Shop/Business place [61.1 per cent and 57.9 per cent respectively].

11. A perusal of the study makes it clear that 67.4 per cent victims adhering to view point that negligence causes crime were predominantly belonging to cool spot and hot spot [27.1 per cent each] of Sagar city. There was only little variation about these locations in Bhopal.
12. The study examined the victims avoiding of visiting crime prone places and their belongingness of hot and cool spot locations in the selected cities. The victims subscribing to the notion [34.3 per cent] were mainly hailing from hot and cool spot areas [37.2 per cent and 27.0 per cent respectively] of Bhopal city. The victim feeling otherwise [61.4 per cent] hailed from cool spot and hot spot locations [30.2 per cent and 28.6 per cent respectively] of Sagar city.

The findings and experiences gained in the present study lead us to conclude that the quest for 'etiology' in the traditional Criminology has been useful in developing our theoretical understanding about crime but it has seldom helped the policy makers and practitioners in suggesting the workable ways and means to effectively reduce crime in the community. The idea of situational crime prevention was primarily the product of this concern. In fact, the functionality of situational crime prevention has been greatly recognized in almost all kinds of societies in effectively cutting the incident of crime. The traditional approaches of crime prevention have also not been very effective as they undertook to address the fundamentals of human personality or social dynamics and these efforts invariably did not produce any instant result. Whilst, situational crime prevention works immediately and hence in many nations this approach has been adopted with amazing success. While success stories of situational crime prevention are many and they have been adequately discussed in the present study, we may also look at some limitations of this exercise that needs to be addressed in coming days with the help of new research. The following account critically reviews the existing concept and scope of situational crime prevention and offers some new considerations for fresh research.

EVALUATION & CRITICAL ASSESSMENT

The criminologists have avoided any precise definition of situational crime prevention (SCP). There seem to be valid reasons for it. SCP was primarily conceived not as concept rather it was developed as a practice. SCP is about checking the criminal action by making the target resistant through several techniques based on the manipulation of environment and applications of technology. It would be proper here to see how the contemporary criminologists attempted to place the concept of SCP in the theoretical framework of the subject.

The salience of SCP approach is traceable in the way the criminologists have perceived the crime and criminal behaviour. Modern criminologists have also referred to some theoretical fallacies in criminology. Clarke (1997), for instance, talked of two such 'mistakes' of contemporary criminologists. The first relate to the fact that the theorists in criminology did not make much difference when explaining crime and criminals. The factors that predispose a person to crime do not necessarily explain the dynamics of crime (Gottfredson and Hirschi, 1990). The situational criminologists are of the opinion that a motivated offender is not enough to commit crime unless he finds facilitating opportunity and absence of 'capable guardians' checking the offending advancements. Secondly, the issues of crime control and handling of offenders have been confused with each other (Willkins, 1990). Apparently, responding to the criminal behaviour (treatment, prison, correction, rehabilitation etc.) and reducing crime could be two separate matters.

The above understanding leads us to conclude various matters. First, the agencies of criminal justice can only have a partial role and limited capacity to prevent or reduce crime in their traditional manner of performance. This is mainly due to the fact that the setting of crime and opportunity factor based prevention is hardly included in their agenda.

The Emerging features of SCP

The objective in this section is to highlight some significant features of SCP approach. The following characteristics emerged clearly in this exercise.

1. *Matured progression:* SCP did not take place abruptly. It was the result of innovation and experimentation carried out in the UK in the last three decades. A brief account of history of crime prevention efforts, as provided earlier in this report, in the UK makes it clear. It was largely the result of realization that much crime can be avoided by simply targeting the opportunities. The opportunity reduction model of crime prevention got significant amount of official support in the UK.
2. *Focused and target oriented:* The reason of the preference and popularity of SCP amongst policy makers and practitioners is due to its practicability and specificity.
3. *Problem oriented:* The law enforcement agencies applied it successfully as it aimed at specific problems.
4. *Tactical and Managerial:* It's also about skills based on aptitude of wide varieties.
5. *Pro active:* Being pro active in nature, it carries capability to reduce crime significantly.
6. *Evidence based crime reduction:* Earlier efforts in crime prevention were not certain in terms of amount of crime cut by them. SCP is evidence based that works on pre decided target and shows in the end the extent of crime reduced by it.
7. *Technological inputs:* The use of technology is the highlight of this approach.
8. *Efficient and quick:* SCP is efficient. The result starts coming, the moment it applies.
9. *Stake holder based:* It effectively caters to the requirements of the stakeholders.

Theoretical Evaluation

In this section, an attempt has been made to look at the theoretical foundations of situational crime prevention in a fresh light. The need to examine the theoretical foundations of SCP stems from several reasons. This is not to deny that the theories that are normally attributed to SCP are invalid. The theories in the framework of SCP-RAT, rational choice, opportunity model, and environmental design are absolutely functional. But what has been ignored is crucial. The all-central concepts in SCP and opportunity reduction drew significantly from the victimological knowledge. However, the acknowledgment to victimological thrust has seldom been made in the works conducted on SCP. The issues like risk, vulnerability, victim recidivism or repeat victimization, victim's role in crime, victim precipitation and victim types are some of the major concepts in victimology that have applied and utilised quite widely in SCP practices. The risk of victimization was the main plank of victimologists in the 80's and earlier. The early victimologists like Hentig, Mendelsohn, Nagel, Wolfgang, Fattah, Schafer in the 1950's and 60's developed many ideas that are clearly attributable to SCP.

CRITIQUE OF MAJOR ARGUMENTS IN SCP

Crime Triangle

The RAT argues that when a crime occurs, three things happen at the same time and in the same space: a suitable target is available, there is the lack of a capable guardian to prevent the crime from happening and a likely and motivated offender is present. This is the core postulate in the RAT theory and the foundation of SCP. Some arguments are being advanced here to look beyond it.

The first issue pertains to the matter of capability of guardians. Needless to state that capable guardian factor becomes crucial in the occurrence of crime. Situational criminologists have not gone further about the dynamics of this factor. Presumably, this factor does not seem to be a static phenomenon and its nature and variation can have bearing on victimization. Following propositions are being presented below to widen the theoretical gamut of this approach.

- Capability of guardians is relative and dynamic. Hence, it would respond differently to the offending advancements. And the likelihood of victimization would also rest on it.

- Capability is specific. This may not respond to all offending initiatives equally. This may prove to be a deterrent to one offence but not the other. The guardian's capability and offender's capability come in to clash in the process of crime. The outcome would depend on who overpowers whom. A security guard with old-fashioned gun at the door of Bank may seem to be capable but he may be a failure in facing a better-equipped offender. This is the case as to how superiority in capability affects the outcome of incident.
- To occur a crime, the suitability of target ought to match with offender's capability. Here the mere 'motivation' may not be enough. Like, a motivated offender cannot do fraud or forgery for want of specific capability to commit the act.
- Capability may not necessarily be the third dimension of the triangle. Sometimes, the capability may relate to target itself. In such case, the target's perceived suitability may be misleading. The 'potential but capable victim' may change the course of the event.
- Target's suitability is perceived and not absolute. This is why some targets cannot be overpowered and some capabilities do not seem to work always.
- The factor of 'motivation' is also dynamic. Sometimes motivation may not be so intrinsic and this may be situationally charged.
- The opportunity creation in the context of behaviour of three dimensions of RAT (target, guardian and offender) may not necessarily follow the conventional route. In other words, this may not be the product of routine interaction amongst the three. There can be extraneous factors that may create, maintain and manipulate the opportunities for crime commissions.

Missing Thrust

The focus of SCP is normally on the target and the setting (space or environment) of crime. The two variables become the major players in the techniques of SCP. The point to be noted here is that the entire knowledge on the behaviour of 'target' stems from victimology. The corollary would then be that all target-based prevention (e.g. target hardening, access control etc.) is of victimological nature. The prevention of this sort is essentially victim oriented. The victim typologies provide crucial data on the personality, behaviour and his/her/its predisposition to criminal assault. The sixteen techniques model of opportunity reduction developed by Clarke (1997) captures all victimological ingredients. The difference is of course that the victim based information and knowledge has been very well translated in 'to practical solutions. All SCP efforts and crime reduction practices, to a great extent, is what is known in victimology- de-victimization. The element of risk was recognized long back in victimological studies. Mendelsohn was a pioneer in developing victimogenesis. The sources of victim-risk were identified in the personality, behaviour and situation or environment surrounding the victim. The environmental designing and crime prevention draws upon the similar notions. Removing, protecting and concealing the target (SCP techniques now) are clearly based on the notions like victim proneness and vulnerability. Similarly, SCP techniques like reduced frustration and stress, avoiding dispute, control of drugs/alcohol etc are based on the concept of victim precipitation. Wolfgang (1958) in his seminal study on homicides in Philadelphia had clearly identified the typology of a class of victims who were assassinated because of their provocative behaviour. Spark (1982) making a victimological analysis found that crime occurs due to precipitation, facilitation, vulnerability, opportunity, attractiveness and impunity on the part of victim. Even the Sutherland's DAT and Merton's strain and deviant behaviour theories could be brought in to the theoretical foundations of SCP. Cloward & Ohlin's Differential Opportunity also did not find mention when the 'opportunity makes the thief' brand notions were being developed. Another theory that was invariable overlooked was that of Hindelang, Gottfredson, & Garofalo's Lifestyle

Theory that talked of situational factors in victimization quite sometime ago.

The argument is simple here. The victimological studies and concept did not find adequate mention in whatever theories developed in the area of SCP and crime reduction. It is therefore a bit misleading to conclude that the RAT or rational choice theories alone are fully attributable to the development of notion of SCP. Of course, the credit goes to a school of criminologists that include Felson, Brantingham and Bratingham, Clarke, Tilley, Laycock, Berry, Pease, Ekblom etc who have commendably translated several ideas in to enforceable practices leading to the development of SCP techniques.

Placing SCP in Criminological Context

While the idea and practice of SCP are getting wider acceptance, there is need to place SCP approach in a proper framework of arrangement in criminological theories. Going by all analysis made above, SCP may be treated as practical way of crime and victimization reduction. Looking at the conceptual and theoretical strands that run through the practice of SCP are essentially based on certain bodies of knowledge that have already made significant impact in contemporary and modern criminological thinking. Following are some prominent approaches or branches of knowledge that contributed a lot on the theories behind SCP:

1. Environmental criminology - the study of crime and criminality as they relate, first, to particular places, and secondly, to the way that individuals and organisations shape their activities spatially, and in so doing are in turn influenced by place-based or spatial factors.
2. Environmental victimology- that looks in to the spatial factors generating vulnerability and proneness for victimization by facilitating the offending practices (Draper, 1995).
3. Security and Risk Management–is also an emerging approach that makes risk analysis in case of varieties

of targets and develop the possible intervention strategies. This approach needs careful consideration as risk generation and management are the acknowledged practices in SCP.

4. Broken window Approach-Many ideas in SCP and later on problem oriented policing were inspired by the broken window thesis. James Q. Wilson and George Kelling developed the 'broken windows' thesis to explain the signalling function of neighbourhood characteristics. This thesis suggests that the following sequence of events can be expected in deteriorating neighbourhoods. Evidence of decay (accumulated trash, broken windows, deteriorated building exteriors) remains in the neighbourhood for a reasonably long period of time. People who live and work in the area feel more vulnerable and begin to withdraw. They become less willing to intervene to maintain public order (for example, to attempt to break up groups of rowdy teens loitering on street corners) or to address physical signs of deterioration. Sensing this, teens and other possible offenders become bolder and intensify their harassment and vandalism.
5. Conjunction of criminal opportunities and offender's resources: These two premises have been proposed by Ekblom and Tilley (2000). The conjunction of several 'immediate precursors' of crime prepares the situational context for crime. The idea of 'adequately resourced offender' is also another facet of the theoretical discussion on SCP. The notion behind this premise is that the resources of a wide range like personal, cognitive, moral, facilitatory, collaborative are equally important on the part of offender who enter to a situation for crime commission.

New Considerations

It may be mentionable here that the researcher in the present study tried to look in to the idea of SCP in its totality. The attempt has been made to place this concept in a proper arrangement of criminological thinking. An attempt has also made in this study to enlarge the concept of SCP by embracing some more pertinent conceptual issues in its fold. This study intends to propose following concepts to look at SCP in a fresh light.

Defacilitation: This can be a renewed thought in the area of SCP. Conceptually speaking, SCP methods do cause a state of 'defacilitation' for the offending behaviour. This may be direct, indirect, implicit or manifest. The argument is therefore that if the paraphernalia and situation necessary for offending are zeroed, the likelihood of crime diminishes significantly.

Disruption of offending process: SCP is intended to work for disrupting the offending process. Presumably, the offending has a chain of sequence and if any link in the chain is prematurely identified and obstructed, crime commission becomes tougher.

Identity disclosure: The fear of identity discloser works significantly on the part of potential offenders. The CCTV is the best example here.

Shaming effect: In Australia some of the studies in a different context have shown that the shaming effect remains quite influential in case of offenders. The SCP's methods are at work some time for this.

Psychic deterrence: The diffusion benefits received by SCP measure confirm the fact that SCP has a capacity to instill a psychological barrier and deterrence in potential offenders.

Socialising effect: This proposition needs empirical validation. SCP measures by controlling the access and specially by setting the rules surely leave a effect on the behaviour of offender in particular and public in general. It's a socialising effect to conform to non-criminal behaviour.

De-victimization: Several measures that are initiated from the perspective of target or victim pave the way for de victimization.

CRITICAL ISSUES

Displacement

This is invariably argued that crime displacement considerably weakens the effectiveness of situational crime prevention measures-for while crime rates may decrease in the area where situational projects have been undertaken, they might increase in other areas where these measures do not appear to exist (Gilling, 1977: 182). The situational criminologists have, however refuted this by citing several studies. Their view is that the displacement of crime may only be partial and insignificant.

Barr and Pease (1990) suggested the idea of 'benign displacement'. They said, "Consequences of benign displacement may either be changes to offending or the more equitable distribution of crime throughout society. In the first instance, while offending may not be prevented, it might change and become less serious as a result of situational crime prevention measures. For example, robbery might become burglary, assault with a weapon might become simple assault and robberies with guns might become robberies without guns. In the second instance, displacement could provide a more even or equal spread of crime and victimisation across the community. The argument here is that some level of crime is inevitable in society but that it is not spread evenly across the social spectrum. Subsequently, the displacement of crime across the community would result in the burden being shared equally by all." (*www.aic.gov.au*).

Fortress Society and 'Big Brother' Syndromes

The British people are said to be the most spied upon people in the world. In many sections of the society, there is apprehension that too much reliance on surveillance measure, like CCTV, in the private and public zones of the community are likely to create a 'fortress society'. Moreover, this may also lead to the unreasonable state intrusion in the privacy of the people. Resultantly, there is also an anti CCTV *website-www.brs.legend.org.uk/cctv/kdis12.htm*

Situational Crime Prevention and Nature of Crime

SCP has been predominantly associated with crimes like burglary or theft of varying nature. The worth of this technique has been proved beyond doubt in such offences. It is often felt that SCP may not be effective in many other varieties of crimes. The proponents of this school however claimed that SCP could be equally effective in several other kinds of crimes. The purpose of this section is to examine the issue.

SCP is always very specific. It is directed to target a particular crime. Hence, no generalisation is possible in this technique that may be made applicable to any other category of crime. Sometimes SCP needs to be reshaped even in the same type of offences. Poyner and Webb (1991) found that the prevention of domestic burglaries of electronic goods may require different measures from the domestic burglaries of cash and jewelleries. Clarke (1997) is of the view that SCP is applicable in all kinds of crime not just 'opportunistic' offences. Applying this to violent crimes, it is said that rates of homicide may have a situational angle as they are often found to be associated with the availability of guns in the society. SCP methods have also applied successfully in many grave crimes like hijacking prevention by strict baggage screening (Wilkinson, 1986) and prevention of robberies in post offices, buses etc by target hardening.(Ekblom, 1988). Clarke(1997) is also of the view that crimes of violence could also be approached by SCP. The use of technique of 'deflecting of offenders' was found useful in some cases. A study conducted in Australia convincingly depicted that SCP could prevent violence. Indermaur (1999) said ' Situational prevention helps to focus on specific situations in which violence occurs and prevent those situations gravitating or escalating to the point where violence is more likely'. This study mainly focused on the prevention of alcohol related and gun related violence.

A publication from Helsinki Institute by Markku and Paksula (1997) discussed the applications of SCP in economic crimes.

New Considerations: As science and technology progresses, new forms of SCP will emerge. If SCP continues to remain effective, they would require keeping pace with the changes. The purpose here is to consider some more techniques in the framework of SCP. The new shape and structure of the SCP may be seen as 'Integrated Situational crime Prevention'. The term 'integrated' is being used here to widen the reach of SCP measure. Notably, many vital measures are yet to be included and practiced as situational measures of crime reduction.

Proposing Integrated Situational Crime Prevention (ISCP)

The knowledge produced in several discipline of knowledge (Crime Science) could be used in SCP. The term Integrated Situational Crime Prevention symbolises the application of multidisciplinary knowledge in crime reduction initiatives. The efficacy of this approach heavily depends on utilising expertise available in all branch of learning. We will talk of couple of such measure and approaches that have been left out in the framework of SCP despite their great preventive value. The study proposes their inclusion in the ISCP.

1. *Geo profiling:* Geographic profiling is an emerging methodology that applies the locations of a connected series of crimes to determine the most probable area of offender residence. It is generally applied in cases of serial murder, rape, arson, and robbery, though it can be used in single crimes (auto theft, burglary bombing, etc.) that involve multiple scenes or other significant geographic characteristics.

   The basis of geographic profiling is the link between geographic crime site information and the known propensities of serial criminals in their selection of a target victim and location. The system produces a map of the most probable location of the criminal's centre of activity, which in most cases is the offender's residence. When linked with additional information relating to the crime incidents, and with additional data sources, such as motor vehicles databases and suspect databases, geographic profiling has been proven to have a profound impact on the effectiveness of a police investigation *(http://www.geographicprofiling.com/geopro/index.html).*

2. *Computer softwares in Crime reduction:* Certain situational and managerial interventions could be carried by the applications of computer softwares.

CrimePoint™ is a new software solution to aid law enforcement and public safety agencies. It provides investigators, analysts and administrators with an integrated data consolidation, analysis and visualization experience. There is software called 'Crime stat' that not only makes a spatial analysis of crime patters in the geographic locations but also prepares 'hot analysis' enabling the agencies to specifically address to the problems of crimes. Another useful software in this chain is 'Crime risk analysis software'. Some further information in this regard can be seen at - *http://www.hightechcrimecops.org*

3. *GIS solutions to Crime Reduction:* The GIS has already become a powerful tool in the hands of crime analyst. The identifications of crime locations, patters, and mapping and hot places analysis become quite insightful with the GIS technology. In several countries, the police have already started using it. This tool needs to be used as an effective SCP measures.
4. *Forensic solutions in situational crime prevention:* This is one of the least explored areas. Forensic aided methods of investigation and detection have an effect on the crime scene in any community. There can be host of situationally effective measures from the angle of forensic science. The developments in voice identification devises, digital imaging, reconstruction of identity devises, forensic mapping, computer aided detection technology etc. could be included in this category.
5. *E-solutions:* In the present age of information technology, the cyber criminality has become a major challenge. There are number of ways within the framework of e-solutions to curb cyber crimes.
6. *Strengthening private sector response:* The private sector has recently emerged an effective resource in the community safety arena. To be able to be more

effective, the SCP thinkers would require to strengthen this sector in all possible manner.

7. Security technology: The recent past has witnessed spectacular changes in security technology. The CCTV, microwave detection systems, portable radios and cameras, magnetic sensors, and laser technology, e-tracking systems are becoming household names in the security world. Recently invented electronic tracking devises do have great potential to become effective SCP measures. Electronic surveillance and computer tracking using radio, satellites, Internet and phone network are some of them. Use of personal GPS and GSM tracking devises and E-mail tracker with police could be extremely effective.
8. Capacity and Capability building for guardians: Speaking in terms of RAT, most criminal incidents have a situational bearing stemming from the incapacity and incapability of 'guardians'. Depending upon the targets, the role of guardians is played by persons, agencies, organisations, security agencies or the police. The offenders often exploit the weaknesses or vulnerabilities in covering or protecting the targets. Therefore, the issue of Capacity and Capability building for guardians assume importance.

The main issues analysed in this section could be summarized as below:

1. The situational crime prevention ought to be viewed as a dynamic application. The need to widen its approach and applications in the newer setting and crimes is therefore imperative.
2. SCP needs to be clearly located in the theoretical boundaries of criminological research. An attempt in this study has been made to this effect.
3. SCP thinkers and practitioners will have to find satisfying answers to displacement factor.

4. SCP needs to be tailored to respond other variety of crime. It can have applicability in cases of certain economic, violent crimes and terrorist crimes.
5. Almost no research exists as to whether SCP would work in the changing context or not. The most SCP practices were carried out and evaluated in case UK, USA or Australia. The applicability of SCP in developing countries, diversified regions, and relatively lesser techno-oriented societies etc. is yet to be explored.
6. SCP has many success stories in the UK and USA where the crimes rates have shown visible reduction due these measures.
7. The issue of sustainability of SCP in long term is also crucial.
8. The personnel applying and evaluating SCP needs to have adequate training orientation.

Implications for India

One of the objectives of this study was to assess the adoptability and applications of situational crime prevention and crime reduction measures in case of India. Obviously, it could be an independent and vast study in itself. The idea is only to make a preliminary discussion on this issue.

An exercise of this kind would need to take in to consideration a range of factors. These may pertain to the socio-geographical and criminal justice performance based issues. The state of India offers a context highly diversified in terms of all basic profile factors. Its geography is extensive and cultural context is heterogeneous. The population is more than one billion. The economy is vibrant and open. The police and law enforcement agencies have to work hard to cater to such a huge population. Crime scene in the country is critical. Its not the routine crimes like property offences every where but also serious violent crimes, organized crimes and particularly terrorist incidents in certain areas pose real challenges.

SCP can in fact contribute to reduce the incidence of theft, burglary, vandalism and street crimes in case of India. Most strikingly, several types of terrorist incidents that occur due to security lapses or lack of vigil can be responded by SCP. The methods like target hardening and access control and other could be made applicable in such cases. This can be achieved by undertaking some pilot project in any particular area. The results of measures applied in this case may be studied and crime reduction plans may be developed focusing upon the local requirement. The crime reduction partnership is another idea that can be given thought in India. The involvement of multi agency partnership in India can address to problems like crimes of everyday.

If the findings and discussions held in this exercise result in directing the attention of criminal justice personnel towards reducing crime by applying SCP and also by generating a debate in criminological circles for undertaking research in this area, the study will have served its purpose.

References

Abagnale, Frank W. (2002), The Art of the Steal: How to Protect Yourself and Your Business from Fraud, America's #1 Crime: USA, Broadway.

Allen, J. (2000), Community Survey of Willingness to Receive Stolen Goods. *Crime and Justice Bulletin,* No. 51. Sydney: NSW Bureau of Crime Statistics and Research.

Anderson D, Chenery S and Pease K (1994), Biting Back: Tackling Repeat Burglary and Car Crime, Crime Detection and Prevention Series Paper 58, London, Home Office.

Anderson, D., S. Chenery and K. Pease (1995), Biting Back: Tackling Repeat Burglary and Car Crime. Crime Detection and Prevention Series Paper 58. London: Home Office.

Atkins, S., Husain, S. and Storey, A. (1991), The Influence of Street Lighting on Crime and Fear of Crime. *Crime Prevention Unit Paper* No 28. London: Home Office. *http://www.homeoffice.gov.uk/*

Australian Institute of Criminology (2005), The Market Reduction Approach to Reducing Property Crime. AICrime Matters 32. *http://www.aic.gov.au/* (accessed 8 April 2005). Also available from Canberra: Australian Institute of Criminology.

Bennett, T. and L. Durie (1999), Preventing Residential Burglary in Cambridge: From Crime Audits to Targeted Strategies. Crime Detection and Prevention Series Paper 108. London: Home Office.

Blake, L. and R. Coupe (2001), The Impact of Single and Two-officer Patrols on Catching Burglars in the Act. *British Journal of Criminology,* 41 (2): 381-396.

Boyce, P. R., Eklund, N. H., Hamilton, B. J. and Bruno, L. D. (2000), Perceptions of Safety at Night in Different Lighting Conditions. *Lighting Research and Technology* , 32(2), 79-91.

Brown, B. (1995), CCTV in Town Centres: Three Case Studies. *Crime Detection and Prevention Series,* Paper 68, Police Research Group. London: Home Office. *http://www.homeoffice.gov.uk/, or* available through ICOLE (2002)

Bullock, Karen & Tilley Nick (2003), Crime Reduction and Problem Oriented Policing: Devon, UK Willan.

Casey C. *et al.* and Segessenmann, T. (2003), Evaluation of the Target Hardening Pilot Programme. Wellington: Ministry of Justice.

Clarke R. V. (1999), Hot Products: Understanding, Anticipating and Reducing Demand for Stolen Goods Police Research Series Paper 112.

Clarke R. V. (1997), 'Introduction' in RV Clarke (ed), Situational Crime Prevention: Successful Case Studies (2nd ed). Harrow and Heston: Guilderland, New York.

Clarke, R. V. & Eck John (2003), Become a Problem-Solving Analyst: Devon, UK Willan.

Clarke, R. V. and M. Felson (Eds.) (1993), Routine Activity and Rational Choice. *Advances in Criminological Theory,* Vol 5, New Brunswick, NJ: Transaction Books.

Clarkc, R. V. and Lester, D. (1989), Suicide: Closing the Exits. Springer-Verlag; New York.

Cohen, L. E. and M. Felson (1979), Social Change and Crime Rate Trends: A Routine Activity Approach. *American Sociological Review,* Vol. 44, Pages 588-608.

Cope, N. (2004), Intelligence-led Policing or Policing-led Intelligence? Integrating Volume Crime Analysis into Policing. *British Journal of Criminology,* 44 (2): 188-203.

Dean Southall and Paul Ekblom(1985), Designing for Car Security: Towards a Crime Free Car. London-Crime Prevention Unit Paper (Home Office).

Di Tella, R. and Schargrodsky, E. (2001), *Using a Terrorist Attack to Estimate the Effect of Police on Crime* . Draft, 2001-04-30.

http://www.people.hbs.edu/rditella/papers/using_terrorist_%20attack.pdf

DiLonardo, Robert L. and Ronald V. Clarke(1996), "Reducing the Rewards of Shoplifting: An Evaluation of Ink Tags." *Security Journal,* 7 (1): 11-14.

Draper, Roderick (Rick) (1995), Security Risk Management: A Considered.

Ekblom P. and Tilley N. (2000), 'Going Equipped: Criminology, Situational Crime Prevention and the Resourceful Offender' in *British Journal of Criminology,* 40, 376-398.

Ekblom, Paul (1987), Preventing Robberies at Sub-post Offices: An Evaluation of a Security Initiative. Crime Prevention Unit Paper 9. London, UK: Home Office.

Farrington, D. P. and Welsh, B. C. (2002b), Effects of Improved Street Lighting on Crime: A Systematic Review. *Home Office Research Study 251.* London: Home Office. *http://www.homeoffice.gov.uk/rds/pdfs2/hors251.pdf*

Felson M. (1994), Crime and Everyday Life: Insights and Implications for Society. Pine Forge Press: Thousand Oaks, California.

Felson, M. and R. V. Clarke (1998), Opportunity Makes the Thief. Crime Detection and Prevention Series, Paper 98. Police Research Group. London: Home.

Forrester, D., Chatterton, M., Pease, K. and Brown, R. (1988), The Kirkholt Burglary Prevention Project, Rochdale. Crime Prevention Unit Paper 13. London: Home Office.

Forrester, D., S. Frenz, M. O'Connell and K. Pease (1990), The Kirkholt Burglary Prevention Project: Phase II. Crime Prevention Unit Paper 23. London: Home Office.

Gilling, D (1977), Crime Prevention Theory, Policy and Politics, London: UCL Press. Gilling, Daniel (2003): ' The Audit Commission and the Ills of Local Community Safety: An Accurate Diagnosis?' *Community Safety Journal,* Vol. 1, No. 1 (pp. 4-11).

Goodman, D. E. (2002), *Midsize Cities and their Correlates with Crime: An Empirical Investigation.* (Cited with the author's permission.) Department of Economics Working Paper 97-1. Tacoma, WA: University of Puget Sound, Department of Economics. *http://www.ups.edu/econ/working_papers/97-1.pdf*

Gottfredson, Michael R. and Travis Hirschi (1990), A General Theory of Crime. Stanford: Stanford University Press.

Hearnden, I. and C. Magill (2004), Decision-making by Burglars: Offenders' Perspectives. Home Office Findings 249. London: Home Office.

Hirsch, Andrew Von Garland, David & Wakefield Alison (2000), Ethical and Social Perspectives on Situational Crime Prevention: Oxford, Hart Publishing.

Indermaur David (1999), Situational Prevention of Violent Crime: Theory and Practice in Australia, Published in Studies on Crime and Crime Prevention, 8, 1, 1999, 71 -87 Crime Research Centre, University of Western Australia.

Jeffrey, C. Ray (1971), Crime Prevention Through Environmental Design. Beverly Hills, CA: Sage Publications.

Jordan, P. (1998), Effective Policing Strategies for Reducing Crime. In Reducing Offending: An Assessment of Research Evidence on Ways of Dealing with Offending Behaviour. Home Office Research Study 187, eds. P. Goldblatt and C. Lewis. London: Home Office, 63-81.

Kelling, George and Catherine Coles (1996), Fixing Broken Windows: Restoring Order and Reducing Crime in Our Communities. New York: Free Press.

Kodz, J. and K. Pease (2003), Reducing Burglary Initiative: Early Findings on Burglary Reduction. Home Office Findings 204. London: Home Office.

Lab, S. P. (1997), *Crime Prevention. Approaches, Practice and Evaluations.* 3rd ed. Cincinnati, OH: Anderson Publishing Co. (Extract from its Chapter 3 'The Physical Environment and Crime' seen at *http://www.securitymanagement.com/library/000484.html*

Laycock, G. (1985), Property Marking: A Deterrent to Domestic Burglary? Crime Prevention Unit Paper 3. London: Home Office.

Lewis, E. B. and Sullivan, T. T. (1979), Combating Crime and Citizen Attitudes. A Case Study of the Corresponding Reality. *Journal of Criminal Justice* , 7, 71-79. (Not seen, cited by Farrington and Welsh (2002a,b) and Lab (1997).

Liz Curtin, Nick Tilley, Mark Owen and Ken Pease (2001): Developing Crime Reduction Plans: Some Examples from the Reducing Burglary Initiative:London- Crime Prevention Unit Paper (Home Office)

Martin, D. (2002), Spatial Patterns in Residential Burglary. *Journal of Contemporary Criminal Justice,* 18 (2): 132-146.

Marvell, T. B. and Moody, C. E. (1996), Specification Problems, Police Levels, and Crime Rates. *Criminology* , 34(4), 609-646.

Masuda, Barry (1997), "Reduction of Employee Theft in a Retail Environment: Displacement vs. Diffusion of Benefits." In

Situational Crime Prevention: Successful Case Studies, Vol. 2, (ed. Ronald V. Clarke). Guilderland, NY: Harrow and Heston. pp. 183-190. *http://crimeprevention.rutgers.edu/resources/ - harrow*

Masuda, Barry (1996), "An Alternative Approach to the Credit Card Fraud Problem." *Security Journal*, 7 (1): 15-21.

Newman, Oscar (1972), Defensible Space, Crime Prevention Through Urban Design,: Macmillan, New York

Nigel Hill. (1986), Prepayment Coin Meters: A Target for Burglary. London-Crime Prevention Unit Paper (Home Office).

Painter, K. (1990), Women's Experience and Fear of Crime and the Scope for Public Lighting as a Means of Crime Prevention. Paper Presented 1990-06-06, Leeds City Conference on Crime and Lighting. (Not seen, cited by Quinet and Nunn (1998).)

Plant, Martin and Harrison, Larry (2003), Prevention and Harm Minimisation in the UK, Alcohol Concern Research Forum Papers.

Poyner, B. and Webb, B. (1997), Reducing Theft from Shopping Bags in City Center Markets. In Clarke, R. V. (ed.), *Situational Crime Prevention: Successful Case Studies*, 2nd ed., pp. 83-89. ISBN 0911577-38-4 (or -6) Monsey, NY: Criminal Justice Press or Albany, NY: Harrow and Heston or Guilderland, NY: Clarke, Harrow and Heston.

Poyner, B. and Webb, B. (1991), Crime Free Housing. Oxford: Butterworth.

Poyner, Barry and Barry Webb (1997), "Reducing Theft from Shopping Bags in City Centre Markets." In Situational Crime Prevention: Successful Case Studies, Vol. 2 (ed. Ronald V. Clarke). Guilderland, NY: Harrow and Heston. pp. 83-89. *http://crimeprevention.rutgers.edu/resources/ - harrow*

Read, Tim and Tilley Nick (2000), Not Rocket Science? Problem-Solving and Crime Reduction, Home Office Crime Reduction Research Series Paper 6.

Redding, Stan & Abagnale, Frank W. (2000), Catch Me If You Can: The True Story of a Real Fake: USA, Broadway Response to Crime Against Business, Australian Institute of Criminology.

Sallybanks, Jonna & Brown, Rick (1999), Vehicle Crime Reduction: Turning the Corner, Police Research Series 119: London, Home Office.

Schneider, Todd, Walker, Hill and Colvin, Geoffrey (2000), Crime Prevention Through Environmental Design in Schools. Eugene, OR: University of Oregon.

Scott, M. (2003), The Benefits and Consequences of Police Crackdowns. Problem-Oriented Guides for Police Response Guides Series No. 1. *http://www.cops.usdoj.gov/* (accessed 19 January 2005). Also available from Washington, DC: US Department of Justice.

Sherman, L. W. and Weisburd, D. (1995), General Deterrent Effects of Police Patrol in Crime 'Hot Spots': A Randomized, Controlled Trial. *Justice Quarterly*, 12, 625-649. (Not seen; quoted by Taylor (1998) [106].)

Sherman, L., D. Gottfredson, D. MacKenzie, J. Eck, P. Reuter and S. Bushway (1997), Preventing Crime: What Works, What Doesn't, What's Promising. Washington, DC: National Institute of Justice.

Skogan, W. and K. Frydl, eds. (2003), Fairness and Effectiveness in Policing: The Evidence. Washington, DC: The National Academies Press.

Smith, M. S. (1996), Crime Prevention Through Environmental Design in Parking Facilities. *NIJ Research in Brief Series* . Washington DC: National Institute of Justice. *http://www.ncjrs.org/txtfiles/cptedpkg.txt*

Stockdale, J. and P. Gresham (1995), Combating Burglary: An Evaluation of Three Strategies. Crime Detection and Prevention Series Paper 59. London: Home Office.

Sutton, M., J. Schneider and S. Hetherington (2001), Tackling Theft with the Market Reduction Approach. Home Office Crime Reduction Research Series Paper 8. London: Home Office.

Sutton, M., J. Schneider and S. Hetherington (2001), Tackling Theft with the Market Reduction Approach. Home Office Crime Reduction Research Series Paper 8. London: Home Office.

Sutton, Mike, Jacqueline Schneider and Hetherington Sarah (2001), Tackling Theft with the Market Reduction Approach,, Crime Reduction Series paper 8, London, UK: Home Office.

Taylor, R. B. (1998), Crime and Small-scale Places: What we Know, What we can Prevent, and what else we need to know. In Taylor, R. B., Bazemore, G., Boland, B. Clear, T. R., Corbett, Jr, R. P., Feinblatt, J., Berman, G., Sviridoff, M. and Stone, C. *Crime and place: plenary papers of the 1997 conference on criminal justice research and evaluation* , pp 1-22, July, NCJ 168618. Washington, D. C.: National Institute of Justice. *http://www.ncjrs.org/pdffiles/168618.pdf*

Welsh, B. C. and Farrington, D. P. (2002), Crime Prevention Effects of Closed Circuit Television: A Systematic Review. *Home Office Research Study 252*. London, Home Office. *http://www.homeoffice.gov.uk/rds/pdfs2/hors252.pdf*

Welsh, Brandon C. and Farrington, David P. (2002), Crime Prevention Effects of Closed Circuit Television: A Systematic Review, Home Office research study: London.

Williams, R. (2004), The Management of Crime Scene Examination in Relation to the Investigation of Burglary and Vehicle Crime. Home Office Online Report 24/04. *http://www.homeoffice.gov.uk/rds (accessed 27 March 2005).*

Witte, A. D. and Witt, R. (2000), *Crime Causation: Economic Theories.* (Preprint, 2000-07-19, Encyclopedia of Crime and Justice). *http://www.econ.surrey.ac.uk/WorkingPapers/econ300.pdf*

Website

http://www.cpted.com.au/)

http://www.crimereduction.gov.uk

http://www.crimereduction.gov.uk/cctvminisite28.htm

http://www.crimereduction.gov.uk/cctvminisite28.htm

http://www.homeoffice.gov.uk

http://www.geographicprofiling.com/geopro/index.html

http://www.hightechcrimecops.org/

http://www.geographicprofiling.com/geopro/index.html

http://www.uncjin.org

INDEX